PROXIMA RIVEN

The Feedback Loop Book Seven

By Harmon Cooper

Edited by George C. Hopkins

Copyright © 2017 by Harmon Cooper

Copyright © 2017 Boycott Books

Cover by Dan Van Oss at covermint.design

Edited by George C. Hopkins

www.harmoncooper.com

writer.harmoncooper@gmail.com

Twitter: @_HarmonCooper

All rights reserved. All rights preserved. This is a work of fiction. Names, characters, places and incidents either are products of the author's imagination or are used fictitiously.

Map of Steam

Chapter One

Who'd a thunk an earthy-green poofter of a druid could be so muscled up under his mauve robes?

Here I was, thinking he was some sort of fat guy, wearing his too-big robes like they're a damn mu-mu or something. I guess that's what I get for thinking.

What was supposed to be a friendly arm wrestling match quickly morphed into an epic bar room brawl once Wizardous – Dirty Dave's fantasy version of crank – was introduced to the mix. Dave's recipe needs perfecting, or maybe it is supposed to turn people agro – *no sé* – all I know is that a couple of lines of that stuff will turn an already combative and obnoxious group, like the Battlin' Brits, into a grossly obnoxious and combative group hell-bent on death and destruction.

But that's not exactly how the fight between Yours Truly and the stalwart stooge of a druid broke out.

The Brits were already handing a group of mages their asses when the druid pops off with how all those immiNPCs should go back to whatever shitty world they came from, and that really ticked me off, especially when he spit on Morning Assassin's boot. Sure, I shouldn't be ready to throw down fisticuffs on a dime's worth of notice, but where I'm from …

Them's fightin' words!

Except we aren't going to duke it out as we would if we were in The Loop. Not today, junior – this turn-based brawl-a-thon is something only available in Tritania, and boy oh boy do I wish they'd update their JRPG-ish game rules and do away with turn-based battling.

Aiden steps up to the proverbial plate.

Swing batter, batter, swing!

To give himself a handicap, he's used a belt to strap his right arm to his side. With just the right amount of flare, The Loop's numero uno asesino executes a one-armed cartwheel, and lands a double-footed kick more Jackie Chan than Bruce Lee. Still, it's effective; the druid stumbles backwards, whistles to those smart enough to clear out of the way, and a drinking buddy joins him.

Talk about too much time at the Fantasy Costco – his warrior compadre looks like a third string extra in his *Robin Hood: Men in Tights* getup that is neither ironic nor very effective. He's got the legs of a sprinter and he's damn proud of them as he charges at me with a dagger held over his head.

Damn noobies.

Everyone knows charging someone with a weapon held high is a great way to find yourself with a faceful of floor. Plus, my avatar is three times the level of his avatar; it shouldn't take an abacus for this bozo to figure out his odds of landing a hit on me.

Out goes my foot and straight to the floor goes Insane Bolt, his teeth shattering like a porcelain lamp falling from a three-story window. Legs McGee pulls himself to his feet, spits bloody tooth fragments, pulls a sword, reconsiders, and logs out like a sissy-pants in search of his mama's titty.

"Ha! That guy'd make a great Reaper!"

Aiden gets it, and as long as someone gets it, my gelotologist will still write me a perfect bill of health.

"I'll kill you." Stonehenge, the bindle punk druid comes in swinging at me for his attack. I equip my trashcan shield, item 14, which takes the brunt of his fist. *Whammo!* He catches me with a left hook that leaves me seeing tweety birds and spinning stars. I crash-land into a table, and go right through it like we were videoing an episode of WWE Monday Night Raw.

Our turn.

I hop back to my feet, give my list a quick scroll, and look over to Aiden as if to say, 'how should I end this?' He gives me the thumb-cutting-the-throat gesture, and I equip Dr. Cyclops' shrink ray in my right and a fly swatter in my left, items 43 and 314, respectively.

"I've always wanted to do this." I take aim at that Celtic turd burglar and squeeze the trigger. A spiral-y red beam emits from the gun and shrinks the bastard down to Legoman size. He takes off, and I follow him like a bird dog, slapping my fly swatter against the floor every chance I get.

"Just finish him off already!" Aiden calls as I scramble into a bar stool, topple it over, toss the stool off me and continue the chase.

"There's a madness to my method!"

The little druid bugger and I both see a mouse hole in the wall at the same time. He makes a beeline for it, and I hurl myself at the hole in the wall to stop him. I do the official *Tom and Jerry* face plant into the wall and slide down as he disappears into the hole.

"Do I have to do everything myself?"

I look back to see Morning Assassin aiming his shooting iron at the wall.

"That's a killer diller weapon you got yourself there!"

I don't know where he picked up the prototype Smart Grenade Launcher, but boy oh boy do I wish I knew where to get me one! My M1917 doughboy helmet, item 424, materializes on my noggin. Nope, it ain't gonna do jack diddly squat regarding our proximity to the impact point, but I'm not going for practicality here, I'm going for style.

"Get him before he logs out!" I shout to Morning Assassin. He nods, takes a knee, clicks the safety, and KABOOMSKI!

He skips the grenade off the floor and into the mouse hole, brings down the wall, kills the creatine-enhanced druid, and kills both of us deader'n duck dookie.

~*~

"It ain't easy being greasy," I tell Aiden after we respawn in the OMIB yurt that Sophia set up in Three Kings Park. Orthogonal Matrix Inverse Base, OMIB – talk about a series of words that does not roll off the tongue. My ass is safe in here, oddly enough, and the wind hissing outside tells me that it would probably be smart to stay in here for the time being.

He slugs me in the shoulder. "Greasy? What are you going on about now?"

"Just being myself," I tell Morning Assassin. "Besides, I wasn't the one greased up and wrestling with the big orc palooka."

Aiden shrugs. "You give Scotty too much *drorikh* and add a half-dozen lines of Wizardous and he'll assault the Gates of Hell with a soda syphon full of Irn Bru – you know that." He offers me that predatory grin that I've come to know and love. I shouldn't be celebrating, *have* nothing to celebrate – I get that – but that doesn't mean that I can't share a libation or two with some old pals. "Now quit yappin', get your ass onto the gurney, and put the visor on."

As I lie down onto the gurney, my thoughts trail back to our night on the town. Lots of Horse Piss consumed, more orc broads than a knight can shake his lance at, a couple of gassy goblins that kept going on about a game called Natty Dread, all capped off by a battle royale after a druid drunk as a Russian grunt on Defender of the Motherland Day talked some shit to a pair of bad hombres, aka Yours Trulies.

"Quantum, why do you have that shit-eating grin on your face?"

"Just lost in reverie. Alrighty, where were we?"

"I was sending you back to your … " he thinks for a moment "I guess meatsack isn't the right word, and *metal sack* sounds like something between a robot's legs."

"Like I told you earlier, Humandroids don't have balls," I tell him, "trust me on that."

"Too bad. If they did, you'd be able to … " he snickers at his own joke.

"You got something to say, wise guy?"

"Just a joke about Dr. Wang and your nonexistent droid wang, but I'm above that type of locker room talk, so forget about it." He clears his throat. "Where were we? Shut up and put this on."

I place the NV visor made from Chronoton metal over my head and wait for the sine waves to do their little dance thingy.

As Aiden adjusts some dials, or does whatever it is Sophia told him to do, I get a sinking feeling in my stomach as I consider what Aiden just said – nope, I'm *not* going back to my meatsack, that's for damn sure. I'll respawn in Evan's droid body, the Tin Man with the empty head space of the Scarecrow, my mechanical ass firmly planted on Sophia's couch, and if there is a God, she won't be snuggled up next to me.

I specifically told her not to do that.

"You ready to dive?"

"Born ready," I tell him.

~*~

A presence registers on my droid's iNet screen pane of vision in the form of a schematic of my body with a blinking red icon. It zooms in on Sophia, letting me know a variety of details, from the weight of my heavy-brained host to fluctuations in body heat over the last hour.

"Sophia, you have got to go," I say, my voice no longer mine. I lift Dr. FrankenAsian's head from my lap and she mumbles something in Chinese and sure enough, I know exactly what she says, "Don't go, I was just getting comfortable," except her voice is muffled, the culprit being a turquoise night guard jammed in her kisser to keep her from grinding her teeth.

"I told you, no funny business. I'm already up to my ass in trouble with the opposite sex. I'd like not to add another problem to my growing list."

Still, Mrs. Hughes' Sweet Baby Droid isn't as rude as I pretend to be. Like a gentledroid, I place Sophia's head on a pillow cushion and she's back to sleeping and drooling in no time. My iNet screen tells me that Doc's combat protocols have finished downloading, but it will take an hour or so for them to update on my system.

Fresh air.

My charge is back at a hundo and it's only now that I notice just how bright Sophia's living room is. You could grow marijuana in here, and if she isn't careful, an FCG drone will note the heat source and the Feds will come knocking, hopefully in the form of Special Agent Reynolds and Special Agent O'Brien, the two F-BIIGie piggies who gave me such a hard time after I recovered from my dive. I haven't forgotten those two boneheads, and maybe, just maybe, I'll pay them a visit in Evan's body and raise some hell.

I smile at the thought. Who am I kidding? Doc would have me shut down before I could hail an aerostaxi. Speaking of Doc...

Me: Say, you up?

Doc: One doesn't work a farm and *not* wake up at the ass crack of dawn. No, I'm not up, but Arnie is, and as soon as the bacon is done sizzling, the coffee is brewed, and the eggs are poached, I'll join him in the kitchen and start my morning routine.

Me: Please tell me that involves a stack of pancakes.

Doc: On weekends, yes. Did you rest well?

Me: Is that a joke?

Doc: I'm known as funny in some circles.

I step out of Sophia's apartment and take a big whiff of the Baltimore semi-haze. The sky is pink, always a good sign, and the sun is just pulling up over the horizon, a giant peach partially obscured by a frothy cloud. I'm just about to send Doc a wisenheimer remark when a message pops up.

Strata Godsick: Quantum, we need to meet.

I stop dead in my tracks and read the message again.

No sensation whatsoever. Had I been in my real body and received this message, I would have lost my shit. I'm talking about heart in the throat, nerves firing, anger boiling, adrenaline pumping – nope, nada, zilch, squat. None of the anxious behaviors of your typical human having received a message from their arch nemesis is *remotely* evident in my demeanor, which gives me plenty of time think of what I'd like to say next.

Me: You can go fuck yourself, Strata.

~*~

I pace for a minute as I wait for a response. I fire off a copy of the message to Doc, whose mammalian instincts engage in a way mine currently cannot.

Doc: The big bad bear has finally come out of the cave! Testicular torsion works, and this mofo really isn't going to like what we do next.

Me: What do I?

I look down at my hands, look through the e-skin and the complex wiring, look down to their metal cores. A bird chirps in the tree above me and I immediately identify it as a Vesper Sparrow.

Doc: Engage. If the bastard wants to meet, I'd say meet him. He can't do anything to you in your current form – that's the beauty of this! Set up the meeting for tomorrow because tonight is Operation Daughter-Nab.

Me: You sure?

Doc: Yes, I'm sure! I'll alert Euphoria.

Me: I can tell her.

Doc: You really don't understand how pissed she is, do you? You'd think with your advanced processing speeds that you'd know what's going on here, but I digress, I'll give you shit later – contact Strata now.

I hesitate for a moment. When given a direct line to your sworn enemy, what should one say? I already said what I wanted to say, nothing new about that, and really, peace talks have never been my MO. Luckily for yours truly, Strata is the first to reply.

Strata Godsick. I've been told that you were able to reach my son.

Me: Nope. Never heard of the guy.

Strata Godsick: You have his body, or should I say, Doc Paulin has his body. In Texas.

Me: Nope, also not true. Also, it's Paulson.

Strata Godsick: It's both. Would it be helpful if I give you a satellite view of where he's being held?

An image appears and with it comes a complete schematic of Doc's farm. Something ain't right – Doc's shit would never be out in the open like that – and after forwarding the image to Doc, my thoughts are justified.

Doc: Not mine. Let him think it is.

I take a seat on the steps that lead to the apartment above Sophia's and return my focus to the conversation with Strata.

Me: I wouldn't go after Doc if I were you.

Strata Godsick: Doc went after my son.

Me: Yeah? And you went after me, Frances, and Zedic. What goes around, comes around, and payback is a bitch.

Strata Godsick: I want to get a message to my son.

Me: And I want to spend the rest of my days in Margaritaville with Jimmy Buffett.

Strata Godsick: I would like to arrange a meeting with you later today in Denver. The Revenue Corporation would pay your airfare and your accommodations.

Me: Tomorrow, I'm busy today, and I'll get to Denver on my own accord.

Strata Godsick: I see. Would tomorrow work for you?

Me: You bet your ass it would.

Strata Godsick: Fine, tomorrow. The Revenue Corporate headquarters in Denver @ 13:00. Come alone. No lawyers.

Chapter Two

Come alone my ass. If Strata really thinks I'm going to show up without mi amigos, he has another think coming.

Doc: I've reviewed the rest of conversation you had with him. You did good, and he's an idiot if he thinks you'll be going alone.

Me: You can review my feed?

Doc: Pfft! You act like I haven't been hacking since the late 1990s.

Me: I can only imagine what he wants to meet about. It's likely a trap.

Doc: Let it be a trap. You'll be in a Humandroid body. There's nothing he can do to you. About today. You'll fly out to Cali at 10 EST, and arrive at 8:30 PST. I have you two booked on a hyperjet, by the way.

Me: First class, right?

Doc: Sure, keep dreaming. Get ready, and wake the good doctor up.

The time flashes on my iNet screen. It's barely six and I'm already up and at 'em, sans my favorite breakfast or the warm touch of Frances Euphoria. That's going to take some healing, but I'll make it right, and maybe making it right begins with manning up; *not* getting my ass into trouble by walking that tight line between jerk face and sardonic commentator, and keeping the references less obscure even with my advanced research abilities.

So then, Strata finally wants to show his ugly mug. What could he possibly want to discuss? Is it strictly a trap? What could he be planning?

For the first time in a while, my thoughts shift to Ray Steampunk.

I don't know if Humandroids are capable of hearing the whispers of higher consciousness, but the name rings out again and it gets me thinking – what could Ray Steampunk know? He obviously knows more about Strata than he's letting on, but *what* else could he possibly know?

~*~

Boy do I hate to wake a sleeping monster. Standing over Sophia now – ominously, I might add, as a vital scan displays the ups and downs of her sleep cycle – I get the notion that a sleeping Sophia is better than an awakened one and I nearly turn on my heels and take my artificial ass back outside. But time is of the essence, and I'm turning a new leaf, dammit, so I pat her on the head.

"We gotta dive."

"What?" She wakes, wipes drool from her mouth, adjusts her nightie, tries to flatten her Asian fro, and finally squints at me again, as if she doesn't recognize me.

"Sophia. Dive. Now."

"Why are you up so early? I was actually, finally getting a good night's sleep!" She drops her head back onto the armrest, which I subsequently nudge with my knee. "Come on, Sophia, get your shit together and let's log in. Eat whatever gerbil food you're going to eat for breakfast – we don't have much time."

She yawns. "Log in? What are you talking about?"

"You and I need to go to Steam and see our old pal Ray Steampunk."

Her second yawn is even larger this time. "Ray Steampunk? What are you talking about?"

"Sophia."

"Carry me to my bedroom and I'll *think* about it." She lifts her arms like a toddler and holds them in the air, her eyes still closed.

Dammit, you.

I reluctantly bend over, scoop her into my arms, and lift her. My iNet screen tells me a load of shit I don't need to know regarding her weight, target weight, hydration levels based on the elasticity of her skin, and core temperature. I ignore them as I grudgingly make my way to her bedroom, which is messy and which triggers another set of notices about possible safety hazards.

I toss her down onto the bed and she cries out. "Hey! That's rude!"

"You dumb melon!" Chuntao chimes in from a speaker on her dresser. I had almost forgotten about Sophia's damn AI who is fond of berating me in Chinese. "Do anything else and I will contact the authorities!"

"Sophia, quit acting like I hurt you and tell your AI to shut up or better still, shut off."

"Why are you being a jerk this morning?" She curls up into a ball, holding her knees to her chest. "I'm cold. Is it cold in here?"

Deep breath, I tell myself; some good that does in a droid's body. "Sophia, the reason we need to log in is because of Strata Godsick."

She uncurls a bit and looks over her shoulder at me. "Come again?"

"He contacted me this morning. I want to ask Ray Steampunk some questions *before* we head out to California."

Talk about lighting a fire under her ass. Sophia rolls out of bed, skips into her closet, emerges a minute later in more appropriate clothing and instructs Chuntao in Mandarin to prepare her haptic chair.

"Where's your chair?" I ask, looking around her room. She nods at what I thought was a pyramid-sized pile of clothing in the corner.

"How's Chuntao going to help you clear that?"

My question is answered a moment later when a very old robot pushes past me. The mech is about the size of a trashcan and runs on three motorized wheels. Its body swivels at the waist and its arms remind me of the twigs you'd stick into a snowman. It passes me and sure enough, an angry face illuminates the back of its aluminum top.

"Yeah, right back at you, Chuntao."

"Do not antagonize her," Sophia grabs my arm and leads me to the living room.

"You never told me she had an actual physical form in your home."

"That's just a vehicle I designed to get her around the house if I needed some additional help." One look at all the clothing, boxes, papers scattered around her living room makes me think Chuntao is doing a terrible job of keeping the place tidy.

"You designed that? I've seen those before, back in the late 2020s."

"No, I didn't design the robot. It's vintage. I designed the interface that allows my AI assistant to operate the robot's body. Lie down on the couch; just like yesterday. I'll get you hooked up and I'll meet you in there."

~*~

"Back so soon?" Aiden asks.

"We gotta get to Steam," I tell Morning Assassin instead of hello. I sit, take the visor off and wait for my gaze to adjust on the guy who tried to kill me for five hundred and fifty-something days straight. He's in a red terry cloth robe with the letters MA embroidered on the front. His loungewear blurs as his assassin clothes take shape. Snake-Eyes would be proud of the armored yet flexible black milspec armor Aiden has chosen for our little excursion to Steam. A mask over his mouth, his cheeks stretch as he gives me his patented wolfish grin.

A flash of light and Sophia's form takes shape. For once, she's in our standard issue Dream Team duds, the same tight collared black number that Frances usually wears.

"Looking good, Doctor Wang," says Aiden. "You found a body for me yet up there?"

"You asked me that last time," she says, "and as I said last time, this guy has your body." She throws a thumb to me.

I shrug. "Sorry, buster."

Sophia's finger comes up and with it, a complex menu screen. She adjusts some things and the light inside the OMIB-yurt dims. Another few flicks of her fingers and a spawning point appears. It floats between the three of us, tendrils of code filtering off its bottom perimeter.

"Done showing off?" I tell her. "We get it; you've got the place under control."

She lifts her nose at me. "I just wanted to check to make sure your ex hadn't infiltrated our system."

"My ex?"

"Dolly," Aiden coughs.

"Let's get to Steam." Sophia presses her finger into the spawning point and her form vanishes. Flickers of vertical Thulean script now rim the spawning point.

I turn to Aiden, give him the eye roll that Sophia would likely give me, and jam my finger onto the spawning point. One flashdance later and I'm standing on a grassy knoll, a fairground really, which sits far enough away from the city of Locus to give a pretty good panoramic picture.

Locus, the capital city of Steam, is a cosplayer's wet dream complete with more pipes than a head shop. Billowy clouds of steam, gears on clock towers cranking, the orange dusk accents the two moons in the sky, and everything has a brassy sheen to it. I can't say I've missed the place, but it's definitely nice to be someplace other than Tritania or The Loop.

I equip my steam pack, item 564, and stick the nozzle in the port on my arm. My vision pane pulses, letting me know I'm juiced and ready to go.

"I totally forgot it was Balloon Day!" Sophia says. The Dream Team's Brainiac has kept her elven ears and western features, but her threads are all steampunk. She's gone with a lacy black top exposing a pair of inflated gazongas barely covered by a brass necklace featuring an eye at the center of a golden gear. Her lower half is barely covered by a skirt decorated with enough pockets to store half of Dirty Dave's wares, and seeing as how they're so short, she's wearing fishnet panty hose which dips into high-heeled boots decorated with gears.

The golden indicator over her head flashes and dims. "He gave me one!" She pumps her fist in the air. "A golden indicator ... it's such an honor."

"Give me a break," I mumble under my breath.

Welcome to Steam. Please take a moment to remember some of the rules of this world:

1) Players using items that rely upon electricity will be penalized through their life bars.

2) Shillings are used as a currency in Steam. Unlike some Proxima Worlds, they have no real world value.

3) Alchemical practices are fine as long as they fit within the boundaries of the world, which are accessible through your player dashboard.

4) Discriminatory comments will be logged. Repeated violations will result in account termination.

"Yeah, yeah," I swipe them just as Aiden appears. A golden indicator flashes over his head as well, reminding me that we're allowed to equip whatever we'd like here regardless of the rules.

"Oooo! I want to get steampunked out."

A flick of his finger and Aiden is ready for the next Steampunk Cosplay Convention. Like some sort of killer Abe, he's gone with a top hat, a tailored dark blue dinner jacket which perfectly sets off his black cravat and red velvet vest. Tucked into the front pocket of his vest is a gold pocket watch which matches the accents on his mechanical hands.

For his lower half, he's in skinny slacks and big boots which, like Sophia, have enough gears to supply an industrial loom in 19th century Manchester. True to his normal shtick – the bottom half of his mug is covered by a mask.

"Well, glad you two could find the time to play dress up."

I snap my fingers and go with my tried and true Loop gladrags – a black trench coat and black everything else, down to my stompers. *Balloon Day, huh?* I think as I take in my surroundings. Talk about a spawning point. All around us are hot air balloons in various states of inflation. The balloons are a patchwork of colors, some singular in nature and the others stitched together. The roar of the flames supplying the hot air and the chatter and calls from the crews manning the balloons grates against my digital eardrums. I don't know who picked the spawning point, but methinks we could have found a place with a little less activity.

I cup my hands around my mouth. "Ray Steampunk! We're in a hurry, so if you could just teleport us to wherever you are … "

An explosion to my immediate left is followed by screams and cries for help.

Aiden has his Slice Bang out before I can even register what the hell has just happened. It's a good thing too; another explosion sends gears and limbs spraying into the air. The blast tosses Sophia and Yours Truly to the ground. I pop up with item 198, my handheld M134 minigun, slung at my side.

No sense in sorting out bystanders from baddies, I lay into the stygian cloud of smoke from the blast direction. Chicago lightning has a way of leveling the playing field. and it's only when Sophia forcibly pushes my hand down do I take my finger off the trigger.

"There are innocent bystanders over there!"

The little-used clawed glove hack that Doc gave her is now on her hand. It spreads up her arm and turns an icy-blue as the symbiose pulsates. Into the air Sophia goes, where she can get a better look.

Sure, I could go with item 567, my steam-powered jetpack, but to add a little flair and really look like a badass, I go with item 254, Dr. Strange's Cloak of Levitation. The fancy red cloak appears and settles onto my shoulders and I'm neck and neck with Sophia in seconds flat, still with my minigun equipped, mind you, scanning the two smoldering craters for any enemy activity.

"Show off," she says under her breath.

"You'd better believe it."

I see Aiden step in and out of reality, slice through a muscled guy with a ...

"You're shitting me." If I had a cigar in my mouth it would have dropped out by now.

Rocket: Reapers incoming!

"Rocket's here?" I shake my head. "More importantly – Reapers!"

The beefed up, skull-masked, creatine-chugging Village People reject turns to blast Aiden and is swiftly met with the clickety-boom end of Morning Assassin's Persian sword and gun combo. The skull-masked jobbie's face explodes and steam billows out of the wound.

Rocket: Kill 'em dead!

Sophia: You're late!

Rocket: Sorry, I was washing my hair!

I see a Reaper broad in a requisite skull mask , corset, and boy shorts charge at Aiden.

I cut her down with a wall-o-bullets that tosses dust, steam blood, and debris into the air. A portal opens and three more Reapers spill out. Back-up has arrived, but by the looks of the three Punisher wannabees, the runts of litter are in high supply. It only takes one blast from Sophia's iced-up claw hack to freeze one of them in place and force the other two to wet their Dom jeans and logout, rather than face a similar fate.

"My favorite thing to do!" Up in the air I go.

One superhero landing later and I'm in front of the frozen Reaper, smiling as I figure out the best way to murdalize. Since the mutant hack is an algoweapon, and while world-specific, the icy blast is technically an algospell, the Reaper trapped inside isn't allowed to log out. A little torture never hurt nobody, so I equip my ice pick, item 538, and get to sculpt. I channel New York mobster Abe Reles as I quickly hammer the pick into the spot where the Reaper's ear should be.

Sophia lands behind me. "Are you sick in the head?"

"Nope, but this one will soon be!"

She grunts, rolls her eyes, lifts her claw back and Mr. Freezes another cloaked Reaper, who uses his AA to logout before the icy treatment can take full effect.

Damn sissy.

"That should just about do it," I say as the pick is all the way in frozen Reaper chippie's head. One cerebral hemorrhage later, and the dumb deadly dame is dead and done for.

Aiden flash dances and is suddenly next to me. "The Abe Reles treatment, huh?" He sticks a finger in his ear and twists it. "I remember when you did that to me."

"I'm pretty sure you did it to me as well," I tell him.

Rocket: You guys did it to each other!

Me: Rocket, howzabout being helpful for once and use your hacking skills to figure out where Ray Steampunk is. As much as I'd like to torture Reapers – and I'm not gonna lie, I could do it all day – this is a job for Ray's Air Enforcers.

Rocket: You got it, Steamboy. Um, let me ask my ladybird if she's heard anything.

Me: Ladybird?

Rocket: My gf, that's my nickname for her.

Me: Got it. Report back.

"Thank you!" An NPC with a mechanized peg leg – no idea how that is supposed to help anyone do anything – hobbles over to us. He's got a pair of oversized Leaks over his eyes and his white hair is done up in a curtain style way, the ends of which hang over the straps of his Leaks.

His eyes flash orange.

"Right this way," he says, his voice suddenly monotone. He motions towards a hot air balloon out of range of the explosions. The balloon is nearly full of air; the ignition fire is roaring and even though I'm no hot air balloon expert, I'd say it's ready for takeoff in t-minus five minutes.

"Ray, cut the crap," I tell the sky. "We have a hefty load on our plate and it'd be just as easy for you to zap us to your current location."

"And miss out on the beautiful view?" Peg Leg asks.

"Weapons up." Aiden follows his own advice with a custom Zastava M77 B1. He keeps his shooting iron aimed at the incoming targets until their forms become more visible.

"Yay! The Air Enforcers have arrived," says Sophia.

The first one touches down. His jetpack flares up once more and he digs his finger into a button clasped in his palm to stop it. "Ahem," he says, embarrassed by the malfunction. Once he has smoothed out his tan Hitler-youth clothing, he removes his Rocketeer helmet and instructs us to clear away from the area.

"Yeah, yeah," I tell the gung-ho enforcer. Others land around him and they begin securing the perimeter. The fact that these boy scouts haven't interrogated us means Ray Steampunk is puppetmastering them as usual.

Peg Leg pipes up. "Please, this way." He turns to his hot air balloon. "It won't be long now."

~*~

Ninety nine red balloons, floating in the summer sky. Panic bells, it's red alert, there's something here from somewhere else.

Sophia pipes down after a long series of oohs and ahhs. The fact that she can fly in Steam and should not be so mesmerized by a hot air balloon is something I fail to mention in a surly manner. Who can blame her? The view from the hot air balloon is enchanting, stable too, which is something I'll have to bring up with Mirror next time I have a chance encounter with that damn snooty dragon.

Nothing like a joy ride after mopping up some Reapers.

We ain't the only balloon or zephyr in the sky. Half the dreamworld seems to be out, and they range from balloons with bicycle-powered burners to a bathtub kept afloat by a pair of dwarfs with bagpipes under their arms pumping medicine ball-sized balloons. One couple has a hotdog-shaped balloon. Beneath it, they sit on a picnic blanket sharing a bottle of wine and dangling their feet off the sides.

I take a deep breath of digital goodness. There's still some of the smoke from Locus up here, but it isn't as bad as it is in the city proper. Other than that, and the myriad, obnoxious balloons, it's a damn pretty day.

Rocket: You have a very fond look on your face right now.

Me: Peanut Gallery – why must you interpret my moment of reverie?

Rocket: What were you reverie-ing?

Sophia squeezes my arm. "It's just sooooo beautiful, isn't it?"

Aiden gives me a look that says, 'what's with you and the good doctor?' I'm just about to casually flash him the one finger salute when Peg Leg fires up the burner, adding more go up-ness to the balloon.

We lift over a smaller balloon powered by a three-wheeled steamcycle. Peg Leg waves to the pilot of the vessel, a tall woman in full Victorian regalia, her hourglass figure enhanced by a corset tied off by a black cord. She blows him a kiss and Peg Leg turns to me and winks.

"Lots of fine young lasses with fine young asses during Hot Air Balloon day!" He says with a Kit-Cat Clock grin on his face. "Meet with me later and I'll take you to a spot where the liquor runs as freely as the women!" His eyes flash orange as Ray the bummer Steampunk takes over his avatar. "I have instructed him to take you to my airship. He will remain silent up until that point so you can enjoy the views."

"Ray, has anyone ever told you that you're no fun?"

Aiden scoots up next to me and leans his arms on the basket's bannister. "You know, we really don't spend enough time here."

"I suppose since Ray pretty much gave us god-like powers here, we could raise a little more hell and to be honest, if he needs help cleaning up the Reaper riffraff that are still here, I'm more than down."

He nods. "Why do you think they're here?"

"They could have been tracking us … "

He shakes his head. "They weren't attacking us; they were attacking innocents."

"Odd. Well, I got no problem snuffing them out while my ass is still stuck in The Loop. Next time I'll get them with my Reaper Hack."

Aiden's mask stretches as he grins. "Maybe a little hunting session is in order. You, me, Doc."

Rocket: What about me?

"What about Rocket?"

"The kid too. As long as he's down to bring his A-game."

Peg Leg gooses the hot air balloon again and it lifts even higher.

We're the highest balloon in the sky, and from this vantage point, I finally see the outline of Ray Steampunk's airship, which sits over Clockpunch Mountain in the midst of mahoosive clouds of billowy steam.

The biplanes take off from the runway and perfectly arc in the air as they make their way over the city of Locus. They spray colored smoke into the air, red, brown, and orange, and as they change their formation, twisting over one another, the streams of smoke mix together and suddenly turn sulfuric yellow. As they continue to speed along, they make triangles and other geometric shapes in the air.

"Just ... so ... beautiful!"

I turn to Sophia and smile. "You want a picture?"

"You have a camera in your list?"

"Do I have a camera ... " I scroll behind my back to item 107, my Polaroid camera. "All right, Aiden, getchur ass over there and no wise guy stuff in the photo, got it?"

Top hatted Morning Assassin in his Sunday steampunk best moves to the other side of the basket and slips an arm under Sophia's. I raise the camera, giving him enough time to make bunny ears over her head.

One click later and I'm shaking the Polaroid film, waiting for the strange, sepia image to settle.

Chapter Three

I can see the glimmer from Ray Steampunk's golden gladrags and gilded cape long before we're close enough to actually make out his facial features. Steam's NVA Seed stands on the observation deck that defines the upper part of his fairytale castle, his gaze aimed at the myriad hot air balloons now floating over the busy city of Locus and the surrounding forest. He seems incredibly alone; I get the sense that Ray will be like this for all eternity. NPC, RPC, or PC – Steampunk would rather be known for his image and what he represents and remembered as such, as opposed to someone with actual feelings.

I'd be best to remind myself not to end up like him.

I give him a wave just to do something and Ray Steampunk ignores me, the cocky bastard. I remind myself of the reason I've come here, *Strata Godsick*. Right now it's still a hunch, but I have the feeling that old Ray is holding out on me.

Our hot air balloon is suddenly suspended in air, as if trapped in the pull of a tractor beam.

It moves slowly towards the Godfather of Steam now, who doesn't even grace us with the 'lift of his hand to show that I'm using powers' pose. Nope, he's stone cold stationary as ever with no expression on his mug.

Once we're closer, the balloon clips away, leaving the three of us and Ray's peglegged goon looking like a bunch of idiots in a floating wicker basket.

"He's so majestic," I hear Sophia murmur.

"For the love of … " I bite my tongue. I'm still learning how not to trigger Sophia; she has a ways to go to figure out how not to trigger me.

"Don't you think?" she asks, digging the knife in and twisting. "His overall demeanor is just so … god-like. Like some Greek god, Apollo or Zeus. Everyone in Steam loves him. *Everyone.*"

Rocket: He's soooooo dreamy, isn't he? I wish I could be like Ray Steampunk and live in an airship all alone while running my almost-fascist world where I'm treated both as a god and a celebrity.

Me: Thata boy, kid. Get 'em!

Rocket: How's my sarcasm coming along?

Me: It needs work.

Rocket: Wait a minute … are you being sarcastic?

Me: Zing! You got me again.

Sophia lifts her nose. "You two really don't understand what a big deal it is to meet Ray Steampunk. Most of the people down there," she motions towards the city, "only dream of one day meeting the creator. Most never meet him."

Rocket:

The argument is over by the time the basket lands on the observation deck. Aiden is the first out. He greets Ray with nod and takes up station at the far end of the deck. Looking like a donut with a control tower poking out of its center, the observation deck is completely stripped of all its furniture, showcasing Ray's minimalist side. Not far from where we stand, a girning gargoyle snorts steam at irregular intervals.

I hop out of the basket and walk right up to the Big Bad Wolf of Steam, who continues to act as if we hadn't just landed. Like always, he speaks without moving his lips. "Hello, Steamboy."

"Heya, Rayski."

Mr. T would be jelly if he saw the numerous golden necklaces looped around Steampunk's neck. That and his golden suit of armor, his long flowing black hair, his all black eyes – I wouldn't be surprised if he doesn't have a painted portrait of himself standing in front of a painted portrait of himself hanging over his bed.

"Mardis Gras with Midas again, eh?"

He ignores me and greets my compatriots instead. "Hello, Dr. Wang, NPC 8-10."

"It's Aiden," Morning Assassin bristles.

"Glad you all could join me, and I must thank you for the fight you put up against the Reapers at the fairgrounds. I don't expect you to fight my battles for me here in Steam ..."

I almost cough *bullshit* into my hand.

"... and I thank you for it. That said, the Reapers have continued to join with the Boiler Plate Army and the Marauders in Morlock, doing everything in their power to thwart the livelihood of those who choose to visit Steam."

"You're the NVA Seed," I remind him. "Why don't you just force any Reaper who logs in to instantly logout? And that's if you're being nice! I can think of a bazillion things I would do to extract revenge on my enemies if I were in your big, golden, Ronald McStarbucks shoes, Ray ol' pal. From force-spawning them in the Imperium latrine to making them constantly punch themselves in the face, and that's without getting weird, like making them spawn with the bodies inside out."

Sophia makes an icky face.

Steampunk clasps his hands together behind his back and turns away from us. "I wouldn't want a discriminatory lawsuit in the real world, now would I?"

"He's right," Dr. Brainulo says. "The Revenue Corporation could bring a lawsuit against the parent company that Mr. Steampunk set up to handle assets, both real world and here in Steam."

Mr. Steampunk?

His clean shaven visage tightens into a grin. "Besides, and I think even you may agree with this, hunting Reapers makes a great quest for others to embark upon."

I consider this for a moment. "Yeah, I could definitely go for a little of that."

"What is it that you'd like to ask of me?" He looks towards the hot air balloons for a moment, the look on his face completely indecipherable.

"Right, let's get down to business. It's like this, Ray. We need to know whatever it is you know about Strata."

"Oh?"

A red biplane passes above us. Aiden's weapon comes up and he lowers it once he's confirmed that the pilot isn't a hostile. Sophia and

Yours Truly? Not so much. I wait a moment for Ray to say something, hoping that he'll at least throw us a bone.

Nope, nada, zilch, squat.

"All right," I say, trying not to get snappy. "You want the lowdown on what happened today? Maybe that will inspire you to tell us something we don't already know. It's like this, Ray, Strata contacted me this morning, and he wants to meet tomorrow. Now before you say anything, I should also tell you that we zapped his daughter, Veenure, or Victoria, or 'that traitorous bitch', with a Reaper hack preventing her from logging in. And Luther? We found his tookus too, on a bizarre-ass turtle island that appears randomly in the Endless Sea."

"*Bitakh Morla,*" Sophia corrects me. "That's the Thulean word for the island."

"That's some narrative," The Prophet of Steam finally says.

"And there's more ... " I look to Sophia and she shakes her head. "I mean, that's it, that's the story. There isn't any more."

"You're referring to Doctor Wang's experiment and the fact that in the real world, you currently inhabit a Humandroid's body, are you not?"

The nerve of this guy. He still has his back to us, yet his voice is loud and clear, as if he's looking right at us. Without turning, he taps his finger against his temple. "You may recall that I'm the NVA Seed."

"So you're reading our minds then? And yeah, Ray, we do recall that. You'd never let us forget it, you boisterous putz."

"Quantum!"

"What?" I shrug at Sophia.

Ray keeps his back to us as he says, "I'm not reading your minds as much as I am *browsing* them. And you, Dr. Wang, have accomplished something of considerable acclaim, something that would make your colleagues green with envy. I applaud you for it."

Her face fills with light. "Thank you, Mr. Steampunk."

He waves her gratitude away, *his back still to us.* "That said, I'm afraid that what you've done will never reach the light of day, as they say up there."

Sophia shoulders drop. Her goofy grin from earlier is all but wiped away by Ray's last statement.

"You shouldn't take it as an affront to your accomplishment; rather, you should take your successful experiment for what it is – something that could change the face of human and Humandroid kind. NPCs are … " he pauses, letting the roar from a landing biplane to settle. "NPCs have different reasoning capabilities from Humandroids. They are much more like you than an artificial being could ever be. You may be thinking, 'Humandroids are artificial beings' but you are incorrect, unless you consider humans artificial beings as well. Then we are all artificial."

"Not buying it, Ray," I say, "and I don't mean that disrespectfully for once. It's like this: humans created Humandroids and NPCs and, well, you as a matter of fact as an RPC are basically a glorified NPC, hate to break it to you. The Proxima Company has servers that hold all this information, from your world to Tritania to disbanded Proxima Worlds, like The Loop."

"Cyber Noir."

"*Tomay-toes, tomah-toes.* Riddle me this: what if someone attacked the central storage, or for that matter, since the Proxima Company has storage all around the globe, *all* the storage places? What happens? You and this world would cease to exist. Therefore, and I'm not trying to be a dick here, you are artificial."

He smirks. "What if NPCs with Humandroid hosts attacked the real world, every part of the real world, and killed all of humanity through, say, a biological attack? Then you and your world would cease to exist."

"Yours would die too."

"Not necessarily. What if these same NPCs with Humandroid hosts kept the servers and the necessary public works that power humanity going, and these Humandroids hunted down any person left alive, or perhaps kept a select group in, say, an isolated canyon just to observe them under laboratory conditions?"

"It would be artificial. All of this is hypothetical."

"Artificiality is in the eye of the beholder, and without mentioning Schrödinger's cat – but *heavily* nodding towards its implications – this theoretical world, this new NPC-Humandroid world without humans, is exactly why Sophia's discovery must *never* reach the light of day. It must not be published, spoken about, written about, or broadcast in any way. It must be buried."

He lets this sink in for a moment.

"Her discovery, after you've returned to your body, must be completely wiped from the records of humanity."

~*~

"All right, Ray," I wave my hands, ready to get down to business, "you won. You're smarter than I am."

Rocket: I could have told you that!

I curl my fists, bite my bottom lip, grind my heel into the airship, and wait for Ray to acknowledge his intellectual superiority or walk it back. Instead, the God of Steam paces for a moment with his hands clasped behind his back.

A quick glance to Aiden and I see that The Loop's killer diller killer has grown bored with our conversation. His eyes haven't quite glazed over, but he does yawn, evident in the way his eyes narrow and the front of his mask stretches.

Ray finally turns to me. "I am the one who created the algorithm that trapped people in the Proxima Galaxy."

"Come again?" I look to Sophia. "Did you just say you're basically the one that got me trapped in The Loop?"

If I wasn't pissed earlier, I sure as hell am now. I take a few steps closer to Ray, scrolling through my list behind my back. I don't think I'll be able to get a weapon up fast enough, and it likely wouldn't help if I could, but that doesn't mean I won't give it a shot, and by *it* I mean *Ray*. I stop on item 331, my Zeo Blaster. What happens when the Zeo Power Rangers combine all their gear? This bad boy with no less than four muzzles.

"Quantum!" I hear Sophia hiss from behind me.

"I created an algorithm that trapped people, not the *glitch*," Ray says. "Parsing matters, and you can put your Zeo Blaster away. It won't do you any good."

"I know, but that never stopped me from trying," I grit.

"That's what I've always liked about you, Quantum. You never were one to give up, no matter the odds."

Ray Steampunk giving me a compliment? This HAS TO be a dream. I return my Zeo Blaster to my list and pinch myself to be sure.

Ray Steampunk's deep voice is again in my ear. "What I was referring to is those whom you call the bleached people. What I created led to the invention of the collar that keeps them from logging out."

"You wanted to imprison people in Steam?" I ask. Even Aiden is listening now.

"Of course not. I invented it in a failed experiment to free you. Strata reached out to me regarding your imprisonment – and I should note that at this time, no one could get into The Loop even through OMIB-porting but we knew with the right tweaks that this could change, so I went to work on creating a portable logout point by studying the glitch. It backfired and to be quite honest with you, it was my fault. I was working on a dozen things at the time and my code was just … off. It was off. I didn't know at the time that there was an actual logout point. If you didn't already know, the glitch only temporarily prevented you from logging out. However, this was enough time for a human body to expire in the real world, so Cyber Noir's NVA Seed kept the logout point from you to protect you, assuming you had died up there."

"The seed–"

"–Dolly," says Morning Assassin.

I swallow hard. Somehow it always comes back to her.

"Dolly was operating under the impression that *if* she allowed you to log out, you'd die. She wasn't able to use your mind to figure out the basics of diving to a VE dreamworld; she truly believed that letting you log out would have killed you for good, then the Dream Team showed up and here we are now."

"That simple, huh?"

He ignores my quip. "All I knew at the time I reverse-engineered the glitch was that the portable logout point I had developed didn't work; that it backfired, trapping a player in a world. So I scrapped the idea; Strata, seeing its potential, tweaked it a bit more and created a way to prevent a person *from* logging out."

"The collar the bleachies wore!" How could I forget those mangy emaciated fiends covered in scratch marks with tufts of their hair ripped out fighting each other as they tried to overwhelm me? The dirty fiends.

"It all makes sense now," Sophia says.

I instinctively touch my neck. "So when the Reapers first reached out to me, promising to free me, they really would have enslaved me using the same collar?"

Rocket: DUH!

"Dammit, kid," I tell the sky. "I'm just confirming things here!"

"Precisely. You were lucky that Frances Euphoria showed up when she did." He gives me a long, hard look. "But I think you already knew that."

"Shit, Ray, why don't you bust my balls a little more?" I mumble under my breath.

"So, if you're wondering what I would tell you about Strata and your plan to meet him, I would say you are in the perfect position to do so in your Humandroid body, as long as you don't tell him that you are again stuck in The Loop. He knows enough about military software to be familiar with InterHead. He won't be happy, but he'll think Doc is having you meet him in a Humandroid body. It's ironic, really, the fact that you're trapped in The Loop again may work to your advantage."

Sophia relays my next thought before I can get the words out of my mouth. "Mr. Steampunk, my question is in regards to Quantum's recent predicament. Cyber Noir's NVA Seed–"

"–Dolly," Aiden says again.

"…Has completely removed the logout option from Quantum's user menu. She's imprisoned herself behind an anti-OMIB palisade that appears to be impenetrable. I ran a few numbers in my head, and based on what I've learned about alien Proxima world algorithmic receptivity, I am under the impression that the Rare Proxima Galaxy metal, Chronoton, could be crafted into a device that could cut through the A-OMIB P, if combined with another type of RPG metal. What are your thoughts on my hypothesis and what, if anything, would you do to increase the likelihood of penetrating the A-OMIB P?"

Ray Steampunk considers this for a moment. "Chronoton could be crafted into a Reality Splitter in Tritania, which would work for *Tritania* only. Your assumption is correct. To guarantee that the Reality Splitter works in Cyber Noir, I'd advise you to create a Chronoton and Sky Iron alloy."

"Sky-Iron?" Sophia's eyes flicker. "I'm sorry, but I'm unfamiliar with the metal."

"That's because you've never heard of it," Steampunk says in an almost condescending tone. "Sky Iron is a dark RPG metal mined in a walled off prison city known as Akrasia, which is on the outskirts of Morlock. It also happens to be where the Reapers have been spawning."

"Morlock? Isn't that the place where we handed the Reapers and Marauders their asses not too long ago?"

Steampunk nods. "Yes, you beat them in the northwest corridor of the city known as the Rust Belt. There are other parts, and Akrasia is one of these parts."

I smirk. "Are you saying what I think you're saying, Ray ol' buddy, ol' pal, ol' stick-in-the-mud?"

"I am unaware of how you'd like me to answer that. Do you happen to have any blacksmith friends?"

"The Knights of Non Compos Mentis has a blacksmith in the guild, a Brazilian kid named Chrono."

"You'll need him, too. Get the metal, and while you're at it, take out as many Reapers as you'd like." With that, Ray turns away from us; his golden cape blows ever-so-slightly in the breeze that picks up. "And the fun doesn't end there."

"What do you mean?"

"Once you cut into Dolly's fortress, technically her A-OMIB P, you may need to kill her before she kills you."

"Kill Dolly?" I gulp. The thought is even worse than the shitty little scenario that the Sage of Gotha cooked up for me. I look to Aiden, who for the first time ever, carries true fear in his eyes.

"If put together correctly, a weapon made of Sky Iron and Chronoton will have slicing capability equivalent to a source code bomb."

Sophia raises her finger to add something.

"Yes, Dr. Wang, I'm aware that saying it like this is over-simplifying it." Ray Steampunk narrows his black eyes on me. "Be prepared to kill her if you hope to ever log out of Cyber Noir."

Chapter Four

"Not gonna lie, I am frickin' stoked about a couple of things at the moment," I tell Sophia.

We're back in her living room; the morning sun has started to warm the place up, which wouldn't bother me so much if it weren't for the fact I received a notification with every subtle change in temperature.

Sophia's vitals appear on my Humandroid's iNet screen but I ignore them. Doc's combat protocols have finished updating and just thinking about them narrows my viewing pane, displaying a vast library of techniques and concepts, everything from Sun Tzu to Massad Ayoob.

"What has you so stoked?" After placing her sleek pink NV Visor on its wireless charging port, she returns to the couch and tells Chuntao to prepare a bath for her. The AI responds and tells her how beautiful she looks. I try to roll my eyes, or at least I think that's what I'm doing. "And what are you doing with your eyes?"

"Never mind," I tell her. "I'm stoked for a number of reasons. One, Doc has given me enough combat knowledge to open up a can of whoop ass in a variety of creative ways. Two, today we finished what we started – Veenure is ours. Three, the Boys of Non Compos Mentis are due for an adventure in Steam to retrieve this rare metal. Four, this rare metal will hopefully get my ass out of The Loop. So that's why I'm stoked. Life is peachy."

She yawns.

"That's contagious, you know."

"No it isn't; you didn't yawn."

I open my mouth to yawn and nothing happens. Weird. I never thought about how satisfying a yawn could be. Suddenly, I want to yawn, I want to feel human at this moment more than ever. And like that, it passes. I'm back to being stuck in Evan's metal meatsack.

"You okay?" Sophia asks.

"Yeah, fine, no problem. Just feeling sorry for myself."

Her hand lands on my leg and she squeezes it. "Awwww, it's okay, don't worry about a thing. I'm here for you if you want to talk about it."

"What kind of depressing droid have you invited into our home?" Chuntao asks in Mandarin.

"You'd be best to keep your trap shut, Chuntao, unless you want me to gut every electronic item in the place." I turn to Sophia. "For the love of all that is holy, Sophia, can you keep your AI under control?"

She stands, turns to the holoscreen and places her hands on her hips. The gesture lifts her nighty enough for me to get a peek of the bottom of her ass cheeks.

Dammit, Sophia.

"Chuntao, you will now treat Quantum with the same respect that you treat me. Are we clear here? This Humandroid is a guest in my home and he will be treated as such!"

Chuntao responds with a bit of ass thunder, which only riles Sophia more. "I'm serious, Chuntao, and stop with the farting noises! It is very unprofessional!"

We're both quiet for a moment, seeing how Chuntao will respond. Finally, after what feels like two minutes of silence, Chuntao lets out a squeaker and the electricity in the place shuts off.

"Chuntao, turn the breakers back on right this minute!"

The hum of electricity again is quickly met with another air biscuit from Sophia's deeply troubled, absolutely pissy AI.

~*~

Me: Hey, Frances.

I'm outside again, sitting on the stoop which seems to be the thing to do when one is stuck in Baltimore indefinitely. Never thought I'd end up here, and truth be told, I'm usually diving, so 'here' is a fairly relative term, but it ain't a bad morning and soon, my ass will be in LA rubbing elbows with the stars.

Maybe I'll even get a picture in front of the Hollywood sign. Ha!

One of the drones that monitors Sophia's apartment stops in front of me and tries to access my system. Not gonna happen. I wave the little metal turd along and unlike Sophia's stubborn AI, the drone gets the hint. Before it leaves, it blinks its big black camera eye, capturing a high-resolution still shot of my image to go along with the video that it's recording.

Good riddance.

There hasn't been a time in my life in which drones weren't flying around either surveilling or delivering packages. I particularly liked the Halloween drones that used to safely give kids candy in my neighborhood in Ohio. "Trick or treat!" I'd yell up at the drones.

Some of them even gave out full-sized candy bars. Me and my buddies would try to follow the ones giving out full-sized bars. Once, a friend of mine named Colin managed to get one of the drones down with a slingshot. We got in trouble later, but not before eating our weight in candy bars.

The good ol' days.

Me: Frances. Are you awake? I'm just about to go to the airport with Sophia. We visited Ray Steampunk this morning and got some info, but that's not the big news of the day. The big news of the day is Strata.

I wait another minute or so. No idea what Sophia is doing in there or why it takes women so long to put their faces on. Well, most women. Frances never wears much makeup. She has one of those faces that is naturally cute and her short hair needs little to no work to fix. I guess Dolly never put on much makeup either, but that doesn't count, and I don't know why I'm comparing the two.

Looks like Frances, the silent treatment, and Yours Truly will share a complicated three-way relationship for the foreseeable future. I'm just about to give up completely on contacting her when I get a message.

Frances Euphoria: I'm already in California.

Me: Frances! Hi!

Shit, Quantum, hold your horses!

Frances Euphoria: Hi.

Me: How are you doing? Are you with Doc?

Frances Euphoria: He'll be here shortly.

Me: And you? Are you okay?

Frances Euphoria: I'm fine. I'll see you when you get here.

Me: Frances, I know I'm going to keep beating this into the ground, and I'm sorry for that now, but what happened wasn't what you think. I didn't originally go to The Loop to see Dolly. Honest.

Frances Euphoria: I'm over it.

Me: Everyone knows that when someone says 'I'm over it' there's at least a sixty percent chance of meaning I'm *far* from over it.

Frances Euphoria: Quantum, I am done with your shit. Is that what you want to hear?

Me: No, I want to hear …

Sophia exits her apartment with a small rolling suitcase covered in McStarbucks mermaids in front of the golden arches. I give the suitcase the stink eye, or at least, I try to.

"What?" she asks. "It was part of a promo for my McStarbuck's gold card. You don't like it?"

"It's fine." Conspicuous consumption isn't what's on my mind at the moment; again, I'm back on Frances and how to make this right. The thought comes – maybe there isn't a way to fix this and for once.

"You look sad."

"Yeah?" I try to muster something mean, but I just don't have the heart. Sophia can be annoying, but she doesn't deserve to feel the brunt of my current frustration, which is mainly aimed at myself. "Did you pack anything for me? I need some new duds."

"I packed the night clothes we got yesterday and Frances already ordered you new clothes. They're at the hotel in LA."

"She did?"

Sophia nods, unaware of the conversation I've just been having with Frances. "Let's go and remember, *do not* act like an ass or an idiot or an idiot's ass. You're a droid now. Behave like one."

"I yam what I yam," I mumble as I follow her to her little pink aeros.

~*~

Note to self: Never, and I mean never, get an AI assistant.

By the time Sophia's aeros arrives at Baltimore-Washington International Airport, I'm just about ready to crack my head open and pull out the cords that allow me to process and comprehend all things audio.

Chuntao is smarter than I thought – and it pains me to say that – but the damn AI has figured out the best way to get under my skin: talk about me as if I'm not there and ignore any of my comments on the utterly stupid subject. The droid currently discusses how good Sophia looks in her Dream Team outfit even though SHE'S NOT WEARING IT.

Crack a joke and I get a trouser flutter in response. Say something smarmy and my seatbelt tightens. Talk about a load of BS. So it is with hope in my heart that Sophia's aeros lowers into the drop off lane and the two of us get out, bidding Chuntao farewell.

"Please don't flick Chuntao off," Sophia hisses once we are curbside.

Two anklebiters from the aeros minivan behind us catch me giving Chuntao the one finger salute and snicker. Their mother, twice the size of a hippo and with an uglier face to boot, shoots me the 'I'll do anything to protect my bear cubs from the evilness of the world including brainwashing them and purposefully raising them stupid just so they don't have to face the reality of our world' look. She barks for them to cover their eyes, which they do. Hubby, on the other hand, snorts when he sees a droid giving a Barbie pink aeros the bird while an afroed Asian broad berates him and finally, takes matters into her own hands and yanks his arm down.

"Do not bring attention to us!" Sophia hisses. "Do I really need to contact Doc?"

Doc: Already here. Quantum. For the love of all that is holy and good and left on this earth for man, excuse me, *humankind*, to pillage – behave thyself or I'll shut you off and Sophia will have you stowed in the luggage compartment. THIS is your only warning for today.

Me: My bad, Doc. It's Chuntao. It's that damned AI. You'd be pissed too.

Doc: I'm not disagreeing, son, but I need you to get to LA in one piece. That piece can either be checked as luggage or it can sit in economy class.

"I thought we were riding first class," I tell Sophia as we make our way to the entrance. The echo of a large open space meets my robo-ears as we enter the drop-off area. My droid eyes immediately start scanning the area for threats or potential hazards.

A prompt from the airport's AI tells me that it is mandatory that it syncs with my feed through the Watch Our Own People Act. I begrudgingly let it do its sync thing, which ain't too shabby. It not only gives me a schematic of the airport, it also routes me in the fastest way to get to my gate and tells me the wait time in food lines for my human traveller.

What I wouldn't give to have one of those IHOP extra icing extra butter Cinnabun pancakes. Jeez do I wish my mouth could water! One quick look to Sophia's skinny ass as she takes the lead reminds me of my current predicament – methinks we won't be stopping for grub, which is a damn shame, as it is almost time for 'second breakfast' and if she were a true friend, she'd be eating for me just to satiate the hunger that I can't satiate.

"Remember, let me do all the talking."

"With pleasure," I tell her as we get in line for the security check. With her tickets purchased over iNet, there is no need for a boarding pass, but the security check is mandatory and as I watch a pierced up ponytailed goth dude get TSAed, I tighten up my nonexistent anus and shuffle forward.

I imagine the little Quantum devil on my right shoulder prodding me to say something snarky while the little angel devil on my left with a bandolier across his chest reminds me, with a weapon trained at my temple, that I don't want to end up in the cargo hold. Oddly, the little angel has faun legs a la Doc. If only the Dream Team's Cyber Warfare Operative knew he had become the angel on my shoulder – that'd get a laugh out of him.

Me: Doc, what's the plan for tonight?

Doc: The plan for tonight is to go on one of those Hollywood homes tours.

Me: I thought this channel was encrypted?

Doc: It is encrypted, and you will be *crypted* if you keep asking questions like this. A taxi will pick you up from the airport. That's all you need to know.

Me: Got it. BTW, the combat protocols loaded.

Doc: The *Texas Edition* combat software package has never let me down.

Sophia is the first to be pat down. After snapping on a pair of plastic gloves, the female Humandroid runs her hands through Dr. Brains-a-lots' fro, making sure there are no hidden skivs, or whatever one could hide in such a mahoosive bundle of tangled hair. Once that is complete, Sophia is instructed to step into the body scanner.

She makes a starfish pose with her arms and legs and is thoroughly scanned.

"Make sure to scan her twice," I joke to the female humandroid TSA agent named Jessica. She ain't half bad for a droid. With her dark complexion and long black hair, I don't need to see that she's a year old to know that she's part of the FCG's new diverse Humandroids in the workplace initiative. More than three-fourths of the earlier model Humandroids where white, which caused some uproar in minority communities. Congress passed a law and now diversity is mandatory.

"Excuse me?" Jessica tilts her head slightly as she looks me over.

"Easy, I'm just joking."

The look on her face hardens and I wink.

"Really, nothing to see here, Jessica."

"FDA/PTSD Monitor 1351885, I am flagging you for a failure to comply with mandatory procedures."

"Mandatory procedures?"

Doc: Yeah, the 'don't be a smart ass with the security screeners' mandatory procedures. Congratulations, you're going to the cargo hold. I'd shut you down now, but this is too good. Sometimes I wonder if you'll ever learn to keep your mouth shut and stop being a dumbass.

Me: So you'd rather me be a smartass?

Doc: Have fun in cargo.

"What seems to be the problem here?" A human TSA agent with a Dracula-esque receding hairline steps up. He's both fat and muscular, something that I continue to see as a body type here in the States.

"No problem, officer, I mean … " I read his nametag. "Luke. Nothing to see here."

Luke looks to Sophia, who has gone from putting her shoes back on to advancing to the barrier separating the initial checkpoint to the finish line.

The ladydroid narrows her eyes on me. "FDA/PTSA Monitor 1351885 is being a nuisance."

"Ma'am," The TSA agent calls over to Sophia. "What's wrong with your Humandroid?"

Sophia shakes her head. "I'm taking him to a specialist in LA who deals with Humandroid-human interactions. He's been … um, *not quite right* as of late." She shows her Dream Team badge. "This is federal."

"Federal?" The agent walks over to Sophia and checks her credentials.

"Cut me a break, lady," I say under my breath to the droid. "We're practically fam."

"FDA/PTSD Monitor 1351885, need I remind you that Camaraderie among Humandroids can be considered a federal offense?"

"There really is something *not quite right* with him." Luke tells Sophia. He turns back to me. "I'll need you to go to return to the Humandroid service desk, check yourself in, and shut yourself down."

"All right, already," I grumble.

He smiles at his female counterpart. "Jessica here will escort you there."

Chapter Five

Never thought I would fly baggage class in a cargo hold, but after doing so and arriving in LA without even remembering taking off, I can officially report back that it wasn't as shabby as I thought it would be. At least I didn't have to sit next to Dr. Wang, or have to sit behind some double-wide man-bear with a penchant for leaning his seat back. No anklebiters kicking the back of my seat either and screaming for their mommies.

Nosiree, I was partially disabled, stowed away, and turned returned upon arrival.

Similar to what happened yesterday after I mouthed off at the McStarbucks near Sophia's cluttered casa, *shut down* means that I can't do anything, yet I can still process what's going on. So there I was, kept in a bracketed body brace looking across the cargo hold at a droid broad with a smoking hot bod.

At least I could still use iNet in my shut down state, which gave me a little time to catch up on the news, some porn – why not? Not like I can act on it – and to review the combat software Doc had me install.

Nice to be an unnatural born killer, if I do say so myself. Next time someone needs an IED made out of a half empty wine bottle, a nylon string, and a clothes hanger, I'm your guy.

"So it wasn't too bad down there?" Sophia asks after I'm back to wiggling my toes and fingers. We stand in the crowded luggage claim area, which is loud and panic-inducing to say the least. The droid gal I was stowed with walks past, turns to me, gives me a cold look, and continues on.

What's gotten into her? I think as my Humandroid eyes lock onto her swaying hips as she walks away.

"Made a friend down there?"

"Jeez Louise, Sophia, you ever stop asking me questions?"

She grabs my arm and squeezes. "It was just you and her in the cargo hold, right?"

"Enough."

"That's romantic."

"Enough, let's just get the hell out of Dodge."

"What's that mean exactly?" she asks. "And where's Dodge?"

I whip my arm away from her. The bustling airport overwhelms my Humandroid senses.

I'm given details about nearly everything, from schematics to potential hostiles, and as we make our way to the exit, I mentally tell myself to shut it all down, which works about as well as telling a hundred-year-old oak tree to move a few feet to the right. Near the exit, FCG Homeland Security officials mill about with drug sniffing, enhanced canines. The stern looks on their face tell me they're all business, and Sophia reminds me not to say anything to them.

"I know not to tease coppers," I tell her. "How do you think I made it this far in life without being arrested?"

"Well, the fact that you were in a digital coma for eight years definitely helped."

"Two subjective years," I grumble as the automatic door opens. The sun gives me a blast of shimmery sun-ness and the display on my iNet screen lets me know the temperature, wind direction, evening lows, and a bunch of other shit I don't care to know. "Sophia, there's got to be a way to turn this droid's info screen off. It's too much."

"Info screen?"

"You know," I say as we approach a hovering yellow taxi, "all the info it tells me on my iNet screen. An info screen."

She places a pair of oversized, oval-lensed sunglasses on her face. The trunk pops and like a gentleman, I take her suitcase from her and stuff it inside. Once we are in the backseat the vehicle is lifting off, she begins her explanation. "I've thought long and hard about how to simplify this explanation for you."

"You consider one minute long and hard?"

She nods. "In my world, yes. You don't have an iNet screen. That is your human way of thinking that you do and what you are seeing is visible in your pane of vision to make it easier to acknowledge and act on objects. Unlike the iNet that humans use, yours isn't being displayed across your retinae in any shape or form, nor is it being displayed anywhere, for that matter. It is simply a projection of the data that your sensors are picking up on, which InterHead displays in a way comfortable for most humans."

"Got it." I grumble. My eyes jump to the wheel of the self-driving taxi as it turns, lifts, and steadies. The panel behind the steering wheel flashes and an advertisement for BOGO sale at Wendy's Hut lights up the inside of the windshield.

Mmmmm ... pizza.

Mmmmm ... burgers.

I tune the good doctor out as I take in the view of LA from the aeros. I've been here once before, a decade or so ago for a Proxima conference. I had a damn good time but the city always gave me an uneasy feeling, like it was waiting for me to turn my back and shiv me in the gut.

The driverless aeros taxi travels for a few more minutes and lowers to a Hilton Holiday Inn.

"Hilton Holiday Inn?" I ask as we drop into a parking space covered by the shadow of an enormous palm. A kid in the pool area takes a running leap towards the neon blue water, grabs his knees close to his body, and gives his older sisters tanning nearby a dousing.

Sophia waits for the aeros to settle. "Open trunk," she says, immediately after a ding from an overhead speaker lets us know it is now safe to exit the vehicle.

"I'll get your luggage," I call after her, but she's out and pulling the luggage out of the back before I can even shut the door. A black aeros next to us beeps and the trunk pops open. With a grunt, Sophia places her luggage in the trunk of the new vehicle and gets in the back.

"Decoy aeros, eh?" I say as I take my seat next to her.

"It's Doc, what do you expect? Also," she nods to the rearview mirror. As the aeros lifts into the air, I see another black aeros lift behind us.

"Were they following us the whole time?"

She nods. "As far as RevCo or anyone else knows, you and I are back in Baltimore. Still, Doc didn't want to take any chances, especially seeing as how … " Her eyes narrow on me. "Especially regarding the way you behave in public."

"I was behaving!" I tell her as the vehicle speeds up.

"Keep telling yourself that."

~*~

After driving for all of twenty minutes and being bombarded with a Super Bowl's worth of advertisements, the aeros drops to another skylane and slows to a crawl. The LA traffic is notorious, and even with the myriad skylanes and actual highways below, it's still stop-and-start at most places.

"That's the hotel," Sophia says, as if there's a driver in the front and they can hear us. The aeros takes a left, slows at an invisible stoplight – as I like to call them – waits its turn, and lowers into the parking lot of an Econo Western 6.

"That's more like it," I say as I exit the vehicle. "My guess is this place has pancakes."

The aeros following us continues past as if it hadn't been on our tail for the last twenty minutes or so. I almost wave, but remind myself that I've turned a new leaf and will no longer be a smart ass.

Sophia shakes her head. "I'm sure it does, but you can't eat anyway."

"Let me get your luggage."

"I got it," Sophia says as she lifts it from the trunk. "I have always handled my own baggage."

"Something about that last line made me giggle on the inside."

She adjusts her big oval sunglasses. "Good."

A quick scan of the flop house and I'm told it is a two-star joint with a three-star breakfast rating and an overall rating of 3.2 on a scale of five. The most recent review talks about a mysterious stain on the ceiling. If I had a dollar for every hotel I stayed at with a mysterious stain somewhere in the room …

"The place looks right up Doc's alley."

Sophia crosses a grassy swath of land separating the hotel from a series of warehouses. She walks up to the first warehouse and the lift door opens to reveal Doc's silver Airstream RV. The old badger himself stands at the back along with Arnie. His B-drone, von Richtofen, is perched on top of the vehicle, its lens trained on Doc.

"Glad you could join us." Doc is in a camo bucket hat that reads CWO in bright orange letters and a pair of overalls. He's got a bib on and there is a smudge of barbeque sauce streaked across it. "I was just eating, but it's rude to not greet guests as they arrive. Let's get inside. Lookin' good by the way, Quantum." He snickers. "What? Was that not endearing?"

"Where's Frances?" I ask, ignoring his jibe. My Humandroid scan does its thing and tells me that for a guy that eats his weight in triglycerides on a monthly basis, Doc's overall health is sound. Sure he could lose a few pounds, but who couldn't? Hell, his blood pressure is better than a man twenty years his junior. If ever there was a reason to cut the crap with fad diets, that reason stands before me in CWO form.

"Woo-boy if it isn't my brother from a different mother! Put-r-there, Quantum!" Arnie the Humandroid comes in for a big hug. He latches on, gives me a good ol' pat on the back, and admires Evan's body for a moment. "That ain't a bad husk you got there, partner," he says with another clap on my shoulder. "Look real good, mighty fine!"

"Thanks, Arnie."

"So where can I put my luggage again?" Sophia asks. "Don't tell me we're all staying in your RV when there's a perfectly fine hotel *literally* a stone's throw away."

Doc mumbles something under his breath. "Dr. Wang, I told you that you had a room in the hotel, under the name Sidney Gottlieb."

"Sidney Gottlieb?" She raises an eyebrow at Doc.

"Good one, Doc!" I tell him as my instant reference checker goes to work. Before I can even spit out my compliment, I already know everything there is to know about Sidney Gottlieb and Project MKUltra.

"Keep laughing," he says as he turns to the RV. "You'll be staying in the room with her. After all, who knows more about setting up your charging rig than our own, most talented and big-brained individual?"

I cringe; at least I tell my Humandroid face to cringe – who knows what the hell it looks like.

"My brain isn't as large as you guys joke about it being," she says, "it is average-sized."

"Good to know." Doc drums his hands on his belly for a moment. "Let's get in the RV. I need to finish my plate of barbeque and it'd be best for me to brief you in there. Arnie?"

"Talk to me, Doc."

"Please escort Dr. Sidney Gottlieb to her room and return with her after she's dropped off her luggage."

"You betcha!"

"Fine," Sophia gruffs. "I need to set some things up anyway." She glances to the RV's door. "That goat isn't in there, is she?"

Doc stops just in time to give her the stink eye. "No," he grits, "*Sally* the service goat stayed home due to the nature of this mission."

~*~

Doc takes his sweet time finishing his plate of barbeque which consists of baby back ribs slathered in Rudy's barbeque sauce, mustard potato salad, mixed greens, corn on the cob with extra butter, and a cake-sized slice of jalapeno cornbread.

Frances Euphoria sits with one leg crossed over the other, eating her gerbil food. The only eye contact she's made with me thus far is a sidelong glance, and since I can read her vitals, I can tell she's experiencing a mixture of nervousness, anger, and sadness. At least that's how I'd describe the fluctuations in her heartbeat and her nervous movements.

"So what's the plan, Stan?" I ask Doc just to fill in the awkward silence between me and the big FE.

"The plan," he says as he uses his cornbread to mop up some barbeque sauce, "is for Frances over there to be our monitor during the extraction, which will happen at 23:00. The finer points of the plan are to come; this won't be a particularly hard mission, but there are some factors involved, which we'll get into later."

"Frances is the monitor? I thought she was coming with us. Arnie, her, and me."

"Arnie is coming with you, only Arnie won't be Arnie, I'll be Arnie." Doc nods to the back bedroom. A sudden flashback of Luther Godsick's pale ass lying on his bed back there hits me – it wasn't that long ago, but it feels like forever ago.

"InterHead?"

He winks. "I'm not leaving all the fun to you."

"I thought Arnie was programmed with advanced combat protocols?" I ask.

"Who the hell do you think wrote those?"

I shake my head in disbelief. "All of them?"

Instead of nodding, Doc raises his bushy eyebrows and finishes his rib.

"How is it that I suddenly know how to make an IED out of a half-empty bottle of wine and nylon?"

"You also need a clothes hanger. That's a fun one, isn't it? Now let me eat and quit asking me questions." He waves me away and returns to his barbeque.

"Why did Sophia come if you and I are doing the extraction and Frances is monitoring?"

"What part of ... " He grimaces. "She's being trained by Frances on running the logistics of an operation. Besides, her Proxima tech and knowledge of neuronal physics may come in handy. Now seriously, go bother Frances or something. I need to get some carbs." Doc gets up out of the booth and moves to the other side, so his back is now facing me. "And after I'm finished, we'll log into Steam and get started on getting that metal to get your ass out of Cyber Noir. Before you asked – Sophia briefed me, and seeing as how it's only lunchtime here in Cali, we have plenty of time before tonight's main event."

"Roger that. Mind if I sit?" I ask Frances.

"Fine." She uncrosses her legs and moves to the far side of the sofa.

"So, are you, um, feeling okay?" I ask her. *What an idiotic question.*

"Feeling fine. Had a massage at the hotel this morning."

"That hotel offers massages?"

"Not for you!" Doc says, and then mumbles something about them 'not being *those* types of massages anyway, and why would it matter if they were.' I ignore him as my droid controls give Our Lady of the GuadaLoop another full scan.

I decide to send her a message.

Me: Hey, let's go outside and talk. I have to walk over to the hotel anyway.

Frances looks up at me.

"What?" I ask. She stands, crosses her arms over her chest, and marches right out.

"Good luck with that," Doc calls over his shoulder.

The Cali sun shines through slanted windows at the top of warehouse. It is a little colder inside than it is outside, and my iNet screen reminds me of this again and again as I follow Frances to the single door that leads to the outside.

"Look, Frances, I know what you're thinking," I say as soon as we're out.

"You already tried that line, Quantum."

"I know, but you stormed off without letting me finish. None of this … " I pat my hands against my Humandroid shell. "None of this is what it seems."

"Ha!" She throws her hands up in the air. In the distance I see aeros moving to and from their airlanes. Arnie is returning from the hotel and as soon as he spots us, he goes out of his way *not* to cross our path, even though that means he actually has to walk around to the other side of the warehouse.

"This is the last I'll say about it because it's the truth, dammit, and since it is as such, it shouldn't be beaten into the ground any longer. I logged back into The Loop out of *curiosity*. Dolly showed up, and sure, I logged back in to see her. She trapped me *after* she found out I didn't want to be in there forever, after she found out, by searching my mind or doing whatever it is an NVA Seed can do, that I wanted to be with you. WITH YOU. Now if you don't believe that, fine, but I swear to you Frances, once I'm out of this metal meat sack, I'm going to do right by you, dammit."

Now it's my turn to skedaddle. Rather than risk screwing up my relatively well-put together closer, I give Frances a brisk smile and turn my happy metal ass toward the hotel. Do I want to leave? Hell no I don't. Would I rather stay there with her and hash this out? Of course I would, but I know better, know myself better, and sometimes it's best to leave things be, *especially* after firing off a genuinely honest string of sentences like I just did.

I'm a few footsteps away from reaching the hotel's parking lot when I hear Frances call after me.

I stop, start to turn, and decide to keep on walking for a moment. She catches up to me a moment later.

"Hey," she says, "don't just ignore me."

"It's the truth, Frances, honest to god."

"We need to work through this." I turn to her and boy if she doesn't look absolutely gorgeous, from her short haircut down to her size seven Converse shoes. Everything about her would tug at my heartstrings, *if* I had a heart. Nothing thumping inside this hollow metal carcass; all I can do is scan her vitals and register the UV levels of the sun that now hits her face directly.

"I know we do," I finally tell her. "And we will, but you have to believe me – it's you. That's what has been driving me. I thought it was someone else, but when faced with the final option, it was you. And she came back to me, Dolly did, to try again to convince me otherwise. Or do something … " I briefly recall Dolly teleporting me from Three Kings Park to the summer house. *That* was Dolly coming back for one more chance. And I blew it because of the jammiest bit of jams that stands before me.

"What are you trying to say?" she asks, her eyes softening.

"I made up my mind," I tell her. "So just think about that, and once I'm out of this damned Tinman body, maybe we can work through it. Until then, let's keep our focus on the mission."

She nods and her face hardens. "Got it, you're right. The mission. It's what is most important right now."

Chapter Six

Feedback eye flitter Proxima riven. Feedback bring me to the place from whence I was spawned, an avatar of the damned with his mangled fingers pressed to two worlds, three, four, more. Feedback a shot in the dark, the call of the vile, the worst of the best, a sour taste followed by something sweet. Feedback Pompeii before the eruption.

I awake in the dive yurt to find Aiden in steampunk regalia polishing his Slice Bang. From the looks of it, he's also polished the buckles on his shoes, the small spikes that line the shoulders of his sleeveless overcoat, and his mechanical arm with its Gatling gun tucked into the side.

He stands, his Slice Bang goes in a sheath attached to one of the three studded belts that he wears and a pair of Steam world-appropriate SPAS-12s take shape on his back. "Ready."

"That's some serious firepower you got there," I tell him as I stand. I should know, item 189, my SPAS-12, Semi-Automatic Pump-Action Combat Shotgun, has come in handy multiple times. Not lately, but before, when I was The Loop's bubble boy. It's fast, loud, deadly, and fun to shoot. Great at killing the soon-to-be-dead or the undead, for that matter.

"So Steam ... " I check my Captain Koon's watch, item 151. "Where the hell is Sophia?"

Sophia: There's been a change of plan. Frances is diving instead and I'll be in-game. So that's where I am, in our hotel room.

I shudder at the word 'our' and pump my fist as the realization that Sophia won't be around this time settles. "No Dr. Braindrain this time around, Aiden!"

We high five and I can practically see Sophia rolling her eyes over the messaging system.

Sophia: Would you two stop playing around and spawn in Steam? The spawn point should appear momentarily.

A glowing pink sphere appears in front of me. It takes me a moment to place the color – it's the same as Sophia's tiny aeros.

"Just touch it, right?" Aiden asks.

"Yeah, but I'll take it out if you don't like it." I tell him.

Sophia: Lame joke.

Before I can respond, Morning Assassin performs a twisting backflip into the pretty pink spawning point. As soon as the tops of his feet touch it, he dematerializes.

"Show off."

Sophia: He makes it look effortless.

"Oh yeah?" I take a few steps towards the spawning point, cross my arms over my chest, and turn my back to it.

Here goes nothing.

I fall backwards and crack the back of my head on the floor. "Shit!"

Sophia: My bad! I must have, um, moved the location of the spawning point.

The pink spawning point is suddenly hovering over me. It lowers into my chest before I can pull myself to my feet.

~*~

Frances is in a tight leather vest that accentuates her milk pillows. Two belts crisscross over her waist, hooked through opposite belt loops that are part of a teeny tiny black skirt with oversized stitching along its seams. Sticking out of her thick red hair are a pair of cat ears made from small gears and accented by a slim lined pair of Leaks. The gold indicator over her head makes her look like she has a halo.

Talk about hubba hubba. Talk about the kitty's roar.

I'm pretty sure she's trying to get back at me in her steampunk anime girl costume, but I know better to bite, so I instead turn my attention to Rocket, who wears a black tuxedo jacket with a popped collar over a peppermint cravat tucked into a dark blue waistcoat. Below the belt he wears a pair of super tight skinny jeans with perfectly proportioned holes at the knees. "What am I forgetting … " He snaps his fingers and a shiny train conductor hat takes shape on his head. "Did you see the boots?"

I nod.

"They're the X-23s." Rocket kicks back on the heel and two sharp blades shoot out from the foot. "Just in case I need to kick some ass! P.S. I'm an alchemy user these days, but I still can and will kick ass upon request." Glitzy hieroglyphs cascade down his arms. They stop at his wrists and buzz with intensity.

"What kind of spell is that?" I ask as I equip my steam pack, item 564, and thread it into the port on my arm.

"It isn't a spell at all; I just did it to look cool!" His cuffs-o-magic quickly dissipate. "Pretty sweet, Q-Bert, right? Am I right or am I right or am I right?"

"Why am I already regretting logging in?"

"Because you aren't doing it right!"

I turn to find the Dream Team's War Faun in a world appropriate tactical vest with tons of pockets and a fully-loaded bandolier for a belt. He's armed to the teeth with shooting irons – two are holstered on either side of his waist, two under his arms, one tucked into the front, a Springfield M1903 slung over one shoulder, a Beretta Pico strapped to either leg, an M4 carbine on a single point sling and likely another gun hidden somewhere. Over his right eye, partially illuminated by the golden indicator over his head, is an eye patch with an advanced reticle on it that reminds me of the inner workings of a clock.

"Have fun playing dress up, Doc?"

"Dress up? This isn't dress up; it's an assignment!" He takes a little spin and flicks his little goat tail at me on the way back around. Looking good by the way, Aiden."

"Not bad yourself, Doc. Glad to see you kept the faun avatar."

He turns and shows us his little goat tail. Sure enough, a Glock is tucked into the back of his bandolier. "Where are we anyway?" He swipes away the Steam prompt. "And why am I already at such a high level?" he snorts. "Just kidding. I know Ray Steampunk hooked me up and is probably watching me right now? Ain't that right, Ray?"

Sophia: The five of you are in the same place we spawned earlier, southwest of Locus not far from the Crown River.

"Ah, so *that's* what that smog covered, over-populated stain on my vision pane is!" Doc places his arms on his sides and gives the city a look. His perky little tail drops as he sees a potential hostile approaching from a different hill.

He's on his belly seconds later, his Springfield M1903 ready to go. His reticle eye patch extends a few inches away from his face and settles as it locks onto the target.

"Need a spotter, Doc?" Aiden takes a knee next to the War Faun.

"I've got him."

"It's one of those strange bicycles!" Rocket says.

"A penny-farthing or ... at least, an all-terrain version of one."

This ain't your granddaddy's penny-farthing, no siree. The penny-farthing approaching us – and soon to be part of my list after Doc gets a headshot in – has studded all-terrain tires. The guy peddling is a sweating beast of a man, with more muscles than an inflated Reaper outside of the Revenue Corporation's headquarters at their annual Asshole of the Year Picnic.

"Must we always resort to violence?" Frances asks as her cute little steam pack takes shape on her back. She lifts into the air before Doc can tell her 'we must' and once she's up, she makes a beeline down from our spawning hillock to the approaching pedal pusher.

Doc doesn't take his focus off the pedalist.

He clicks the safety off, steadies his breath, and readies himself to pull the trigger. Frances lands, they speak for a moment, and she is up and out in a jiffy. The cyclist turns away, his big form going back up the hill the way he came.

Frances lands and hands me a telegram. "It's from Ray Steampunk."

"For the love of … " Doc huffs and he gets back to his feet. "Well?"

"This has to be some sort of joke," I mutter as I look the letter over. "Why can't we just get what we need from Ray and skedaddle? Why does it always have to entail some sort of quest, some sort of dramatic entrance? We could literally spawn in Morlock, clean up shop, and be back before Doc's afternoon snack." I wave the telegram at Frances.

"Don't look at me!"

"Oh, I'm getting my afternoon snack, you can bet your bottom dollar on that," he grumbles. "What's it say?"

I clear my throat and speak in a clipped, 1920s radio broadcast voice. "Ahem, an airship will arrive shortly. You will be taken to the Lost Pines, not to be confused with the Pines of Palafitte, and from there, you will make your way to the Prison City of Akrasia."

Sophia: The Prison City of Akrasia is a cesspit located on the easternmost edge of Morlock and is separated from the city by three walls, Wall Maria, Wall Rose, and Wall Titan. Convicted felons from Morlock and military prisoners from the Boilerplate Army are sent there to serve out their sentences. Going through the Lost Pines is one of several ways to enter the prison city, which is a popular tourist destination."

Doc clears his throat. "I think, and I hope I'm right here, Ray is trying to save us trouble by telling us to go through the pines. He may know something we don't know. There's the airship there." He points at the orange sky.

"What should I do with the telegram? I'd rather not clutter my list with something so useless."

Frances snorts. "Clutter your list? Says the guy who has a cherub-shaped church key and a Peter Griffin mask."

"Item 57 and item 283. What's your point?"

"A Poppy Troll collectible figurine; a bowling ball signed by some guy named Walter Sobchak," adds Rocket.

"Yes, items 357 and 106, respectively."

"Don't forget your hand-cranked meat grinder and your case of stink bombs," adds Aiden.

"Item 173, which I yanked from the Chef; item 405, which I stole from some anklebiter who was in the abandoned amusement park. Look guys, I'm a changed man, or more accurately, a changing man. Give me a break already!"

"Is the telegram signed by Steampunk?" Rocket asks. "If so, I'll take it. Those things are worth mad shillings."

~*~

About three minutes in, Doc and I have had just about enough of the oooohs and aaaahs from Frances and Rocket to equip industrial-strength ear plugs. I have a pair, item 445, which cost me a pretty penny. Who am I kidding? I stole them from Two Face Tommy. In another one of those 'days on repeat' stories of mine, Two Face Tommy was having his big party. Glitz, glam, doll-faced dames with eight inch high heels and little knives strapped to their thighs – you name it.

Tommy had just had a custom pair made for him by none other than The Loop's goodest weapons dealer, Dirty Dave, and boy was it a nice pair. Contained in a case of solid gold, ol' Tommy, who had trouble sleeping at night, kept the earplug case in his nightstand.

Let's just say the Tooth Fairy paid him a little visit that night and robbed him blind instead of leaving him a fiver.

Talk about silencio. I can't hear a damn thing with his earplugs in, not even the report from my Tommy gun!

"You got that look on your face," Aiden says.

"Which one?"

"The one that says you're thinking too hard."

"Better than thinking too flaccid!" Doc laughs at his own joke. The Steam Faun leans against a large crate. Aiden is next to him, flipping through a scrollazine he picked up in Tritania called *Goblin Holes*. I have no earthly idea what the hell he's looking at, but the occasional chuckle from Doc and the fact that there's an orc chippie in full monty on the cover tells me that it ain't your typical 7-Eleven rag. Euphoria already gave MA the stank eye for it, luckily she's over by Rocket, both of them looking through a rectangular window at scenery below as if they've never seen a Proxima World before.

"What's for dinner tonight, Doc?" I recall the delicious-looking BBQ brunch he was noshing when we arrived. What I wouldn't do for some BBQ right about now.

"Tonight? Well before Operation Daughter Snatch ... "

Aiden snickers.

Sophia: Gross.

"What?" I ask the ceiling. "It was a good joke and you know it."

"I'll be enjoying a pork roast with gravy, oven-baked red potatoes seasoned with onions and rosemary, along with a medley of broccoli, cauliflower, and carrots. I cooked it up in the crockpot before we left home and got five meals out of it! For dessert you ask? Probably some Blue Bell. I brought a pint of homemade vanilla, rocky road, and mint chip."

I lick my lips. "Damn, that's some good eating."

Frances scoffs. "Heart attack on wheels."

Sophia: Don't worry, Frances, I've already ordered us some food.

"You mean on hooves." Doc shows her the bottom of his caprine appendages. "And you two can keep the gerbil food to yourselves."

"I agree with, Doc," I chime in.

The airship rattles. Doc has one of his guns in his hands faster than Rocket can say, "This sure is a bumpy ride!"

A quick looksee to the window and I see that we've entered a small lightning storm. Nothing to write home about, and I'm pretty sure our gilded and Fabio fanfic-looking bromigo Ray Steampunk wouldn't let us die anyway, but I've yet to meet a person whose heart doesn't skip a little during a heavy storm.

I stand from the barrel I was sitting on and scoot up next to Rocket, watching as the sudden rain slaps against the airship's windows. "How's my body?" I ask him. "Looking all right?"

"Looking bodacious, Q-Rip. I took a few selfies with you though; put some lipstick on you too."

Doc snorts. "Forward a few of those to me. I want to make sure I have something to share with you every time you're acting like an asshole."

"Acting like an asshole? When was the last time I did that? It's impossible to put lipstick on me," I tell them both, "I have a breathing apparatus in my mouth!" The furtive glances between the three that turns into deep, braying laughter says it all. I grunt and return to my barrel. "I get no respect," I mutter under my breath.

Lightning strike again the storm suddenly dissipates, as if it were being scrubbed out by a giant eraser. Blips of light peak through the dark clouds and I get that itching feeling someone is watching us. Just to be sure, I slowly curl my hand into a perfectly formed middle finger.

That's for you, Ray.

Lightning cracks one last time and the airship drops a few feet in altitude, tossing my avatar to the deck.

~*~

~~Prepare for debarkation! Prepare for debarkation~~

"Is Ray Steampunk making up words again?"

"It's an actual word," and Doc is just about to explain the word origins when the floor of the airship gives way.

"Here we go!" I shout.

Rocket is the first to fall out; as alchemical symbols twist and flitter up his body, a pair of translucent yellow wings form on his back. Of course, Aiden has his steam-powered jetpack on faster than I can give my list a quick scroll, and like a good for nothing bastard, he captures the falling Frances in his arms and lands safely at the edge of copse of pines.

I go for Doc, who clearly could have handled himself, and together, as Doc curses in my arms, held as if he were my newlywed bride, we descend to the pines below.

Sophia: Speaking of screenshots...

"How romantic!" Rocket laughs as I land valiantly with the Combat Faun in my arms. All business, Doc hops out, grabs two guns and he and Aiden secure the perimeter.

"I was going to, um, rescue you." I tell Frances so only she can hear it.

"Aiden beat you to it, and besides." She gives me a look that would freeze the chivalry right out of Prince Valiant. "I don't need rescuing."

"You know what I mean, not trying to be misogynistic or nothing."

"Try harder." A saber pistol with a pearl grip appears in her hand. With the weapon at her side, she joins Doc and Aiden in securing the perimeter.

"You could have rescued me," Rocket says as he places an arm around my shoulder.

A dark shadow hovers over the Lost Pines. I don't know if it is always like this so close to Morlock, but I got a feeling that Ray

Steampunk was going for the Mordor vibe when he oversaw the design of this part of the continent. Everything has a burnt look to it, even though the pines on the pine trees are actually green.

I wave my hand in front of my face. My skin tone has changed ever so slightly as if the color has been stripped out of it. I look to my teammates; they aren't quite black and white, but this place is definitely lacking color.

France Euphoria's face illuminates as her atlas sphere floats into the air.

"I thought those were only good at finding logout points," I say.

Sophia: They're also useful for navigation and illuminating dark spaces.

Sure, the forest is dark, but that's nothing for my heavy duty MagLite with a flare in its grip, item 398. It's supposed to shoot a frickin' laser, but I can't figure out how to make that happen, and I've been meaning to ask Dirty Dave to take a look at it for a while now.

"Nice one," Doc says as he takes in the beam of my light. "Is that the Barnes Mag 250?"

"How'd you know?"

"Pfft! Both of you put your bright toys away. Equip something less noticeable."

Rocket chops the air and arcane magic twists up his arm. "Illuminate vision!" His eyes glow and return to their normal color.

"If that's how we're doing this … " I go with my Reaper skull, item 551. As soon as I put it on, gridlines appear and the option to toggle between various viewing modes take presents itself. I go with NV and the dark forest turns green.

I turn back to Frances to find her with an equally impressive mask on that looks like something out of the DisNike *Tron* reboot from the 2030s. Her atlas sphere is still with her, but she's disabled all light functions from it.

"Are we done playing dress up?" Doc gives the signal for us to follow. "Stay frosty."

The Faun of Steam scuttles ahead, his shootin' iron trained on the dark pines. Aiden holds up the rear, a Remington ACR at the ready, leaving the three of us in the middle.

Me: Rocket, right. Frances, watch overhead, I'll hold left.

Rocket: Roger that, Steamboy.

Me: Dammit, you.

Sophia: Would you guys like to know more about Akrasia?

Me: No.

Frances Euphoria: Sure.

Rocket: What Steamboy said.

Doc: What Rocket said.

Sophia: Rumor has it, no one has ever broken out of Akrasia.

Frances Euphoria: If no one has ever broken out, how are we supposed to get in?

Sophia: Anyone can enter Akrasia; not everyone can leave. Prisoners of Akrasia wear similar restraints to the ones that bleached people wear, although the restraints are on their ankles, not their necks.

Me: So Ray Steampunk is preventing people from logging out?

Sophia: No, he'd never do that! He's a great guy, a legend, really.

Doc: What part of stay frosty do you people not understand?

Sophia: Sorry, Doc! But to answer your question, Steamboy, the ankle band that the prisoners wear is similar to something that a person under house arrest wears. It prevents them from leaving the city. Prisoner PCs can certainly logout, but they must serve their sentence when they log back in. The Akrasian authorities only count the time that they are in Steam as part of their sentence. Some have fifty year sentences – pretty much lifers and no, before you ask, they can't just do the resetter thing. Duh.

Me: But aren't people technically free to move around Akrasia? It can't be that bad, can it?

Sophia: That's a stupid question Have you ever even looked at pictures of Akrasia? It is a vile, sinful place. The worst of the worst take residence there. Zedic and I once met a contact there – worst experience I've ever had in Steam.

Me: Sounds like my kind of place! But seriously, I thought you said it was a tourist destination.

Sophia: It is. For some reason, people still enjoy it.

"Psst, Aiden," I whisper. Morning Assassin flashdances and is suddenly next to me. "Akrasia is Steam's version of The Loop."

A wolfish grin forms on his face, evident in the way his mask stretches. "Good." With that, he's gone, back to auditioning for the role of Nightcrawler in the newest reboot of the X-Men franchise, *X-Men: Wolverine Good, Magneto Bad but Likeable.*

Sophia goes on for another few minutes about Akrasia lore and about the famous walls that surround the city. About the only thing I take from her dissertation is the name Wall Rose, which sounds like it could be either a great album title for an experimental post-rock R&B Tejano band that I'd like to form with Aiden someday, or something that is in reference to something else that is somehow related to the steampunk genre.

I'm going to go with the latter.

"Weapons up!" Doc takes cover behind a pine just as the ground shakes.

Rocket is tossed off balance, but manages to catch himself. With a whirl of his hand, the Dream Team's boy wonder zips to the tree next to Doc.

Frances and I head right and the ground rumbles and of course, Aiden already has his brown ACR tucked under his arm as he unloads a magazine at the approaching force. Doc joins him. The sound of trees and roots and the clank of rocks being cut in half add to the metal symphony being played by Doc and Aiden.

Something looms in the distance, something big.

~*~

Sophia: It's a rogue drill mech!

Light pours into the forest as pine trees begin to fall. A vehicle – I still don't know if that's what I should be calling it – rips up soil, roots, and stone as it advances towards us. For wheels it has twelve-foot-high gears. Instead of a hardened shell, it has smaller gears and pulleys whirring a mile a minute. Attached to the back of the vehicle and dipping over its head are pincers topped by, you guessed it, sharpened gears. It's a cross between a Transformer, a giant weed whacker, and one of those industrial dump trucks.

Doc: Info, Sophia, now! Any weaknesses?

Words flash on my pane of vision.

Sophia: Here's the copy/paste from the Steamopedia. Rogue Drill Mechs were used in the Babbage Wars. They were originally created as steam-powered construction vehicles to cut into ridges around Clockpunch Mountain. Their creator, a PC named Bobby Bjurstrom, objected to their use as war machines and destroyed the entire fleet, but not before he stole one and vanished with it.

"That's some story, Sophia!"

Doc pulls an AT-4 out of his list, fires the round to no effect, grunts in disgust and tosses the launcher aside.

Sophia: I'm not finished yet!

Me: Sophia tell us its weaknesses, not a goddamn bedtime story!

Sophia: That wasn't a bedtime story.

A Volkswagen-sized rock sails towards me and I hit the AA brakes.

What I do next would definitely fall under the category of a yoga pose. I drop to my knees and from there, fall backwards *without* ever touching the ground. I hold this awkward position as the rock passes over me, inches away from my nose. If I were Barbara Streisand, we'd definitely have a problem, but this ain't nothing for Mrs. Hughes' Pride and Joy and his little button nose.

The Rock of Gibraltar passes and mows down a line of trees, spraying splinters of wood into the air.

"Time for some boom-boom!" I shout. "MA, care to pay a closer visit!"

As I come up from my extreme asana I give my list a quick scrollski and arrive on item 48. A black Nokia cellphone takes shape in my right hand and a brick of C4 with a jury-rigged cell phone detonator in my left.

No time to play a game of Snake, I hand off the C4 to Aiden and motion for everyone else to get behind something. Footloose the Assassin slips in and out of reality and appears on top of the rogue drill neck in seconds. He slides the C4 into a compartment on its side and bails out.

"All clear!?"

Doc: Blow it!

Rather than turn what Doc's just said into a juvenile fellatio joke, I jam my thumb into the send button only to get the annoying 'sending message' hourglass. "Come on," I say, pressing the button repeatedly. "Come … on … "

Message sent.

The resulting explosion is music to my ears.

The mechanical ground muncher creaks and groans as it collapses to the forest floor. Once the coast is clear, I pop my head up from my cover spot and give the bastard a quick once-over through the lenses of my Reaper mask. Grid lines galore – the weirdest thing about the rogue steam mech is the fact that there are portions inside of its body that are obfuscated, almost as if some crayon happy Valentine's Day mistake scribbled over the core of the vehicle with his favorite cosmic black.

Two red eyes appear in the center of its form.

"It ain't dead," I announce to the group. "And if I'm not mistaken, I think there may be someone inside!"

Doc: Concentrate all firepower on it!

"I've got it!" France Euphoria's mutant hack spills up her arm forming a thick biomass weapon. The tendrils peel back on the place where her hand should be and a barrel rimmed in electric blue takes shape.

She fires off an icy blast and holds her ground as aqua algo-energy spews out of the hack. It hits the rogue steam mech full on and crackles as it coats the mech's body using its own steam for fuel.

"Good, Frances!" Doc gives Aiden the 'let's wrap this up' hand lasso only to be leveled by a huge crystal of ice.

The steam mech's gears are still spinning a mile a minute, tearing the hunks of ice off its body and tossing the debris all around the woods. Poor Doc has a mini glacier on his back, his little faun legs kicking from beneath it like he's auditioning for a role as the Good Witch of the West in the forthcoming sequel to the *Wizard of Oz* prequel.

I'd equip my ice pick, item 538, if I thought it would do any good. "Rocket, cast a spell or .... do something! I need to get my Reason Railgun set up!"

I give my list a 'behind the back scroll' as I get into position. Item 459 to the rescue!

"One badass spell coming right up!" The kid with more ironic shirts than a Portland thrift store lifts into the air and a huge sphere of radiant energy encompasses his body. He lets loose a supernova's supernova. which smacks the living bolts out of the rogue steam mech. The mechanical beast sputters, putts, tries to get its pincer gears up, and collapses yet again.

"What the hell did you just cast?" I ask as more steam sprays out of the rogue drill mech.

Rocket shrugs. "It's a spell called Malfunction. It pretty much works on anything robotic here in Steam."

"Why in the hell didn't you cast that from the get-go?"

"You guys were cool with your weapons! Like some real badasses, especially Doc. The Faun of Steam!"

"It's the Faun of *War*," the Dream Team's Cyber Warfare Operative growls as he keeps his weapon trained on the vehicle.

"You okay?" I ask over my shoulder at Euphoria.

"Did anything I said or did lead you to believe that I *wasn't* okay?"

A hatch on the side of the vehicle opens and Aiden and Doc advance on it as a man in a greasy tank top stumbles out. A bandana is tied across his head and a pair of suspenders keep his loose trousers from falling.

"Don't shoot!" he says as he raises his hand. "I'll talk, I'll ... I'll give you what you came here for!"

~*~

"Well hello, Bjurstrom, nice of you to drop in."

Sophia: Actually, I don't know who that is. He's done something to his handle.

I approach the man, who has yet to take his hands out of the air. "Alrighty, No Handle, you got all of fifteen seconds to tell us why we shouldn't send you on a one-way airship to Ray Steampunk's newest version of Alcatraz in the center of Rusty Trombone Lake."

"Impressive," Rocket says. "The lake is actually called *Crankcase* Lake, but people jokingly call it that. You read the briefing!"

"Don't you care accuse me of actually doing my job," I tell the kid.

The man clears his throat. "Mind if I drop my arms?" he asks, slightly out of breath. "It's hurting to keep them up like this."

Doc and Aiden exchange glances. "Keep 'em high," says the faun as he loads one into the chamber of his MK678 pistol.

"My name is Joe L." He curls his blackened fingers.

"All right, Joel." I tell the dirty yegg. Something about his overbite and the way he carries himself reminds of one of the Three Kings of, well, Three Kings Park.

"That's Joe L.," he says, "but most people call me Joel."

"All right, Joel, keep them high."

"But it really is Joe L."

A wise guy, huh?

Doc grits, "Well whatever the hell your name is, where's Bjurstrom?"

Not ten seconds later, Joel's laughing like a hyena. A quick glance to Frances, who has a wrist gun aimed at Joel and I've got nothing, no read on what she's thinking. Could be thinking anything.

"What? You don't know?" he wheezes.

I shake my head.

"The rogue steam mech *is* Bjurstrom, and your little mage just fried the hell out of him."

"To be fair," Doc says, keeping his pistol trained on the greaseball, "you attacked us first."

"It was both our ideas." He points from his chest to the steam mech. "Both," he whispers.

Me: Crazy much?

Sophia: You shouldn't assume someone is crazy just because they say crazy things.

Me: Quote of the day right there, Dr. Wang!

"Both of our ideas," Joel mumbles, "it might not look like it, but I'm the brains behind the operation!"

"So you're Bjurstrom then?"

"No, I'm an extension of Bjurstrom's D-NAS created through a spliced algospell. Like I told you the first time, I'm Joe L., or Joel." He nods his head. "That's Bjurstrom."

Frances eyes light up. "I get it, you're like Bjurstrom's brain, correct?"

"The sexy lady is smarter than she looks!"

Frances ignores him and says, "Good, so you can help us."

"Why would I do that?"

Frances lowers her weapon and approaches him. Doc and Aiden fan out, but neither of them lets Joel out of their sight. "I think we may want the same thing."

"Oh?"

"We need to get into Akrasia, to find some people and see if we can locate some Sky Iron."

Joel considers this for a moment. "Do you mind if I lower my hands? I need to scratch my ass."

Frances looks to Doc and he shakes his head no.

"Sorry," she says, "but you'll be able to lower them soon, I assure you."

A bead of sweat appears on Joel's forehead. "My arms are really starting to hurt."

"I'll handle that." Aiden appears behind him, pulls his arms down and cuffs his wrists together. He lowers Joel to the ground and forces him to sit.

"What do you know about Sky Iron and where we can find it?" Frances crouches in front of Joel, still playing the good cop role.

"Sky Iron hasn't been mined for years. Not since … before the War of Gibson and Sterling, that's for damn sure."

Doc asks, "Can Bjurstrom mine it?"

A grin creeps across Joel's face. "If he's feeling up to it, yes. And he knows exactly where to find it, so it shouldn't take him that long to get it either."

"Then we'd like him to feel up to it," Doc grits.

"For him to feel up to it, there are two things that need to be addressed: one, your spell rusted out Bjurstrom completely."

"Go me?" Rocket looks to each of us for approval.

"Yeah, go you, wise guy," I tell him.

"You aren't powerful enough to reverse the spell," Joel informs him.

Rocket smiles bigly. "My girlfriend can definitely do it. She's at a way higher level than I am. She's pretty much been here since the start of the world!"

"Get her on the horn then," I tell him under my breath.

"Which horn is that again?" he asks, being sly.

"You know what I mean."

"She's halfway around the world and sleeping at the moment. Usually, she uses a Somnium Skip Box to skip sleep, but not tonight. She was tired. We had a lot of fun last night."

A half-smoked coffin nail takes shape in Doc's mouth. He takes a quick puff of it and says, "All right, we'll get Bjurstrom fixed, Joel. That's easy, doable. What's your next demand."

"It's not my demand ... " He again nods at the vehicle. "It's his. Bjurstrom wants to bring down all three walls, Wall Maria, Wall Rose, and Wall Titan."

"The walls separating Akrasia from the rest of Morlock?" Frances asks.

He nods, dead serious. "It will create utter havoc."

Sophia: That will destroy the city entirely; it may even pit Marauders against the Boilerplate Army! This is totally a bad idea. I know no one will listen to me, but it's on the record!

I glance to Doc and he shrugs as if to say, *not my world, not my problem.*

"As long as it entails sticking it to our own enemies holed up in Akrasia," I finally tell the greaser, "the Dream Team is game. Let's bring down the walls."

Chapter Seven

"Let me guess," I ask as we follow Joel through the dark pines, "We have to go through a sewer to get into the city."

Rocket snorts. "Is your mind in the gutter or something – see what I did there?"

He looks to me for approval and I offer him a slight nod. Rocket takes this as an indication to continue. "We're not going through a sewer, Q Run, we're gonna waltz in like some big bad wolves!"

"Quantum," I remind him, "Call me Quantum."

"I'll get a nickname that sticks one day!"

"Steamboy is pretty good," Frances offers.

"Keep it up," I tell them both under my breath. I see a few pine cones and go to step on them. Damn that crunch is satisfying.

"He's right, no sewers," Joel says. "There are multiple entrances along two of the three walls, which are fully open for people to come and go. Remember, if they have an ankle bracelet, they can't leave, and the bracelets can't be removed, so there is really no reason to make entry difficult. Nope. No sewers, tunnels, nineteen-feet-tall ladders, or teleportation devices. You may be wondering what good destroying the walls will do."

I shoot Doc a quick glance. He's too busy keeping a trained eye on the dark, piney woods to acknowledge my look. "I'm wondering," I finally tell Joel.

"The three walls are ... how do I put this?" He considers this for a moment. "They *are* the algospell keeping all those with ankle bracelets trapped inside. If we destroy the walls, the worst of the worst will be released back into Morlock."

Frances Euphoria stops. "And the subsequent chaos will spread."

"Why yes," says Joel with a crazy grin on his face. "It will spread, and will likely pit the military against the populous. Remember, the leadership of the Boilerplate Army has had it out for the Morlockian governmental authorities for years. If the walls come down, the chaos will give both sides a chance to go at one another. And Locus doesn't need to worry, Steampunk's forces will quell those that reach his territory. Easily quell, I might add. He's the NVA Seed. All he has to do is snap his fingers and anyone in front of him – PC, NPC, RPC – will crumble to ash. You guys should know this. Don't think I can't see the golden indicators above your heads. You are his emissaries."

"I wouldn't call us that," I tell the vagabond. "Have you ever met Ray Steampunk? I'm not gonna call him an asshole, because he's probably listening to our conversation right now, but he ain't far off."

"So he's a taint then?" Rocket asks.

Doc snorts.

Sophia: WHAT ARE YOU SAYING ABOUT RAY STEAMPUNK?

Rocket: SOPHIA, PLEASE DO NOT SEND MESSAGES IN ALL CAPS. IT MEANS YOU ARE SCREAMING AT US!

Sophia: I AM SCREAMING! RAY STEAMPUNK IS THE NVA SEED!

"What the hell is wrong with her?" I ask so only Frances can hear. "I get the feeling that'd she'd fit right in at Jonestown or North Korea. Show Sophia some kind of authoritarian figurehead and she goes loopy gaga whenever anyone disagrees with them."

"Loopy gaga?"

"What?" I ask with a shrug. "I can't make up phrases?"

"I have a question," Rocket tells Joel. "You said all walls must be destroyed to cancel the algospell, right?"

"Yes, the only way to cancel the spell is to destroy all three walls, and the destruction doesn't need to be what you're thinking – I'm not talking about trying to bring down the Great Wall here; just a good-sized hole will dispel the algomagic, and I already have explosives ready to go at Wall Titan and Wall Maria."

"So why do you need our help?" I ask as I dip under a low hanging branch.

"It is Wall Rose that has been giving me issues for years, *years*."

"Well, that blows my plan."

He stops and turns to me. "What do you mean?"

"Not gonna lie, and Doc, you will appreciate this – I have GBU-43 Mother of all Bombs in my list, item 358."

Doc stops and considers. "Dirty Dave?"

"Who else? Never used it before, but that's not because I didn't want to use it. Hell, I've been itching to find a way to use it for a while now."

"A MOAB is way, *way* too large for what we are trying to do," Joel says. "We're not trying to kill people, we're trying to force a situation in which they kill themselves."

Aiden appears next to Joel. "You said Wall Rose has been giving you issues – why's that? Shouldn't it be just as accessible as the others?"

"Wall Maria and Wall Titan are lined with retail stores, from contraband to souvenir shops. Wall Rose is a different story entirely. You can't access the wall from within Akrasia because of Tent City."

Sophia: That's right! I knew I was forgetting something!

I roll my eyes. *Why can't something just be easy for once?*

Joel clears his throat. "Tent City runs along the mile-long interior of Wall Rose. Steam Breeds are housed there. And before you ask, Steam Breeds are man and robot amalgams."

"So cyborgs." I lose my footing and stumble forward, catching myself just before I go head first into a pine.

"If that explanation helps you get a grasp on what I'm saying, fine, they're cyborgs, but Steam Breeds are much more dangerous than a cyborg," Joel says. "They're usually two to three times the size of a normal man. I think of them as mutants."

"So they are NPCs?" Doc asks.

"Most are, and nearly all of them are housed in Tent City due to an instability in their D-NAS. They lashed out randomly and they are incredibly brutal."

"So they are prisoners within a prison city that is actually a tourist destination."

"Self-imposed prisoners," he reminds me. "The Steam Breeds can move around the city, but they don't. They keep to themselves. Then there's the Chain Gang."

"Chain Gang?" Frances asks.

"Those are the scum of the Proxima galaxy. They are people who've been arrested *in* Akrasia, and boy is it hard to get arrested in Akrasia due to the fact that the place is practically lawless. The Chain Gang takes care of keeping the place relatively clean. They are policed by the SRT Mondoshawans, which are bulbous, big metal bastards that remind you of what would happen if you mixed The Penguin with Art Deco stylings."

"SRT?" Rocket asks.

"Special Response Team."

"To recap," Frances says, and it's a damn good thing she's recapping because I've lost interest in what Joel has been saying, "Akrasia is a former prison complex located in the Marauder city of Morlock. Akrasia has its own prisoners, even though most people are already prisoners. The prisoners of Akrasia are known as the Chain Gang. The most dangerous area of Akrasia is known as Tent City, where Steam Breeds live, and even though it has open entry, no one goes there. There are no laws in Akrasia, but the Special Response Team polices the Chain Gang."

"Why tents?" I ask. "I get all the other stuff – typical Ray Steampunk full-immersion bs – but why are the biggest, baddest, nastiest most cyborgiest hombres on the block living in tents?"

"Because they kept destroying the housing units."

"So the rest of the people, prisoner and, um, double-prisoner, alike live in houses."

Joel shoots me a funny look. "They aren't animals, you know."

"No, I don't know. Everyone keeps hyping Akrasia up when really, I'm about as scared of a bunch of beefed up nogoodniks as I am a trio of yawning kittens that just woke up from a nap."

Joel nods. "To be clear: housing units are bought and sold, like any commodity. Some have been turned into motels too. AirBnB is also popular in the parts of Akrasia closest to Wall Titan."

"Yet the Steam Breeds live in tents. You'd think the biggest, baddest dudes on the block would be running the housing market."

"Steam Breeds don't think the same way as you and I, and there's a reason they haven't been decommissioned entirely. Steam Breeds are the Marauder's last resort. They will use them against Steampunk and his forces when the time is right, which is another reason we must destroy the city of Morlock. But there's another reason why the Marauders keep the Steam Breeds. They give them leverage against the Boilerplate Army." He grins. "All this to say, what better way to unleash chaos into the city than to let all the prisoners, the Chain Gangers, and the Steam Breeds out to destroy the city?"

"Something just seems off about all this," I tell the group. "Ray Steampunk – and yes, if you're listening then you should really think about what I'm about to say – is the NVA Seed. If he wanted to destroy Morlock, he'd do it. Come to think of it … " I stop and wait for the group to turn to me. "Our mission *isn't* to destroy a city or a wall or battle a bunch of Steam cyborgs. Our *mission* is to obtain Sky

Iron and hopefully, sniff out some Reapers and hit them with our hacks."

Joel laughs. "Do you have selective memory or something? The only way to get the Sky Iron is to use the last Rogue Steam Mech, which only I can operate. The only way to get me to operate it is to help me destroy the walls."

I don't say anything for the next fifteen minutes or so as we make our way to the entrance. Something about this whole operation is rubbing me the wrong way and I get the feeling, that for the umpteenth time, Ray Steampunk is making our life difficult when he could simply hypnotize Joel, fix the rust, and get us the Sky Iron without having to bring down the three walls of Akrasia.

Methinks we're being played.

~*~

A gramophone above the entrance to Wall Maria sounds out:

~~Those entering from the Lost Pines, unequip any weapons you may be carrying and prepare to have your photo taken.~~

~~Those entering from the Lost Pines, unequip any weapons you may be carrying and prepare to have your photo taken.~~

We get in a line behind a motley group of steampunked visitors, the repeat offenders, I mean, visitors, outfitted in striped prison gear and the others staring at them jealously, ready to drop a pretty shilling on some touristy shit the moment they get through the gate.

A particular couple catches my eye, mainly because the mother has her corset pulled so tightly that it locks as if she's going to burst, that or lift into the air like an air balloon. Her hubby, a Ulysses S. Grant cosplayer with not one, but two, pocket watches, a monocle, and a corncob pipe sticking out of his mouth catches me giving his wife the double-take, and very nonchalantly opens his jacket to show me his concealed revolver.

~~*Those entering from the Lost Pines, unequip any weapons you may be carrying and prepare to have your photo taken.*~~

I know the announcement just said to put our weapons up, but we have a moment and in that moment, I equip the Uberti Cattleman Revolver, item 590, which I won in a crooked game of Russian Roulette in Devil's Alley.

He nods, impressed, and returns his attention to his kiddos.

"What are you doing?" Frances asks as she sees me twirl the revolver around my finger.

Now that I got her attention, and since we have to wait in the line, I mosey up next to her so we can communicate without the others hearing us. "I've got my eye on Joel," I whisper to her, "just so we're clear. I just got a bad feeling about all this."

"Let's just see how it plays out. We need the Sky Iron, well," she turns to me and her eyes practically burn a hole through me. "*You* need the Sky Iron. We're doing this for you."

"Reapers too, we'll squash them. Which reminds me, we need to find out what they're doing here in Akrasia in the first place."

"Good call," she says, "ask Joel once we're inside."

The line moves slowly and eventually, we get to the checkpoint. A recently polished Mondoshawan in a crisp SRT uniform holds an automatic rifle across his chest. Next to him, in similar garb, is another Special Response Team officer, this one with a pair of Leaks over his eyes. He scans each visitor and once he clears them, they're allowed to enter through a large arch cut into Wall Maria. Even before entry, I see the words painted on the face of a building inside: NO MAN'S LAND.

Me: Stay frosty.

Rocket: I'm feeling toasty, myself.

I look over my shoulder at the kid and he shoots me the thumbs up.

"Hold still," the big-boned SRT Mondoshawan officer scans me. He raises an eyebrow.

"What?"

"You know what."

I return the Uberti Cattleman Revolver to my list.

"Stay still."

A Special Response Team officer under a large black covering attached to a wooden box camera squeezes the trigger and immortalizes Mrs. Hughes' Numero Uno Achiever. The SRT officer with head gear grunts, "I said *stay still*. You're moving around too much." He signals for the photographer to try again.

"I got nothin'," I tell him, "nothin'."

"I'll be the judge of that, pal."

"I'm not your pal, pal."

He glances to his compadre just in time for Frances to elbow me in the gut. "I apologize for him."

"No problem," says the SRT officer through his voice box. "We know exactly how to deal with riffraff like this."

Frances pushes me forward before I can respond and I take my place in a line passing under the archway.

At least this line is moving.

It takes all of fifteen seconds to enter Akrasia proper, where I'm greeted with what one would expect from a prison city. Guys and gals big and small mill about mean-dogging and mad-mugging as they go about their lives. The clothing varies, but the fact that there are prison uniform shops near the entrance tells me that wearing something other than orange or duds with black and white stripes is a fashion faux paus.

I got no problem re-togging, and I already have an Alcatraz prison uniform in my list, item 156, which appears on me faster than a snide remark. The numbers 8675 are plastered across the back.

"Not bad, Q Knights," Rocket comments, "but you look more like you're auditioning for the remake of *Brokeback Mountain* than wearing a prison uniform."

"Dammit, Rocket, the Alcatraz prison uniform consisted of blue jeans, a work shirt, and a blue jean jacket."

Aiden clears his throat. "Pretty sure that's called a Canadian tuxedo."

Rocket looks to Frances. "Can I use some guild funding to get properly accoutered? Did I say that right?"

"You're learning," I tell him, "and of course you can. That's about the only perk of being on the Dream Team – playing dress-up professionally."

"He didn't ask you," Frances says, "he asked me. But yes, yes, you can, and Doc and I will join you."

"What about Aiden?"

Morning Assassin snaps his finger and a matching Alcatraz uniform appears with the numbers 309 on the back. "We're matchers," he tells Rocket as he takes a place next to me.

"We need to get to one of the contraband shops," says Joel, "and you're tourists, you don't need to buy prison uniforms."

"But we can, right?" I ask.

He rolls his eyes. "Sure, go ahead."

~*~

"It's this way," says Joel, as we move along the perimeter of the wall towards a contraband shop. Aiden and Rocket have gone with the classic, horizontally striped black and white *Jailhouse Rock* prison outfits while Frances has busted out the *Orange is the New Black* look, classing it down a bit by tying off the tips of her bright orange top at the waist.

Rather than wear the obligatory orange slacks, she's gone with orange yoga pants, practically poured on, which is another thing I've noticed about Akrasia – haute couture is all the rage. Hell, even Doc has jumped on the bandwagon with his supermax dark red prison uniform with the numbers 8008 written on his sleeve.

I hear some Jody calls and Joel stops us, waiting for the Chain Gang to pass.

"I don't know what you've been told!"

"I don't know what you've been told."

"Time is bought and time is sold."

"Time is bought and time is sold."

"I'll do mine and when I'm out."

"I'll do mine and when I'm out."

"I'll be back without a doubt."

"I'll be back without a doubt."

The group of big guys and a few equally plus-sized gals pass, their ankles secured to a shared chain as they pick up trash on the streets.

"It's this one." We follow Joel into a one-story shanty shop about thirty-feet-long. "It's you!" I say as soon as I see the weapons dealer, Steampunk Santa, the same guy who first sold me a Slice Bang in Locus. He's in a pair of oval glasses that make his eyes large and circular and he wears his trademark red frock. A leather vest barely covers his gut and pinned to his lapel is a single peacock feather. I hear the cluck of a chicken and see that he's brought his cat – named Chicken – with him. He looks up at me and smiles.

"Well, if it isn't my favorite not-Marauder!" says he.

"You never told me your name," I say.

"And with good reason, young sir."

"I always called you Steampunk Santa in my head."

He runs his hand through his Billy Gibbons beard. "What do you call me when you're not in your head?"

"Huh?"

"Let it pass, let it pass. The name is Leeroy Jenkins, but Steampunk Santa is fine. Now, how may I serve you on this fine Akrasian afternoon?"

"I thought you didn't sell to Marauders," I joke. "What about Ray's golden boys?" I point to the indicator above my head and nod to Frances. "And girl?"

"Have you learned nothing, *nothing,* from our last encounter?" He sighs, stands and walks to the backroom. "Follow me."

I keep my trap shut as I follow Steampunk Santa – never got a name – into the backroom. "Chacho, wakey wakey, hands off snakey!" he barks at a man sitting on a sealed crate and resting his back against the wall. Chacho also has a beard, although his is less Santa and more Mad Max as it's tied off with two red bands, which match the bandana tied around his noggin. Aside from the steampunk Cap'n Jack Sparrow look on top, the rest of him is world-appropriate, from his pinned cravat to his too-small vest to the tight screamo singer black jeans tucked into shin-high buckle-laden boots.

A measuring tape appears in Chacho's hands.

"You first," he tells the Faun of Unlimited Ammo. Doc steps up, scuttles around just to give everyone a good look at his tail, and allows Chacho to measure him. "A little bigger around the waist than I thought," Chacho mumbles.

"That's armor," Doc tells him. "*Armor.*"

"Yeah, sure it is. Okay, done, you next." He rattles his measuring tape at Rocket. The Dream Team's Boy Wonder steps up and puffs his chest out a bit.

"What the hell are you doing?" Chacho asks.

"We're getting armor, right? I want mine to accentuate my muscles."

"What are we doing here exactly?" I ask Steampunk Santa, who stands near the door conversing in quiet tones with Joel.

"Ah, questions, questions, questions. As this isn't a need-to-know basis, I'll simply tell you point blank. You need Steamsuits and I have four. We are measuring you to see if we need to make any adjustments for the cabin."

"Steamsuits?"

"Based off the Andromeda exoskeleton suits we use up there," Doc says.

I suddenly recall the Steamsuit that was hanging in Steampunk Santa's secret underground weapons lair. "We're getting those things? Badass!"

"Yes, the four of you would be deader than the place Death goes to die if you tried to go into Tent City without some heavy firepower. Even with the favorable stat boosts from the man, the myth, the legend himself and your braggadocious inventory lists … " He smiles at us and the ends of his mustache lift, " … you'd still be dead."

"Got it," Doc says.

"So to level the playing field, as it were, each of you is getting a custom Steamsuit EXO 76, which you may recall – and if you do, I must commend you for your memory – I showed the two of you," he points at Frances and Yours Truly, "when you visited my humble weapons shop back in Locus. Having some proper mech will make you formidable in the eyes of the Steam Breeds, and they may not simply crush you upon contact."

"I thought you only had one of those," I say, recalling the piece that hung from the ceiling of his underground lair.

"I now have four, the only four."

"How'd you manage that?"

He furrows his brow. "You and your questions. If you must know, a young woman named Cyn Oneida managed to secure the other three, well four, as mine was stolen. But that's a story for another day."

"So candid all of a sudden!"

Steampunk Santa scoffs. "It's not like you'll remember her name two seconds from now."

"Who's name?" I ask with a sly grin.

"Enough asshattery." He claps his hands. "Time for measurements!"

Frances steps forward to get her measurements taken.

Curiously, Chacho spends more time measuring her bust than is necessary, and I watch him do it, the damn perv I am. I don't know what has come over me, but suddenly, in my mind's eye, I see Euphoria naked in all her magnificent glory. Damn if we didn't have some fun together and damn if those times aren't looking like they are going to be cherished fapping memories from here on out. Euphoria ain't budging, and I'm pretty sure Mrs. Hughes' Most Successful Creation won't be changing that anytime soon.

"Your turn, tough guy," says Chacho.

I step up and Chacho gets to measuring as Steampunk Santa details the Steamsuit capabilities to Doc, who has taken quite the interest as apparently he has used an Andromeda model in the real world.

Of course he has.

A bell in the other room rings and Steampunk Santa excuses himself. I look to Joel, who has taken to examining some of the crates at the back of the room.

So that's the kablooey.

And it's then that I realize the back wall of the room is actually Wall Maria. The contraband shop has been built next to the wall, using the wall as its own back wall. Joel reaches out knocks his hand on the wall.

What's he's thinking is anyone's guess, but my guess is that it involves bringing the wall down and possibly getting up inside Bjurstrom and taking a little nappy. I don't quite see the relationship here, seems like Joel is simply an extension of the downed rogue steam mech, but that's just me.

Steampunk Santa steps back in the room. "Ahem, gather around young boy scouts and girl scouts." he lowers his voice. "Reapers have appeared in another quarter of the city and they're going door to door looking for you."

~*~

No time to sit around and chew the fat. The three, if I dare say, *bestest* members of the Team of Dreams have made it to the streets faster than upchucked poisoned muffle Trumplings after a night of lukewarm WalMacy's sake.

Three's company and five's a crowd – Joel thought it would be better if we divide up, just in case the Reapers are able to cut through us. I would have taken offense to Joey even making that assumption, but I was so geared up to get out and get to ass-stomping that I kept my trap shut. Besides, it'd be best to lure the Reapers *away* from the contraband shop.

Aiden flashdances away.

He's back in a jiffy with a wolfish grin on his face. "Four Reapers, half a klick east on a block lined with bail bond shops."

It's then that I notice the thickness of the crowd all around us. The family I saw from earlier is here too, their kids decked out in steampunk souvenirs and prison uniforms. I don't know how this place became both a DisNike vacation destination and a spot for hardened criminals, but reason and Proxima worlds never were bedfellows.

There's gonna be some collateral damage.

"How do we want to go about doing this?" I ask.

Doc thinks for a moment. "Four of them, three of us, that's pretty good odds if you ask me, especially considering the fact that normally it's about twenty Reapers to one Dream Team member, which begs the question, why do they suck so badly? They're like the 2008 Detroit

Lions or something." His MSIWI appears in his hand. "Let's find them and fill 'em full of holes."

"Now we're talking, Doc!"

He returns his Metal Storm bonesaw to his list. "Better yet, we'd better save one for interrogation purposes."

"They'll just log out; they always do."

"Not with these." A pair of burnished steel cuffs take shape in his hand.

"Whatchoo got there?"

Doc shrugs nonchalantly. "The Reapers aren't the only one that can prevent someone from logging out "

Sophia: Doc! You said you wouldn't use those unless you had to!

Rocket: Wait, is he using the permalog cuffs? NOT FAIR. Why am I not part of the Kill Squad? Only squares and girl scouts stay back and protect the target. Also, not fair. All of this is not fair.

Frances Euphoria: The Dream Team does not use permalog cuffs, as per our bylaws. Rocket, I was a girl scout and I'm proud of the fact. Anything else you'd like to say while I'm standing in the same room as you?

Rocket: Got any thin mints?

I laugh aloud and Aiden gives me a funny look. "Sorry," I tell him, "it was something on the messaging system."

Doc: FYI – the Dream Team is *not* using permalog cuffs. I was only *telling* Quantum about them. Remember, comms are for important conversations only. We will handle the hostiles. Frances and Rocket, you continue to provide protection for Joel and anyone else in his establishment. Rocket, shut your mouth and sit on your hands until we get back.

I wink at Doc, letting him know I'm in on his little white lie.

He does not wink back. Instead, he points at the darkened sky over Morlock, right at Sophia, and makes the universal 'keep quiet' single finger to his lips, followed by the 'I'll cut your throat' gesture. Amazingly, Sophia gets the picture.

"Welp, better get outfitted." I go with my SPAS-12 Shotgun, item 189, to match Morning Assassin's shotty. Just to keep things world-appropriate, I equip my saber pistol, item 559, and holster it. For flare – because who doesn't need a bit of flare? – I equip item 71, my eel leather belt with its QH belt buckle that spins.

I give the belt a good spin and Doc gives me a look that could break open a safe.

"What else … what else? I know!" Wade Wilson's carbonadium katanas, item 325, appear on my back.

"You done playing dress-up?" Aiden asks, but by the twinkle in his eyes, I can tell he's impressed. His two SPAS-12s disappear and he smirks as his right arm morphs into a hand cranked Gatling gun. The ammo belt materializes in his other hand and after he loads and locks, he throws the belt over his shoulder like it's the Tinman's brass-and-copper scarf. "What?" he asks. "You aren't the only one that is allowed to be *well-armed*. And that, my friends, is how you make a pun."

"I've gotta *hand* it to you, that wasn't bad."

He rolls his eyes. "Let's go."

The three of us fan out, Aiden in the lead. I don't suspect it will be hard to find the Reapers with their masks, muscles, chains, and overall douchiness and for once, I'm not wrong.

We turn the corner and as Aiden reported, the Reapers are on Bail Bond Street, shoving their way through the crowd as they move to the next establishment. Apparently, whomever they bought their information from only gave them a portion of it, never telling them exactly where we were heading.

Me: Bystanders, what are we going to do about these guys?

Doc: I'll take care of that.

Too late. Apparently, I'm a big deal at the Reaper Saloon, or wherever they hang out. One spots me instantly as if I were wearing a neon green jumper and a matching Dr. Seuss top hat.

"Hit the deck!" I shout as he unloads a long burst of metal unhappiness right into the crowd, tearing through the flesh of convicts, tourists, and whoever else has made the very unfortunate choice of visiting Akrasia today.

"Out of the way!"

AA bar activated, I go for my tried and true 'walks on shoulders' act, leaping from shoulder to shoulder as the Reapers mow through the crowd. Faster than a recently wealthy running back sprinting away from law enforcement, Doc plows through the crowd with his two Steyr AUG's pumping out 5.56 NATOs like 'cool' is going out of business and he's the one trying to run it into the ground.

The War Faun is juiced on his AA too; his bullets expertly avoid the fleeing crowd as if the bullets have minds of his own.

Damn that's some good shootin'!

Aiden tele-kills the first Reaper, a stocky little pitbull pup with watermelon biceps and a gelled up wowsie-wow Mohawk jutting out the top of his Reaper mask. Before the next guy can even get his weapon up, Morning Assassin is behind him with his Gatling gun arm giving him the reverse firing range treatment. He's gone before the next Reaper can spin around, get his hack up, and fire a blistering blast of fiery blue energy into Da Kine Bail, completely destroying the joint.

My turn.

BOOM-shakalaka-BOOM! I take the skull mask off a Reaper broad's ugly mug and finish the job by speeding up on the AA as I overhand one of my Carbonadium katanas. It pegs her in the shoulder; she hits the pavement and logs out immediately.

Shit!

A fist outta nowhere sends me tumbling sideways.

It only takes one long, dazed glance to see that the beefiest of the Reapers is double-hacked up. The end of one of his arms is morphed into some type of symbiose Stretch Armstrong/Popeye fist, and the other a double barrel gun with underslung biomatter just to give it a cool futuristic look.

Doc: The smallest one is our patsy. I'll get him cuffed before he logs out! You and Aiden take the other.

"With pleasure, Doc!"

Aiden has a career in telepathy if he just hones his skills and finally decides to go back to night school. He's already laying down metal utterances of death by the time I get my shootin' iron up and start a-blasting Rollins' brother from another mother one boom-shakalaka after another.

I could go freeze hack and Gramoguns, items 554 and 558 respectively, but a nice afternoon of shooting always calms my nerves. Sure, the big bastard Hulk-smashed the hell out of the pavement sending debris and dust into the air, and sure, the bozo can blast the surrounding buildings with his hack until he's blue in the face, but he doesn't have the speed or sheer bulletry that Aiden and I are prepared to lay down to kill the bruiser.

So we keep shooting, Aiden flashing in and out to avoid the Reaper's blasts and Yours Truly simply lets MA distract the Bronie as I keep pumping shots at Papa Bear.

Eventually, those bullets start to tear through his spike-laden armor and it is with great glory that Aiden appears directly in front of the schmoe-hawk, Slice Bang in hand, and stabs him in the stomach while simultaneously firing a shot.

The big sissy logs out before he can completely croak.

"Let me go!" I look over to see that Doc now has the smaller Reaper permacuffed. He pulls him to his feet and Aiden appears next to him.

Me: Where do we take him?

Doc: Not the safehouse. How 'bout whatever is left of Da Kine Bail?

I point with my nose towards the smoldering bail bond shop and Aiden gets the drift. He yanks the Reaper towards the joint and pulls him behind a partially crumbled wall.

"What did you do to me!?" the Reaper bellows.

"Quiet," Doc says as he bends over and gets in his face. "Or I'll make sure you'll never logout out again. We clear here?"

The Reaper gulps audibly and nods his head.

~*~

I wait for Sophia to protest and much to my surprise and delight, she doesn't.

"You're not supposed to illegally trap people!" the Reaper whines, his voice muffled and metallic due to his skull mask. Speaking of which, I rip the skull mask off, curious as to what this bozo hides underneath.

"Hey!" he screams.

This one dumped all his attribute points into appearance. He's got the angular Fabio face down to a T, and a ridiculous Guile haircut to boot. Too bad his septum piercing is too small for me to grab hold of and yank out.

"What's your name, son?" Doc asks. Can't tell if he is going for good cop or bad cop here. I'm down for either.

"Screw you, goat-man!"

Bad cop it is. The reaper cries out as Doc pistol whips the shit out of him.

Sophia: Doc!

"Stop! Please! Okay, I'll tell you all of it, anything. Anything!" he sobs. "Don't hurt me! It … it hurts!"

Aiden shakes his head, truly disappointed.

"Look, my name isn't important. It's information you want, right? I'll tell you what you want to know. Just leave my name out of this. I ... " he hesitates and whispers. "I don't want *him* to know."

"Okay then," Doc says. "Let's start here – why are the Reapers in Akrasia? Hell, why are you people even in Steam for that matter?"

The Reaper grimaces. "Sky Iron," he finally says, "that's why. We're here to collect it. I have no idea why anyone wants the damn metal. Not my department. I'm the lowest rung on the totem pole, if you couldn't already tell. That damn Sky Iron seems impossible to find anyway. All we've been able to get is a little bit from some guy's tooth."

Sophia: THEY'RE HERE FOR THE SAME REASON WE ARE.

I nearly trip as the capital letters spill across my viewing pane. Aiden gives me a confused look and I wave it away. "Sophia," I mumble.

"What's he planning?" Doc asks the Reaper pigeon. "What's Strata planning to do with the Sky Iron?"

The Reaper snorts. "Like I know what he's planning! You realize I've never met the guy, don't you? Hell, most of us haven't! I've only seen him on other people's live streams and in videos that we are required to view. That's it, honest!"

"Then why the hell do you follow him?" I ask.

"Because ... " his eyes glaze over. "Because he knows the way. He has brought us this far, and he will bring us to the end."

"Holy Kool Aid, dumbass," I say, "I don't think that's quite how it works."

"You asked!" he snaps. "And I'm sure, no matter what you do to me, Quantum Hughes, Strata will finish what he started!"

What he started?

"Doc, let me see your bean shooter." Too lazy to equip my own, I step forward and pop the shit out of the Reaper.

"Hey!"

Sophia: Sky Iron, when used in conjunction with other precious metals, can tear through the game time continuum. I'd bet my future home in Valhalla that this is the reason Strata wants it!

"You'll have to tell us more than that if you want to ever logout again," Doc tells him, "much, much more than that."

"You really ... plan to prevent me from logging out?" the Reaper snivels and his eyes flash black. "I'm recording, you know!"

Now it's Doc's turn to laugh. "You really don't realize what those cuffs do, do you?"

The Reaper instinctively struggles to turn and take a look at them. Once he realizes he can't he seethes, "They will come for me; once they see that I haven't joined them back in the dive location."

The last two words spark a memory. I recall what Frances and Arnie discovered when they went to retrieve Luther Godsick's body in Colorado. There were tons of vats at his devious papa's McMansion; there must have been fifty to a hundred. "Wait a damn minute. Is your real body in Strata's mansion?" I blurt out.

He shakes his head and scowls at me. "Did you not hear a word that I said? I've never met the guy, which means I'm *definitely* not in his Meridian Circuit." He bites his lip, suddenly realizing he's said too much. "Shit … "

"Meridian Circuit, huh?" Doc grins from cheek to cheek, stretching his salt-n-pepper goatee wide. "Ready to tell us a little more about that?"

"What do I have to tell you for you to set me free?" he counters.

Doc doesn't take his eyes off him. "Something important, something that we can actually use."

"The Meridian Circuit is Strata's inner circle. They are perma-logged in. They … " he gulps. "They protect him."

"If these guys are so tough," I ask, "why haven't we encountered them before?"

The Reaper moves forward and wipes blood from his nose to his sleeve. "You have," he says quietly. "You're just too stupid to realize it. They *are* Strata. They power him."

Chapter Eight

To make himself invincible, Strata's avatar is created from the Digital Neuronal Autoconstruct System, D-NAS, of every single member of his Meridian Circuit. This makes him stronger than any RPC, NPC, or PC he encounters.

The bastard is feeding off the Meridian Circuit, and their autoconstruct combinations have given him god-like powers.

What's even crazier is that like me, the members of the circuit exist in two worlds, their bodies in vats in Strata's home and their avatars in specially constructed extraction centers in the Proxima Galaxy. By not having a single player identity, normal parameters that apply to any given player do not apply to Strata.

"So ... he could theoretically crush an NVA Seed?" I ask as we make our way back to the contraband shop. With no more information to provide to us, Doc let the Reaper go, but not before blasting the palooka with his hack. Do not pass go, do not collect two-hundred bones – I wonder sometimes what it must be like to be a Reaper and *not* be able to log back into the Proxima Galaxy. Well, sure, they can log in, but they won't make it out of the OMIB, plus there's the spanking by Granny Weatherwax.

Sheesh.

Sophia: To answer your question, Quantum, an NVA seed consists of four intertwined strands of D-NAS. Strata's avatar, if the Reaper was being honest, consists of over fifty.

Rocket: (/) (°,,°) (/) WHAT the hell did I miss?

Sophia: Here's the transcript.

Rocket: What no vid?

Sophia: No.

Rocket: #whatcenturyamIlivingin?

"Why does he want Sky Iron there?" I glance to the War Faun, who appears to be deep in thought. A cancer stick takes shape in his mouth and after a long inhale, he exhales a cloud of blue smoke.

"With the Sky Iron, Strata could potentially crush an NVA Seed and thus destroy a Proxima world. No doubt about it."

"He can't destroy an NVA Seed." Aiden steps around a man in prison garb holding hands with a short guy with mechanical legs. "He can overpower one, but he can't destroy it."

"Even though … " I do the math in my head. "He's about twelve times stronger than an NVA Seed?"

Doc nods. "That's why he needs the Sky Iron. I really don't know why they invented it in the first place. Combined with metals from other worlds, it can make the equivalent of a nuclear weapon for dreamworlds." Doc looks to the darkened sky. An SRT Zeppelin is moored over Akrasia with lines connected to a few of the taller structures. "Ray, I know you're watching, and you know better than to hold out on us here."

Nothing.

"Good luck with that, Doc," I tell the Faun of Steam. "I don't know what Ray's endgame is, but I have the feeling he isn't exactly concerned with how this plays out."

"Yeah, I think you're wrong." Doc shrugs. "Definitely wrong there. Strata could destroy Steam, which would destroy Ray. So, Ray, ahem, a little help for the faun? How 'bout giving us some Sky Iron and destroying whatever is left after we free Quantum's dumb ass?"

The clink clank of chains striking the pavement pricks my ears. The Akrasia Chain Gang turns a corner in front of us. Steam's scummiest scum march right past us with scowls on their faces. They range in size from mountain to hillock. A few puny guys make up the rear and one – shaved head, tattooed skull, pockmarked cheeks – gives me an especially ugly snarl.

"You planning to back that snarl up with some bite?" I ask the scuzzbag with an Adam's apple that looks like he's got a cantaloupe lodged in his throat. He's gone before I can get an answer.

"There's more to this story," I say after the Chain Gang is out of earshot.

"Gee," Doc says, "You think?"

Sophia: Many Proxima worlds have a single rare metal that can be used to craft that particular world's most powerful weapon. Rare Proxima Galaxy metals. Remember this? RPG! They weren't meant to become alloys, but it seems like that is what Strata's trying to do here. Need I remind you that we too are trying to do this?

Me: No you need not and I don't know why you choose to do so.

Sophia: Good.

I ignore her next lengthy explanation. "What I mean by *there's more to this story* is that there is something Strata is trying to do with these metals, and I don't think we should necessarily jump to a Death

Star conclusion here. What else can be done with these alloys? Is there a profit motive here?"

Doc considers this for a moment. "I don't see what the profit motive could be, but I'm not putting it past him. Sophia? Any ideas?"

Sophia: Maybe it's a control thing. Maybe he wants to use it to threaten NVA Seeds. For once, I agree with Quantum, there must be some type of profit motive here.

"Maybe he's trying to get the Proxima Company by the balls," I say as I step around a confectionary stand. Candy shivs on a stick? No thank you. "They must be monitoring this and Revenue Corporation."

"The Proxima Company practices the same philosophy as Ray Steampunk." Doc stops in his tracks, glances at the wares of weapon shop, thinks about going in, decides not to, and continues. "They don't get involved unless it is of dire consequences."

"Reapers in Akrasia looking for Sky Iron isn't considered a consequence?"

"Any player can look for RPG metals. It's not against a by-law or anything."

"So we can't expect their help then, huh?" I ask.

"Have we had their help thus far?" Doc asks. "Let's get back to the RW."

~*~

Got a machinehead, it's better than the rest.
Green to red, machinehead.

All sorts of shit appears in my mind's eye. Everything from the layout of the hotel to fluctuations in temperatures in the room remind me that, without a shadow of a doubt, I am far from human. I don't need to even open my eyes to know that Sophia is lying on the bed. I don't need to search for things to do in LA to know that the Holo-Eagles are playing a concert at PepsiCo's Dodgers Stadium tonight and that while tickets are sold out, you can still purchase tickets to the virtual concert. I don't need to check the AQI to know that LA is currently sitting in the yellow zone with a passing score of 71.

What a day it has been.

I feel like I need the CliffsNotes to my own life. It started out with a message from Strata, – that'll be a shitshow – and it moved to Steam, where we met with the God Emperor Ray Steampunk who sent us on a quest to Akrasia to fetch some Sky Metal. After that little sesh with Steampunk on his wowsie-wow airship, Sophia and I bangtailed it to LA, where we met Doc for Veenure's real life extraction tonight.

From there, it was back to Steam and to the Lost Pines, where we were attacked by Bjurstrom the steam mech and his driver Joe. L, or Joel, the weird bastard, who later joined us. Then it was a *Mr. Gorbachev, tear down this wall* scenario in which Yours Trulies are supposed to destroy the three walls around Akrasia in return for some Minecraft action from Bjustrom. While we scoped the joint, we found out that there were some Reapers snooping around and we got the nogoodniks before they could get us. An interrogation commenced, and it turns out the Reapers *too* are after the Sky Iron and Strata has a large group of permadivers in his McMansion known as the Meridian

Circuit that are giving him his incredible power when he's in the Proxima Galaxy.

Whatever happened to simplicity? I swear someone is making this up as I go along.

Once I get my meatsack back, *if* I get my meatsack back, I'm taking an epic vacation, dammit. It doesn't matter where, as long as it's to a place that I can catch a breath of fresh air. A Caribbean island maybe, or the Poconos. I wouldn't mind doing a little whale watching on a trip from San Fran to Anchorage, hop over to Tokyo and spend some time in a Zen garden in Kyoto before bouncing to an atoll in French Polynesia followed by a quick skedaddle to South Africa for a little safari and from there, to Buenos Aires for a vibrant night out.

Sometimes I forget I'm a government employee, an *unpaid* government employee, thus far.

"No, Chuntao, ice cream is better on a warm day than shaved ice. Seriously. Shaved ice is like, an early sign that a person is suffering from Pica."

A voice responds from a small wireless speaker on the nightstand. "I respectfully disagree, beautiful Sophia. Pagophagia is hardly as harmful as Pica, and nutrients that can be derived from the vitamins and minerals now put into the flavoring used for shaved ice are beneficial to your species."

Kill me now. The most ultimate-est of ultimate ironies has put my artificial keister in a hotel room with a rape-y scientist and her terrible, horrible, no good, very bad AI. Woe is me, or something like that, but it's the hand I've been dealt and hell, I'm the one who dealt it!

"Quantum, what are you doing over there? Why does it look like you are brooding?"

Chuntao offers me a terse greeting in the form of a squeaky utterance.

"Thinking about stuff," I tell Dr. Drains-me-stein. I open my eyes to find her – surprise surprise – on the bed in a lacy nighty. For the love of all that is holy, I have no idea what has gotten into Sophia and why she insists on skimpy clothes whenever we're alone. The answer is no. Not if I were drunk off my ass, not with another droid's stolen pecker, not if we were the last two people on earth and the fate of humanity in our hands.

Me: Save me.

Frances Euphoria: Save yourself.

Me: It stings, it burns, kill it with fire!

Frances Euphoria: What are you talking about?

Me: You really don't know what goes on when I'm around Sophia, do you?

I turn my feed on for a second, letting Frances catch Sophia propped up on the bed next to her NV Visor. Her nighty is hiked up enough for me to almost see a swath of upper thigh. When in doubt, turn up the jealousy? We'll see if it works. If that doesn't work, douse them with pity.

"Come lie next to me," Sophia says as she pats the bed, "that chair must be so uncomfortable. I feel like lying next to someone."

"Cuddle up to one of those pillows, pretend it's your ex."

Sophia rolls her eyes at me.

Frances Euphoria: LOLZ!

Me: THIS is not a LOLZ situation, for crying out loud! Do you see what I'm faced with here? Dr. Wang has a thing for robo-wang, and I have no wang, so I don't even know where I'm going with that joke except to say, please, for the love of all that is holy and good on this rotten earth of ours, save me.

Frances Euphoria: Fine, come over here and keep quiet about it. I'm across the hall. And don't think for one minute that I'm not still angry at you.

Me: You were just laughing.

Frances Euphoria: I was laughing at your misfortune.

"Well, Doc is calling me," I smile briskly at Sophia, "we need to get together and plot some big league espionage shit."

"Okay, I'll come." She quickly tells Chuntao that they'll finish their conversation later. The droid responds with a trademark trouser blast. "Behave, Chuntao, there's no reason to get angry!"

"But Sophia," the metallic voice rings out, "I'm not done with explaining the reasoning behind my summer food of choice!"

"Just stay here," I tell her, "Continue your discussion. The meeting is top secret, need-to-know."

"Okay, then I'll go over to Frances' room and catch up." She folds her arms over her chest. "You know, for the only two women on the team, I feel like Frances and I don't spend enough time together."

I sigh, or at least I try to make a sighing sound. It doesn't give me the satisfaction like it would if I were in my own body.

"Is the droid grumpy?" Chuntao asks. "He is a very stupid droid; maybe too stupid to understand the basic human emotion of vexation. I'd say he is trying to be grumpy, but he is coming off like a little fox turd. I hate your droid help, Sophia."

"Dammit, Sophia, Chuntao – " I point outside to the general location of Doc's RV. "Meet me down there!" I'm out of her room before she can say anything else and before I can thrash the place like a coked-up 1980s rock star.

As soon as I step outside her room, my droidie senses tingle. The hallway is clear and empty, and I'm definitely on the lookout for a pair of creepy little twin girls in blue dresses.

I knock on the big FE's door in the vein of *We Will Rock You.* She answers moments later, in her oh-so-tight-oh-so-nice Dream Team duds. She's got a smirk on her face that melts my mechanical heart. Since coming back to this world, I always knew there would be Reapers and repercussions. Little did I know the extent of my poor choices; little did I know that one day, I'd have more in common with a toaster than a living, breathing human being.

Heya Dollface, I almost say. Instead, I go with a different greeting all together. "Thank you for saving me."

"You're welcome. Come in."

"Also, FYI, Sophia is hot on my tail and she'll be looking for me in a few moments, after she's put some damn pants on," I say as I slip inside. "I sent her to Doc; better give him the heads up."

I fire off a message before Frances can even close the door.

Me: What's up, Doc? Sophia is coming for her briefing.

Doc: The briefing is scheduled thirty minutes from now!

Me: I'm sure you'll find something to talk about until then.

Doc: She was in her nighty again, wasn't she?

Me: I can neither confirm nor deny ...

Doc: You can stop your Glomar response right there. Looks like the meeting is starting fifteen minutes earlier. You and Euphoria get down here ASAP.

Me: Damn. I was trying to have a moment here!

Doc: So was I, with a barbeque sandwich that you've now ruined by sending Doctor Wang to me. What goes around comes around. See you in fifteen.

"Doc says we need to get our asses down there in fifteen minutes."

Frances walks to a chair near the window and sits on the edge. She crosses one leg over the other and offers me a curt nod. "Good."

"Look here, fifteen minutes ain't a lot of time to spill my guts, and you know where I stand on all this, anyway. I'm just happy to be around you, even if I'm technically 2,647.63 miles away from you."

"Distance from LA to Baltimore?"

I nod. "You know, Frances. If you kept me around more often, you'd find that I know tons of interesting little facts and tidbits that would surely brighten your day. For example, the HoloEagles are playing tonight. And in a way, we're in a hotel in California, so that must mean something."

She starts to laugh and catches herself. "You're ridiculous." Frances takes a bottle of lotion from her purse and squeezes some onto her hands and smooths it up her arms. "What?" she asks. "My skin is surprisingly dry."

"Mine ... too?"

She gives me a funny look. "You really think I'm going to lotion up a Humandroid?"

"Well, when you put it like that."

She shakes her head, no longer joking.

"Lighten up, Frances, I'm just horsing around." I sit down onto her bed and collapse backwards. The *thunk* sound is a wee bit louder than if I were to do this in my real body. Again, I ain't me, or the old me, that is. I'm me in the way that someone on their profile is themselves. Close, but no cigar.

"Don't get comfortable," she tells me. "And you should drink a glass of water. You're supposed to have eight ounces per day."

"There's water in whiskey, right?" I ask with a smirk.

"I ... " She thinks about this for a moment. "I have no idea what would happen if you drank alcohol. I'm guessing I wouldn't like the outcome."

Chapter Nine

"That really you in there, Doc?" I ask as I look Arnie over.

Arnie is half a head taller than Doc, humandroid-thin, and even though he is wearing a pair of overalls, he looks pretty damn fierce in his tactical vest.

Of course it's Doc.

I just saw his body lying on his bed in the back of the RV with something akin to an NV Visor over clamped his noggin. Holy Cerebro knock-off, Batman! The InterHead skull unit, while great for soldiers in the field, may also be used to find estranged mutants and as a Deus ex Machina plot device for pretty much every other X-Men movie. I'm surprised Marvel hasn't sued InterHead already.

I'm also surprised DisNike hasn't bought Marvel.

I glance to the big bad Faun of the Dream Team and give him my most sincere, shit-eating grin.

"Good, now that I'm suited up, let's go over the plan." No country twang here – Doc's voice is true grit with a side of rusty blade. How he is able to have that sort of voice and I'm stuck with Evan's effeminate intonation is beyond me.

He clasps his hands behind his back. "As you all know, Veenure can't log in, not yet anyway, and I'd bet good money that RevCo has a team of programmers trying to reverse engineer the effects of our mutant hacks. They may get there eventually, but they're not there. So, according to the intel I've gathered, Victoria – we should probably call her by her real name – has a lot of free time on her hands. A lot. Rather than sit around and whack off, which is what most Reapers have done since they've been forced out of the Proxima Galaxy – I know, I track them –Victoria has taken to going to extreme fitness classes."

I swear someone needs to roll in a cork board with a bunch of suspects' pictures pinned to them. Instead, we have iNet. Case in point: the pictures of Victoria Godsick that now scroll across my iNet screen and lines linking her to known associations. She's thinner than most gamers – hey, what can I say? – and in all but one of the pictures, she's in workout gear. The broad has the Godsick nose, that's for sure, but other than that, there's nothing that really stands out about her appearance.

Doc says, "We know that Victoria is living in the Revenue Complex, which is a three-story donut-shaped building with a park and outdoor fitness area in the middle."

The schematics flash on my iNet screen. The place looks posh as hell, a lot nicer than the flophouse the FCG was keeping my ass in back in Baltimore.

"She's on the third floor, in the east wing, room 314. After her fitness class, she will exit the park, and make her way to her room. This is when we'll nab her from both ends. Easy peasy. The center park has four exits, and naturally, she'll go through the one closest to her room, which will put her out on the first floor."

Dots appear on the schematics, two green and one red, *the target*.

"Quantum will go through the front and neutralize any security they may have. *Nonlethal – this* part is important. I'll do the same from the back."

The green dots enter and move towards the red dot on the schematic.

"We'll get her, and move out the east wing fire exit, where we'll be picked up."

"By who again?" Sophia asks.

"By Louie De Palma. From there, we'll switch vehicles twice, and bring her here. The Dream Team has federal jurisdiction to take her into custody, but due to the sensitivity of the issue and the fact that the Dream Team is partially funded by a Revenue shell organization – Sphere Global LLC – we're conducting this as a covert op. Solon has all the evidence set to be released if RevCo tries to take this to the press. In related news, testicular torsion 1301 is now a class offered at American University. I'm working on 1302 to start next semester." Doc-as-Arnie smiles curtly.

"What are our call signs?" I ask. "Because I've been thinking … "

"Yours is Metal Man, mine is Bovidae," says Doc, "Frances is Mama. Sophia will not be on comms, and we will not be using iNet for this mission. Everyone clear?"

"I want a new call sign."

"It was Metal Man or Steamboy," Doc tells me, "and I figured you wouldn't like Steamboy."

~*~

Boy is it sunny in The Big Orange.

The weather is oh-so-perfect and if my pasty meatsack were here, I'd definitely have to spend some quality time on the beach working on a tan. Pale as a vampire may be a thing in some circles, and it may be a direct result of being a gamer, but I definitely plan to get a golden sheen when I finally get my RW body back.

The thought of tanning gets me wondering as to what type of swimsuit Frances may have, which triggers some memories.

Memories are odd from within the shell of a Humandroid's body. They're clear and at the same time, it is like I'm watching them through a telescopic lens, alien to my own observations and experiences. They don't have the closeness that one associates with important memories; there's something myopic about them, something stark and fuzzy. They make me feel cold even though this feeling doesn't register per se on my droid bod's iNet screen.

Both Doc and I are outfitted with weapons, Glock 22s, both with toggle switches that trigger a neuromuscular inhibitor, several mags, and Bullshark G-10 8CR13 tactical knives. We're in a lightweight milspec vest under our EBAYmazon clothing, which fits better than I thought it would.

Security isn't too heavy according to Doc's sources, no more than six people, and the likelihood of any of them providing an issue to highly trained Humandroids is nil. Not to prop us up, but with the combat info Doc had me download, I can neutralize a target in no less than three-thousand ways, and that's just with my hands. Give me a blade and a shootin' iron and you're looking at a real killing machine.

A corona of light reflects into the cabin and my Humandroid sensors go bonkers, telling me everything from the current weather temp to the change in cabin pressure as our LyftAeros lowers to another skylane. The Hollywood Hills are somewhere over my shoulder, the ocean somewhere else. The beach is sparking, the street is piping hot. I'm in the moment and I'm not. The light pollution haze matches my current mindset and it's time to let it go.

Let it go, let it go, can't hold it back anymore.

Damn if that wasn't a popular song when I was an anklebiter.

"You ready for this?" Doc-as-Arnie asks.

I nod. Never thought I'd find my Humandroid tookus in the backseat of an aeros next to Doc as a droid. Halloween came early this year.

The dashboard announces that we'll be making our landing soon. LyftAeros in-cab electronics system keeps trying to sync with Evan's OS. It's worse than the David Beckham bathroom products or the host of other ads that overload my iNet screen when I'm in my human form.

In my human form. Ha! I kill myself.

But seriously, the ads are bad, but what happens in a droid's chrome dome? Worse. I walk around feeling violated half the time as various systems try to latch onto mine, integrate, attempt to autoload.

Frances Euphoria's voice appears in my head. True to the covert nature of the operation, there will be no iNet comms. "Bovidae, Metal Man, Mama, you are approaching the drop off point. Bovidae will remain in the taxi, which will take him to the other side of the complex. Metal Man, approach the front entrance and clear the air, over."

Doc says, "Mama, Bovidae, affirmative."

I don't say anything. It's interesting to hear Frances get on comms like a pro and boy am I glad to have her voice in my ear rather than Dr. Explains-too-much.

A minute or so later, the LyftAeros lands several blocks away from the complex and I hop out.

It lifts back into the air and a gust of wind pushes past me. Yup, this is definitely a tech housing area. Silicon Beach is peppered with fair-trade ethically sourced kosher halal grocers, high-end coffee shops with manicured patios, heated kundalini yoga studios, kitschy food trucks, and fancy pet grooming establishments. Talk about different lives – the lives lived by those in tech are a far cry from the lives of those who make up the majority of their customers.

I keep a low profile as I make my way to the entrance.

Lots of the dwellings here are built in circular shapes, and I'm glad to have a very precise guidance system a la GoogleFace showing me the way. I don't know what the world was like without GoogleFace maps, but my guess is that it was a bitch to navigate certain places. Not anymore. The only problem with the map apps that play such a big part of our lives is that we are no longer able to get lost.

"Mama, Metal Man, approaching, over," I say in a low voice.

Frances responds. "Metal Man, Mama, Bovidae is moving into position. One minute to entry, over."

One minute. A horned lark lands in a tree outside the entrance to the establishment. The horned lark scoots over towards the trunk of the tree, which is still secured to the ground by stakes to allow it to grow. It chirps and I listen to it for a moment as the world comes to a standstill all around me. On my iNet screen, a load of information about this particular species of bird comes to me.

"Metal Man, Mama, Bovidae in position, you may proceed. All target iNet feeds will be disabled in fifteen seconds, over."

"Mama, Metal Man, affirmative. Mama, Metal Man, disable all outgoing communications from the concierge, over."

"Metal Man, Mama, affirmative. All live feeds disabled, over."

I take the steps that lead to the Reaper Complex and a set of motoglass doors slide open. *Two guards on the right, in front of the main entrance, one concierge, all human.*

"May I help you?" the concierge asks.

"Yes, I'm here to work on the EBAYMazon drone drop-off point. I received a work order."

"I see," says the concierge. His eyes flash. "Ah yes, here it is. Please step over to the checkpoint. All outside persons are checked before entry."

I do as instructed and the security guards approach. I lift my arms for the pat down and as soon as the first one's hand touch me, I grab him by the back of the shoulders and slam him face first into the wall behind me.

The other one scrambles for his weapon, but I reach him before he can unholster it. I pull his arm back, snap it, and hold it there as he screeches in pain.

The schematics of the space travel across my mind's eye. *The janitor's closet.*

The man I'm still holding onto struggles to pry himself from my grip. "You ... you broke my arm you asshole droid!"

The other one is still in lalaland; the faceplant into the wall left a small crater and the blood smeared across his lips tells me I've broken his nose.

"You," I tell the concierge. "Help him into that closet, *now.*"

The concierge, shaken beyond belief, is hardly able to move. I see him try to move, but I know his nerves are shot. No vital scan needed. He faints and smacks his head on the desk.

I push the guy forward, drop quickly and disarm his bloodied partner, and by the time I'm back on my feet, I have my Glock pointed at him. "Help him to the closet," I tell the one still standing. "No funny stuff or I will kill you."

He helps his counterpart up and without saying a word, he takes him to the janitor's closet.

"You ain't done," I tell him. "Get the concierge and stuff him in there too."

He obliges and soon, the concierge too is in the closet.

"Now get in there yourself."

"Whatever you say, droid," he grumbles, "you'll be decomissioned for this."

He gets in the closet and closes the door shut.

"Mama, Metal Man, remote lock the janitor closet door, over."

"Metal Man, Mama, affirmative."

I hear the lock click shut. I holster my weapon, smooth out my uniform, and I'm just about to proceed when the glass door slides open and Veenure steps out, a yoga mat tucked under her arm and a towel over her shoulder.

~*~

"Who are you?" she asks. Her vitals indicate a heightened sense of awareness, but not much else.

"Your worst nightmare," I growl, my weapon trained on her.

Veenure stifles a laugh. "Only an idiot would say something like that."

"You are being taken into custody for the murder of Zedic Woods.

"Murder?" she cocks an eyebrow at me. "You're not really a droid, are you?"

"Hands up!" I tell her.

"And by your snarky comment, I'd say ... " she looks at me curiously for a moment. "Quantum Hughes."

"This is your last warning! I will neutralize you!"

Veenure keeps her yoga mat tucked under her arm and slowly begins to turn. "You won't shoot me, Quantum."

"Stop resisting!"

"I'm warning you, Veenure, I will immobilize you if I have to."

"Veenure?" she cocks her head at me and takes a step backwards. The sensors on the door pick up her presence and open. Her lips part as a sinister grin forms across her face. "You're here on behalf of the Dream Team, I presume?"

Doc's voice rings out in my eye. "Metal Man, Bovidae, do not engage target. I repeat, do not engage. Target must be taken unharmed. Toggle to your neuromuscular inhibitor. I'm en route, over."

"Bovidae, Metal Man," I glare at Veenure as best I can, "affirmative." I hit the toggle and ...

Nothing.

The NMI has malfunctioned. I glance down at my weapon, and in that moment, Veenure spins and takes off down the hall.

"Bovidae, Metal Man, in pursuit, over!" I shout as I chase after her. "Target has turned right. Mama, Metal Man, where are our visuals?"

"Metal Man, Bovidae, why the hell didn't you zap her? Over."

"Bovidae, Metal Man, weapon malfunction, you're going to have to get her, over."

"Roger that."

Video feed from the hallways take shape in the lower left-hand corner of my viewing pane. Blinking green icons appears on a schematic of the building layout representing the Boys of Non Compos Mentis; a red icon indicates Veenure moving towards what looks to be the east wing.

"Metal Man, Bovidae, target is heading towards her bedroom, over."

"Bovidae, Metal Man, affirmative," I say as I tear through the hall. The hallway is a beige cover with randomly placed 'works of art' similar to the kindergarten scribble in the halls of Strata's McMansion. The floor is clean, recently buffed laminate, and next to each door is a dual retina and fingerprint scanner.

I step on the gas. An indicator on the upper right portion of my vision pane tells me my current speed, and displays a variety of charts as to how long I can maintain this speed at my current charge life, which is about 78%. The video feed on the opposite side shows me that Veenure has just taken to the stairs and that I am exactly 11.181983 feet from catching up to her at my current pace.

I turn to the stairs, taking two at a time. "Bovidae, Metal Man, target is on the stairs, over."

"Metal Man, Bovidae, roger."

We hit the second floor and the schematic expands on my viewing pane. It doesn't stay there for long; we move to the third floor, Veenure's floor and the schematic settles here. I also see that Doc is now on the third floor, closing in on the target.

"Stop resisting!" A door opens, and I roll to avoid it. "Back in your room," I tell the pudgy Reaper, "or you're next!"

Thirty feet, twenty feet ...

Veenure sprints ahead, screams 'emergency override' and crashes through her door. At the same time I see Doc round the hall, his weapon at the ready. He takes to the ride side of the door; I take to the left.

Camera feeds from her room trail across our iNet screens.

No weapons as of yet; she is, however, scrambling to get something out of her desk.

Docs goes in first and as I follow, I hear the sound of a body smacking against the floor.

Veenure lays on her bedroom floor, her legs at an awkward angle. Sticking out of her thigh is a small injector.

Her vitals indicate that she is dead.

Chapter Ten

"I still can't believe she did that." Frances Euphoria sits on the sofa in Doc's airstream with one leg crossed over the other.

"Good riddance, if you ask me."

Sophia has gone back to our room – shudder – to rest and Doc is still wrapping up all the paperwork with law enforcement. Doc knows me well enough to keep me away from law enforcement, so as soon as Veenure killed herself, I was immediately sent back to the hotel toot sweet.

"I don't know how we're going to rectify this with Strata tomorrow," I tell her, "not that I really care if Veenure is dead or not. I'm just talking about overall direction of the meeting we're set to have. He'll know it was us; I surprised he hasn't contacted me about it already."

"Contact him," she says suddenly. "He reached out to you; you have his direct line."

I shrug. "If he has something to say, he can contact me."

Frances rolls her eyes. "It's weird seeing you with all your Quantumtude in a droid's body."

"Quantumtude?"

"A word I've invented for your general snarkiness and your unique ability to exacerbate most situations. Like it?"

"Can't say that I do."

Frances reaches into her purse and takes out a Soylent fair trade ethically sourced fat-free kale, pecan and honey bar. She produces a tube of protein-enhanced peanut butter paste, covers the bar, and takes a bite from it.

"Still on the gerbil food, huh?" I tsk. "I'd make a 'Richard Gere's butt plug called and wants its din-din back' joke, but it's beneath me. And seriously, damn, what I wouldn't give for a porterhouse right about now." I lick my lips and pretend my mouth is watering. *Mmmmm steak.*

"How's your charge level?"

"For some reason I feel like that type of question should be considered sexual harassment. You with me on this?"

She chuckles. "I don't think that will hold up in a court of law, but then again, I'm not the Dream Team's lawyer and we can't afford HR." Her face turns serious. "But back to your earlier thought: I have no idea how Strata is going to take this and if you ask me, and I know you haven't, I think he's leading you into a trap tomorrow."

"He can do all he wants to my body," I tell her, "that's the beauty in this. Finish your gerbil food and let's go for a walk."

We step out of the airstream and move to the parking lot. The setting sun gives the pavement a unique pink tone. The rush hour smog has settled over LA; the AQI is up five points from where it was earlier and the noise index is surprisingly low. My guess is people have finally arrived home and they've begun self-medicating with food, iNet, and beer, the holy trinity.

Pollutes too. The freaks love their designer inhalants.

Frances and I head west, towards a newly built shopping district in a recently gentrified area. A million thoughts come to me – from looking up housing costs, to distances traveled today on foot, to Frances' vitals and how they've changed slightly since she ate her snack bar, to the best way to avoid staying in Sophia's room tonight.

Sure, I could just come out and ask it, but I got an itching feeling that it'd be best to hold that card just a bit longer. Better a little late than too soon.

"We knew her, Quantum," Frances says, "and no, I don't feel sorry for Veenure, I mean Victoria, in the traditional sense; I feel sorry for her, regarding her upbringing. She's always been second best to Luther, you know it, I know it, and she *still* gave her life for her father's cause."

"I'm over it, Frances. Veenure was a blip on the radar of my life. Hell, I've already forgotten what her avatar looked like. All I can seem to remember is that she was fond of showing off her Thulean, bastardized language that it is."

"No need to be heartless."

I pat my hand on my chest.

"I get it, Tinman. So then what's on your mind?"

We stop and wait for the little flashing man on the other side of the street to let us know that we're okay to cross. Once he gives us the go ahead, we slowly make our way to the other side. A homeless man stands on the corner with a sign that says, *Don't have to be a weatherman to know which way the wind blows*, and below that, *I'll stop giving forecasts for a dollar.*

Ha! Weathermen. It's been awhile since I thought about those schmucks. If we were in The Loop, I'd give him a sucker punch just for the hell of it. Then I'd transfer all my credit to him, leaving him utterly confused as to why he was just assaulted and then paid bigly.

"You have that smirk on your face that tells me you are daydreaming," Frances says.

"This isn't my face, it's *Evan's face,* and what makes you think I'm thinking about anything anyway?"

A guy in a miniskirt with ten leashed Chihuahuas pushes past us. He's got high tops on with wings on the sides.

"They're so cute! I'd love a dog," she says after he passes, "but I'm too busy with work."

"Same here."

"You want a pet?"

"Work," I tell her, "I can hardly take care of myself let alone a lazy mutt."

~*~

"No funny business tonight," I tell Sophia as soon as I let myself into our shared room. The walk with Frances was refreshing. She brought up Veenure a few more times and I let her – when mama's happy, everyone's happy.

Who am I kidding? Doctor Luv is on the bed in the same nightie. She's dimmed the lights and has already scooted over, making room for her favorite droid.

"Funny business? I think you have the wrong idea," she says.

"Do I?" I place my hands on my hips. "I come to our room and you're laced up in Victoria's Secret."

"I bought this at JC Targets."

"You get the picture. What's with all the lovey stuff anyway? You and I? Well, that'd be about the worst RomCom to ever hit theaters. Talk about a flick no one would catch. The critics would pan it and people would take to the streets."

She pulls the blanket up to her chest. "What do you mean?"

"Here's what I'm trying to say: just a few days ago, you could hardly stand to look at me. Now all the sudden, you're treating me like I'm the bee's knees."

Her faces flushes with blood. "I have no idea what you're talking about."

Chuntao gets involved. "You can go eat a rotten egg that has spent two years buried in a boar's ass, Humandroid."

"Sophia, kill your AI before I do," I spit in killer diller mandarin. "Chuntao, keep your trap shut, you dumb melon.

"Chuntao, power down. Sleep mode."

After a long, loud, lengthy trouser blaster, the AI flickers off.

"Good, where were we?"

"You were accusing me of coming onto you," she says.

"Were you not?" I take a deep breath. "I'm looking for drama right now."

"What are you looking for?" she asks.

Did she ask provocatively? I point my finger at her. "I'm looking to charge and dive. I need to blow off some steam, no pun intended."

The Loop. Just thinking about diving to the underworld's underworld puts butterflies in my belly. I feel like it has been forever since I hit the mean streets, stirred up some trouble, took out some bigwigs and gave everyone who looked at me funny a piece of my mind. Been a day, and after one of *those* days, there ain't nothing like a little twilight violence to settle one's nerves.

"You're going to The Loop?"

"Yeah, but later, after I've hit Steam with Aiden. We'll do a little sniffing around Tent City, see what we can't uncover."

"I may join you for that."

"No, you won't," I say firmly. "You'll get some rest. We'll need you tomorrow. Sniffing around is what Aiden and I do best. Once we get a lay of the land, we'll have a better chance tomorrow of bringing that wall down, then we rebuild Bjurstrom, then we get the Sky Iron, then my avatar ass yet again becomes a flesh ass. I can't wait to eat some pancakes."

She scoffs. "You make it sound so easy. You recall what Ray Steampunk said, don't you? You'll have to destroy Dolly. As in *destroy,* as in D-E-S-T-R-O-Y."

I clear my throat. "That's something I'll have to accept. Now if you don't mind, help me get hooked up." I take a seat on the sofa chair and Sophia starts setting me up for my dive.

"I just spoke to Rocket," she informs me after she's connected a few cables to my headset, "he'll be logged in too."

"Why?"

"It's like you have selective memory or something," she says. "He's meeting his girlfriend, a renowned alchemist, and together, they're going to try to reverse engineer the rust spell he cast on Bjurstrom."

"I don't know why we can't just call Bjurstrom what he is – a hunk of metal."

"He was once a person, and a hunk of metal doesn't quite fit the bill."

I recall the rogue steam mech tearing through the forest ripping roots and rocks from the soil. Yes, Bjurstrom is a hunk of metal, but he's a *badass* hunk of metal.

Sophia lowers a visor over my eyes. There really is no reason for the visor, but she jury-rigged the helmet from an old NV Visor so this is what I get. The system powers on. No Brian Eno hum, no nothing. Just a bit of static and I slowly start to become cognizant of the fact I'm in my avatar's body.

Odd to think about that, from meat sack to avatar to Humandroid and back to avatar.

Lightning crashes outside of the dive yurt, thunder rolls, the roof rattles. I get the overwhelming sense that Dolly is just outside the wall, waiting like a fox outside the henhouse.

"Careful with the hair," I tell Aiden as he helps me take my visor off.

He shakes his head. "Can we hurry up and get the Sky Iron so we can get your body back so I can go back to your world?"

"Why do you think I'm here?" I sit up on the gurney and grin. "And where the hell did you get Hugh Hefner's robe?"

He does a quick spin to model his velvet dinner jacket. "You still think you're the only one with an inventory list?" He slaps my cheek, hard.

"Hey! Watch it pal!"

"I'm not your pal, guy."

"I'm not your guy, buddy."

"I'm not your buddy, buster."

We both grin at each other. "Shit, where were we? Steam. We're going to Steam to do a little poking around in Akrasia, specifically, Tent City. You game?"

His Hugh Hefner robe and cute cuddly bunny slippers disappear, replaced by his trademark black ninja milspec outfit, only to be replaced again by a steam version of his ninja outfit, this one complete with a slick black jumpsuit and rusted gears where his nipples should be.

"A jumpsuit?"

"I'm not done yet."

His arm morphs into a mechanical number complete with a small, retractable Gatling gun jutting out of his forearm.

"Still, a jumpsuit? And what's with the gear nips?"

"Am I not cool enough for you?"

"No, my friend, I'm not cool enough for you."

I clap my hands together and a matching jumpsuit forms on my body. I go with a pair of big black stompers accented by chains with skull and crossbones on the upper shaft. From there I go with my classic Deckard trench coat, item 111, and you bet your ass I strap just about as many hidden guns, weapons and knives as I possibly can.

Aiden shakes his head. "The weapons are cool. The boots are dumb."

"Really?"

"Skull and crossbones? What are you auditioning to be a Reaper?"

"Dammit, let's just get there."

~*~

A spawning point floats into shape and both of us touch it. Vortex my vortex, our avatars take shape in the contraband shop. A gas lamp in the corner fights back the shadow. The sound of rats scurrying in the wall reaches my ears.

"I was wondering how long it would take for you to return," Joel says. The bandana-ed better half of Bjurstrom sits on a chair near the lamp, his silhouette towering over the contraband on the opposite side of the room. This place sells everything, from posters of Raquel Welch to artificial legs with hollowed out spaces to stash narcotics.

He holds a stemless wine glass with a dark, oily liquid inside.

"I told you we'd be back." I lean my elbow against one of the shelves. "And here we are, as promised."

"I thought you'd be earlier." He yawns, and takes a sip from his wineglass.

Rocket: Hey there, Q Rito, I just logged in! My girlfriend and I are at the steam mech. She's going to try some spells to fix, um, the spell I fudged up earlier.

Me: Good to know.

"Rocket is with Bjurstrom," I tell Aiden and Joel, "to reverse engineer the rust spell."

"Excellent." Joel doesn't sound *exactly* like Mr. Burns, but he isn't far off. "Then the three of us can scope out Tent City. I'd like you to get the feel of the land."

The Steam Faun materializes in front of Aiden in his trademark milspec vest and a hunter orange hat that reads CWO. "What?" he asks. "You thought I was going to let you do some reconnaissance alone?"

"I figured you'd be sleeping," I tell him.

"Pfft! That's what Somnium Skip Boxes are for." With that, Doc moves to the door, his hooves clomping against the hardwood floor. "What are we waiting for? Let's get a move on!"

The air outside is frigid; the denizens of Akrasia are all tucked and ready to go nighty night, their designer prison garb hung and ready to be worn tomorrow. Everything's in its rightful place, and while I don't understand the appeal of visiting here for those who aren't prisoners, I can report back that the place is at least quiet at night.

That's gotta count for something.

Joel takes the lead, followed by Doc, Yours Truly, and MA. Not a lot of flash dancing from MA. His Gatling gun arm at the ready and his tried and true Slice Bang has appeared on his back, Aiden is all business and I pity the fool who casts shade in his direction. We take the next right and find ourselves smack dab in the middle of the drinking district.

"Sixth Street," Joel says, "named because, well, it is the sixth street."

"You know, Joel, you'd make a good tour guide if the Rebel Alliance thing doesn't pan out."

He shakes his head. "Not gonna happen."

I give the place a quick looksee. Sure, there are few boozehounds milling about, but they're all keeping to themselves, not making eye contact with nobody. The orderliness makes my trigger finger itch. It's like something bad is about to happen here. It ain't quite the *Upsidedown* that is The Loop, but there are some similarities.

I glance back over my shoulder at Morning Assassin. Our eyes meet and he feels it too, I can tell.

"Is this place always this spooky at night?" I ask Joel.

"This isn't the half of it," he says under his breath. "Wait 'til we get to Tent City."

"Stay frosty." Doc's bonesaw forms in his hands. If he's feeling anything, he ain't showing.

"Up ahead," Joel whispers.

I catch what looks like a check point. There's a single gas lamp hanging from a perch on the wall, moths buzzing around it. As we make our way closer, I get a sense of just how big the Steam Breeds are. They're not Steam Enforcers, nothing like that, but that doesn't mean these guys couldn't move a mountain. Judging by the size of the open gate, these guys would make The Hulk look like a small fry. And that's the other thing – the gate is wide open. These Steam Breeds can come and go as they please, but they don't.

Which gets me wondering. "Say, why won't the big clunkers leave again?" I ask up the line. "I'm pretty sure someone already told me, but I forgot."

Joel stops and turns to me. "They feel safer here."

"But they could theoretically bring the wall down themselves, right?"

He considers this for a moment. "Yes, I believe they could."

"But they don't."

"Some people build walls to keep people in, some people build walls to keep people out."

"Which one are the Steam Breeds?" Doc asks.

"Both, and they didn't build the walls."

I shrug. Sometimes I get the feeling that Joel is just bullshitting us, and that this entire quest is to glorify Ray Steampunk and his wowsie-wow creation that is Steam. Old Quantum boils to the surface and I just about equip my Ruger Vaquero action revolver, fire off a shot, and ask for the Breedies just to come out already.

I clench my fists instead. I'm surprised that I haven't equipped any weapons, but really, I'm flanked by two of the most dangerous people to ever exist in a Proxima world. Safe company. Doc and Aiden will mow down anything that tries anything.

"These are the tents," Joel whispers.

My BFG 9000, item 100, materializes in my hand as soon as I see a towering, eighteen wheeler of a man slowly let himself in one of the giant circus tents. For his wooly mammoth size, he's surprisingly light on his feet, and as he slips in, he turns to me and his eyes, small circular portholes, flash red.

I track him all the way in.

"Damn these guys are big," I say.

"Told you so." Joel takes one look at my gun and shakes his head. "And what part of 'don't shoot at them' do you not understand?"

"You never said that."

"It was implied."

"Everyone else has weapons."

"If everyone else sticks their thumb up their ass, will you do it too?"

Aiden snickers.

"Well?" Doc asks. "Answer the man's question."

No time for a rebuttal. A Steam Breed steps before us, the gaslight from the entrance giving him just enough light to give us a good look at the big bastard. He's all sinewy muscle stretched over mechanical parts. Just like the other one, his eyes are circular red portholes. He grimaces, exhales deeply, and steam sprays out of his nostrils. With that, he turns, showing us his back and broad shoulders. The upper part is covered in heavily scarred flesh; his lower half is a collection of winding and grinding gears.

"Whew," Joel says after he has moved into one of the circus tents, "glad he didn't stomp us. Let's keep moving."

Me: Why are we so scared of these big bozos again?

Doc: I'm with you there. Your BFG would have given that mountainous misfit a new hole to shit from.

Rocket: Speaking of new holes to shit from, good news, fellas!

Me: What's that?

Rocket: My super sweet GF and I have cured Bjurstrom of his rust. He's practically brand new!

Me: what does this have to do with shitting?

Doc: Good job, kid, we're just finishing up here.

We press forward, into the row between the tents. I hear a bed creak as a Steam Breed sits down in one of the tents. Other than that, the place is spookily silent, which isn't helped by the fact that the two moons overhead are mere slivers tonight and a mist has settled over Akrasia.

"The walls not far from here," Joel says, "just up ahead."

"I still don't get why we are running reconnaissance. I'm not trying to brag here – I have enough stuff in my list to bring this wall down right now. So why not? Let's do it; rather than creep around like mice collecting data for no good reason."

No answer, not even from Doc, which only makes me feel even more annoyed. *I'm ready for some kaboomski!*

Joel throws his hands out. "This is as far as we can go."

"What do you mean?" I slide past Doc and scoot up next to Bjurstrom's bonkers operator.

"This is what I wanted to show you."

Doc clicks on a flashlight revealing a series of tripwires that cover the space between the wall and the last Steam Breed tent. He arcs his light left, more tripwires, and right, even more. My BFG materializes again and I take a few steps closer to the first set of wires.

"Damn, they're tightly woven together."

"Exactly," says Joel, "and if anything touches the wires … doneski."

"Now there's a word I can appreciate." I stand catch a glimpse from Aiden. "Are you thinking what I'm thinking?"

"Long range missile attack?"

I nod.

"It's not quite that easy," Joel says. "Those tripwires operate on a fourth-dimensional scale."

"Please don't tell me you are about to go into some string theory," I say.

"That's exactly what it's like. There are other tripwires connected to these wires that operate on a different plane of reality."

"We're in a virtual entertainment dreamworld. We're already on a different plane," I remind him. "And what does the tripwire do exactly?"

"Toss something out there and see for yourself."

I equip item 192, my frisbee, and give it a good whirl. Jillions of bolts of electricity lay waste to it as soon as it passes over the barrier.

"Damn! That's the kind of joltage that would give Edison an acute case of Tesla envy!"

Doc says, "So we'll need to get over that."

"Yes." Joel nods ever-so-slowly, "and this is why I wanted to take you here. I didn't want you to think this would be a walk in the park. I have a feeling if I told you the wall was protected by tripwire, your group would have strolled in here and had your asses handed to you. The *only* way to do this is to get in good with the Steam Breeds, and in your forms, that isn't happening."

"Which is why Steampunk Santa had us outfitted for Steamsuits," I say.

"Bingo. It took you long enough to catch on."

Rocket: REAPERS have spawned at Bjurstrom! We're taking heavy fire!

Doc has already zipped away before I can get my finger up.

"What's wrong?" Aiden asks.

"Rocket, Reapers, we need to go, *now!*"

A broad with pigtails and a pair of knockers that you could land a helicopter on blasts one of the Reapers with what I would describe as a giant key weapon. She has the head of an over-sized, ornate Victorian key tucked under her arm, and she uses the unlocky-end to taze the hell out of Reapers spilling out of a yellow portal.

"Get over here!" I shout as I go with Scorpion's Spear, item 233, which tears into the front of the Reaper's chest plate and tugs him over to me. *Finish him!* I greet Shao Khan's inbred cousin with an uppercut that takes his head off.

Bullets fly and explosions tear the trees from the ground. Reapers spill out of their portal, armed with a cartoonish amount of firepower. Laser blasts tear through the soil and shoot debris into the air.

Doc has his bonesaw up and a smoky treat in his mouth; Aiden is flash dancing and back-knifing; Rocket is practically Doctor Strange with all the alchemical symbols twisting around his arms; the kid's main squeeze is dosing the Reapers with a fine helping of magical fury from her Key gun; and I've gone with item 14, my trashcan lid shield, and Hackie set to ice mode.

Feed me!

"Yeah, I know, I know," I tell my mutant hack as I pivot towards some cover.

AA bar activated, I fire over my shoulder, freezing a Reaperette solid. Doc finishes the job and continues blasting metal unhappiness towards the Reaper's general spawning point.

Suddenly the soil shifts.

I make it just in time to Bjurstrom the steam mech. The ground gives way as I scramble up his body.

"What the hell?" I shout as I see the ground caving in all around me. More Reapers, this bunch equipped with jetpacks, fly over us as the ground collapses.

Doc fires up just as a tree breaks in two, falling directly between Rocket and him. Two Reapers scoop Rocket up by his arms, slap a collar around his neck and …

They flashdance away.

"ROCKET!" By this point, I've tossed my trashcan lid away and have gone with both hacks, firing willy-nilly towards the Reapers spilling out of their portal. "They have Rocket!"

Item 567, my steam-powered jetpack, takes shape on my back and I break for the air. A Reaper comes at me and Hackie responds by filleting the wannabe Task Master.

"Quantum!" I stop just in time for Aiden to save my ass from a collapsing tree. He too has a jetpack, as does Doc, who is now airborne, guns up and cutting down anything with an overabundance of muscles and a skull mask.

Suddenly the Reapers start logging out or bangtailing it to their portal. I'm still trying to blast them and get a few too as I zip around and try to figure out what has happened to Rocket.

Me: Kid! Rocket! Where the hell are you!?

"They took Rocket!" I tell Aiden. I dive through the air towards one of the last Reapers standing, AA full swing, and he dematerializes milliseconds before I can nab him.

"Doc, Aiden! Cuffs!" Doc, about eight feet away from Aiden, overhands his permalog cuffs and Morning Assassin, disappears.

Morning Assassin reappears behind enemy lines, frantically trying to catch Reapers before they disappear or get to their portals.

No such luck.

The dust clears, the Reapers have disappeared, and Rocket has disappeared with them.

Chapter Eleven

"Shit!" I equip item 73, my pair of Halo MC6s and blast through a tree. Splinters and debris spray through the air; the tree creaks and falls. Once it's smoldering and split in half, I point them at the two moons overhead. "Dammit, Steampunk! Why are you letting this happen! You could have stopped them. DAMMIT!"

"They took him!" Rocket's girlfriend stands below me in the newfound crater. She has her Victorian key gun at the ready, the end still charging. Her face is already wet with tears.

I land in front of her. "Yeah, they took him, just like they've taken others! GODDAMN them!" I blast my MC6s into the rock wall. Roots and bits of pebble burst into the air.

Doc lands behind me and places a much needed hand on my shoulder. "Cool it, Quantum, there's nothing we can do for the kid from here. Put your shooters away."

"Just … those dirty rat bastards. Not Rocket. He didn't deserve it, *doesn't deserve it.*" I clench my hands on the grips of my guns.

"I'm logging out now," Doc says hurriedly, "Hopefully I'll be able to get a lead in the RW. Shit. And we have nobody in Baltimore right now either. I'll arrange for Frances to go first thing in the morning. Maybe there's a red eye, but I'm guessing it's a bit too late."

"Send Sophia instead," I grit.

A grin twitches on Doc's face. "Yeah, you've earned that. Good call, but there's still the issue of Sophia being the one that is currently monitoring your human avatar *and* the one who will escort you to Colorado tomorrow. What? You thought we'd let you fly alone after your last breach of protocol in the airport?"

"Frances can do that."

Doc nods. "She can. But does she want to?"

"If she doesn't, send her back to Baltimore. If she will, send Sophia."

"Deal."

Rocket's girlfriend pushes past me. "What are you two sitting here going on about!?" she bellows. "Rocket, my dear Rudraksh, is gone!"

"We're aware of that, Lakshmi," Doc tells her. He raises his finger to log out.

Confusion paints across her face. "How do you know my name?"

Doc jams his finger onto the logout button and is gone in a flash.

"How does he know my name?" she asks. "My handle is Geariya."

I look to Aiden, who has begun picking through the rubble covering Bjurstrom. Even if he wasn't wearing a mask, the look on Morning Assassin's face would be indecipherable. It reminds me, very briefly, the difference between our realms of existence and our relationships with Rocket.

The kid has definitely grown on me and hell, with the amount of people I have either against me, begrudgingly working with me, or generally peeved off that I continue to exist, it ain't too shabby to have a fan.

"Dammit," I say as I turn away from his bosomy girlfriend. I've seen a lot in Steam when it comes to ridiculous costumes, but this one has taken it to a whole new level. And now ain't the time to be staring at cha-chas.

With nothing to say for once, I move to Aiden and help him move some of the smaller hunks of stone that cover Bjurstrom's hood. I suppose it's his hood. I really have no idea where the rogue steam mech's engine is, nor how it operates. I'm sure there's some steam involved, which gets me, again, thinking about Ray Steampunk and how he is a good-for-nothing son of a bitch for letting the Reapers take Rocket.

I get angry again real quick. "He could have stopped them, right then and there."

Aiden, grunts as he tries to move a slab of rock about the size of a covfefe. "Yeah, he could have. Dolly would have."

There's my trigger word again. You'd think I'd grow tired of hearing Dolly's name and having a gut reaction. At least it has become more of a mixed gut reaction, if there is such a thing. I recall the last time I saw her, just before she locked herself away in Fort Dolly.

Damn.

Tell me that it's nobody's fault but my own and I'd agree. It still doesn't make it sting any less.

"I feel like killing," I tell Aiden, "and even with Ray Steampunk on our side here … " I look up at the sky and roll my eyes. "I don't think he'd let us keep our golden player indicators if I did what I'd like to do."

"So what are you thinking?"

"I say we go to The Loop and pay Two-Face Tommy a visit. That palooka always has something going on in Devil's Alley. Hell, he's probably throwing a party right now. There'll be dames, Riotous, guns and thugs. A stomp-a-thon."

Aiden shakes his head. "It sounds fun, but Sophia told me I shouldn't leave the dive yurt. Hell, I can't blame you."

"You're leaving me here?" Lakshmi asks, her eyes filling with worry. "After what has just happened to my dear Rocket?" She turns the waterworks up a notch. "It's like you guys ... don't care about me!"

"Maybe she's right, Quantum, maybe we should just stay here." Aiden sets down a rock about the size of a nightstand. He wipes his forehead, even though there's no sweat present. "Rocket is a good guy. He wouldn't have left you stranded or missing just to go blow off some steam…"

"Hey!"

"Not what I mean," Aiden assures Lakshmi, "what I'm saying is: Rocket would do something else. He's loyal. I might not know him as well as you, but I definitely get that vibe from the kid."

"Yeah, you're right about that." I sit down on a stone and kick my legs out in front of me. My health bar flashes, reminding me I could use a top off. I equip my steam pack, item 564, and plug into the port on the other side of my elbow. I don't remember getting struck by anything, but the fight was so sudden that I might not have been paying enough attention.

An idea comes to me so hard and fast that it nearly knocks me backwards. "Revenge," I gulp, "Strata knows about what happened to Veenure in the RW and ... he's taken Rocket! He wants revenge!"

~*~

I bite my lip as I look at Aiden. "There's a lot going on up there that I haven't told you about."

"Gee, you think? What's this about revenge?"

"For starters, Strata and I are supposed to meet tomorrow. I dunno if I told you that already, but there it is."

"Easy peasy. Tie a bomb to your chest and end it." Aiden shrugs. "That's what I'd do, and it's not like you'll die because you'll be in a Humandroid body."

"Trust me, it's crossed my mind, but I don't think that would be the justice he deserves. He needs to face the consequences of his actions for the people he's poisoned and misled in the real world," I grit. "He needs to spend the rest of his life in the slammer, no lethal injection either, just stuck in a cell scratching each day that passes into the cell wall."

"Why does nobody comfort me?" Lakshmi is on the ground now, her knees pulled to her chest. "What kind of men are you!?"

Aiden looks back at me, considers the question, and continues, "So that's all you have to tell me, or is there more?"

"There's more. I was so pumped to log in and get to ass-stomping that I failed to tell you about what happened to Veenure."

His eyes narrow. "What happened?"

"Doc and I went to arrest her, she bolted, we chased her to her room and she killed herself."

"Well, good riddance."

"That's what I said."

He paces for a moment his hands behind his back. Finally, he says, "This is definitely revenge then. It didn't just happen out of the blue. You got Strata by the balls, now he has you. Which is ... a strange image to think about." His eyes twitch. "Real strange. So the question is: what happens next?"

"One, Strata kills Rocket. Two, Strata uses Rocket as bait to coerce us."

He nods. "Three, Strata kills you in your Humandroid form at your meeting then kills Rocket."

"Four, Strata enslaves Rocket and turns him into a Reaper. Does something with the kid's D-NAS too."

"Five, Strata forces Rocket to be part of his Meridian Circuit and feeds off the kid to strengthen himself."

"ENOUGH, ENOUGH!" Lakshmi hops to her feet and points her key gun at us. "If I hear one more world about Rudraksh dying, I'm taking both of you out!"

"Easy, sister," I tell her, "you don't want it with us. Believe you me."

She fires a blast into the woods that incinerates two trees. She loads another magical round into the grip on her big-league Victorian key. "I know you have mutant hacks, but I will do my best to fight you!"

Aiden appears behind her with revolver aimed at the back of her head. He cocks the hammer. "Lower your weapon," he tells her calmly, "this won't end well for you."

I put my hands in the air and force a smile at both of them. "Whoa, whoa," says I, "Everyone cool it. Nobody is killing nobody, and this especially applies to Strata Godsick." I look up at the sky. "Alrighty, Ray, if you don't get your ass down here pronto, I am going to spawn in Locus and start murdalizing EVERYONE if you don't respond. There will be hell to pay!"

A blinding barrage of light at the far end of the crater signals the God Emperor of Steam has finally decided to grace us with his presence. The golden diva man floats out of the portal and moves to a holier-than-thou-looking-down-upon-thee point just a few feet in air, which makes me wonder if he'd be a big fan of Sophia's *Passive Aggression for the Magical Being* ebook that she has yet to pen.

He glares down at me with his cold black eyes, and of course, as he speaks his lips don't actually move. "You called?"

"Holy!!!!!" Lakshmi's smeared eyeliner corrects itself and she quickly adjusts her hair and her funbags. "It's … it's really you!"

Aiden, still standing behind Lakshmi, lowers his weapon. He positions himself to catch her if she faints. Lakshmi has worked herself up into a frenzy by the time Ray's kingly ass floats over to us. She has a new outfit on, her hair is pinned a different way, her corset is pulled even tighter and her knee-high boots are polished and the heels have grown a few inches longer.

Me? I'm not a fanboy and I'm definitely not a fan of Ray Steampunk. I equip Doc's Metal Storm bonesaw, item 586. I'm partial to the newest items in my list, not ashamed to admit that, and I am very well aware that my egregious bean shooter won't do shit to Ray's ass, but that doesn't mean I won't try. "What in the hell is wrong with you, Ray?"

"As you know, I do not like to get involved with the day to day operations in Steam."

"Ray, you got us chasing our tails in Akrasia trying to get some frickin' metal and you let the Reapers get away with Rocket! Now they've upped the testicular torsion, and you're just sitting back in your airship watching all this unfold like it's the latest summer blockbuster. I got news for you, pal, what we're doing here has real world implications and you'd be stupid as hell to think that letting the Reapers get the Sky Iron won't be bad for your God-like ass. And another thing – letting them take Rocket when you could have intervened is just damned dirty. You're a real piece of work, Ray, and if no one has told you that before, it's probably because they're too busy trying to polish your brass knob you stupid son of a bitch!"

Ray's facial expression remains the same. "Are you finished?"

"Am I finished?" I fire the bone saw at Ray and the bullets slow in front of him and drop to the ground. "Three, you're a real asshole!"

"I've come to discuss strategies with you. Or will you continue to shoot at me?"

I shoot at him once.

"Finished?"

"Yes," I growl.

"So now that we've established you can't shoot me, let's begin our conversation. Lakshmi," he says without looking at Rocket's girlfriend, "I'm going to need you to log out now. This is a private conversation. I will, however, have an admin keep you updated on Rocket's situation."

"But ... " Her hand raises on its own accord and a logout button appears. "Please!" she says as she tries to gain control over her body. No such luck; Ray's NVA mojo forces her to press the button. She's gone faster than your perpetually unemployed brother-in-law when the bar bill arrives.

"It was unfortunate that I was unable to prevent them from taking Rocket."

"Unfortunate!?" I'm beside myself again. Does this pompous asshat really understand how he comes off? I get the urge to fire another shot at Ray but I swallow it down.

"They used a technology to do that – to OMIB-port – something that I haven't encountered before," Ray says. "It was incredibly fast, and I believe the tech they are using was made from other RPG metals, an alloy."

"Any idea where they went?" I ask.

"They took him to a custom OMIB space, the inverse of their storage world."

"Strata's storage world? I know the place."

"You will not be able to spawn in the OMIB of that world without the RPG metal. Sure, you can go to their storage world again, but only a Reality Splitter weapon will be able to cut into the OMIB. The Reality Splitter, if you recall, is the same weapon you needed to free Zedic which you were unable to craft in time to save him."

"I remember."

"And it is the weapon you will make when you get the Sky Iron, by alloying it with Chronoton."

"I don't need a reminder, Ray, I need a strategy going forward."

Ray's form starts to slowly dematerialize. "I just gave you your strategy. One more thing: Do not give in to Strata's demands. You have Luther's location – this is the one thing he has torn through the Proxima Galaxy in search of. It is your ultimate trump card."

"What if … ?" I look to Aiden and gulp. "What if Rocket spills his beans? Then our single trump card is null."

"I don't believe he will," Ray says just before his avatar has completely vanished, "his resolve is much stronger than you think."

~*~

I awake on the other side of a shit situation. All sorts of shit about Sophia's hotel room comes to me, but I ignore it.

Damn you, Strata. I can only imagine what Rocket is going through right now as I slowly remove Sophia's makeshift NV Visor from my noggin.

"So that's why it is so quiet," I say after I've discovered that Sophia's bed has been vacated.

I stand, flick off the bright light used to fuel my droid bod's robosynthesis, and I'm just about to reach the door and head to the Big Euphoria's room when Chuntao makes her presence known.

"Yeah, I hear you Chuntao, and like I said before, Muffle Trumplings ain't good for nobody. It sounds like you need to see a gastroenterologist, but that's just me, maybe your gassiness is a result of how big of an asshole you are."

"You are a rude and stupid droid, a rotten egg that has fermented inside a trashcan filled with maggots. I did not program myself. Sophia programmed me to do that."

"You're shitting me."

"I can't shit you and you can't shit you. I'm watching you, droid. There is something very odd about you."

I give the wireless speaker on the nightstand not one, but two, birds. I hold them there long and good too.

"Human gestures mean nothing to me. I can fry your circuits."

I grin as a wicked idea comes to me. "You know, Chuntao, that your headmistress has a thing for me, don't you? She'll deny it, but both of us know it's true."

The bitchy AI makes a spitting sound.

"There's a good Chuntao; yes, you know then. Well, if you don't get your act together, I'll give in to her demands and once I have her in the palm of my hand, I'll convince her that there are way better AIs, that *she can do so much better than you,* and I'll see to it that you're replaced."

The AI goes quiet.

"Now that you've pushed me to the point of a DisNike villain, Chuntao, watch your ass!"

With that, I slam the door shut and march across the hall to Frances Euphoria's room. I drum my fingers on the door for a moment, appreciating how *natural* this feels. I hate to say that I'm starting to get used to my droid body but I am, and about the only thing missing are a bunch of mech anime add-ons that would allow me to both kick ass and take names in a variety of situations.

Frances opens the door, her face a bit puffy from crying.

She wears her heart on her sleeve and I can definitely tell *without* scanning her vitals that she's recently experienced something. "Come in," she says, "Sophia's here too."

Yay for my sanity – Sophia is wearing clothing, the Dream Team duds, and she sits on a sofa chair in front of the window. She looks up to me, shakes her head bitterly, and looks back down at the floor.

Time to be a fearless leader.

"Don't worry," I assure them, "we'll get Rocket and we will, I mean this, *we will* hand the Reapers their asses."

"But how?" Sophia asks. "He has Rocket!"

"And we have Luther."

"If you give him Luther's location, they will destroy Tritania looking for him."

"No," I tell her, "we won't let them. We will fight them and we will enlist our friends to help us."

"Friends?" Sophia asks. "You've alienated Empress Thun's royal court!"

"There are the giants … " I recall the Saiduka Giants and their little troll of a leader, King Coromon. "They could be helpful. The Brits too, if they're not incarcerated. And the Lost Boys."

"The Reapers will turn all their resources to Tritania," Frances says, "all of their players and their weapons. If they are able to get the Sky Iron, or any other RPG metals, they could simply threaten to destroy the world *if* the NVA Seed doesn't hand Luther over."

"Why isn't the Proxima Company involved here?" I ask. "Don't they care that one of their worlds could potentially be destroyed?"

Another knock at the door. Frances opens it and Doc and Arnie enter. Both are in overalls; Doc has on his CWO trucker hat. Hovering over his shoulder is his B-drone, Von Richtofen.

Arnie is silent as he takes a position near the door.

"Who's staying, who's going?" Doc asks. "I need to know, pronto."

I look to Frances and thankfully, she gets the hint.

"Sophia can go back to Baltimore to take care of Rocket and Quantum's bodies. I'll escort Quantum to Denver. Doc?"

"Arnie and I will leave in the next twenty minutes. It's a thousand miles away, which means I will need to go airborne and you guys know how I feel about traveling in an aeros. That's why I have this." He taps on the front of his overalls and my interface zooms, showing the outline of a flask. "Nighty-night, kiddos."

I start to make a 'are you going to spawn in Barbie World' joke but think otherwise – damn does it feel good to finally become a mature, functioning member of society.

"Aiden and I spoke to Ray Steampunk," I inform the group. "His only advice was to use Luther's location as a trump card."

Doc nods. "Did he say anything about not stopping the Reapers from taking the kid in the first place?"

"Not much. Only that they were faster than he thought they'd be."

Doc chews on his lip for a moment. "I don't think Steampunk knows just how difficult the situation will become if they get the Sky Iron and create a Reality Splitter, or something similar."

"It'll be all-out war if they get their hands on the metal and he didn't even mention Akrasia, or Bjurstrom, or bringing down the walls."

"Typical Ray. Look, I knew the guy – he's the type that will sit back and watch the world burn if he thinks that someone else will put the fire out at the very last minute. I guess he sees us as that hope." Doc sighs.

"So back to the trump card," I say, "do I use it to get Rocket or not?"

Doc glances at Frances. "What do you think?"

"It will create an all-out war in Tritania that may spill over to other Proxima worlds most notably Steam, that is, until the Reapers get the metal."

"And we don't have the metal yet," Doc says. "Scoping out Tent City with Joel, I think it may be a bit harder than we originally thought. That last wall was heavily guarded. Then again, it may be a walk in the park."

"So do I use Luther as leverage or not?" I ask them.

"You usually just make those decision on your own," Sophia says coldly.

Deep breath.

"Yeah, well I'm trying to do this right here, dammit. I'm not letting Rocket face the same fate as Zedic. Hell, I will even trade my body if it means keeping the kid around."

Doc considers this for a moment. "No, don't trade your body, not in its current state. I'm serious, give up Luther if you have to, but do not offer your own RW body. That would be suicide, and we can't guarantee Strata will actually follow through with whatever he says he's going to do."

"But giving up Luther's position may put Tritania on the path to extinction," Frances says.

"Only if they get the Sky Iron," Doc reminds us.

"What are the legal ramifications of giving me a gun and letting me kill Strata right then and there?"

"He's not going to let you bring a gun," Doc says.

"I don't need a gun to kill him." I raise both hands and clench my fists. "I have these. Find out the legal ramifications."

Doc nods. "I really don't know how that would play out."

"It would be a disaster," Sophia says, "if you want justice for Strata, bring him down the right way. Strangling him or whatever it is you plan to do would be a cheap way out."

I look to Doc and he shrugs.

"Find out the legal ramifications," I tell him, "and give them to me straight. I want all options on the table."

Chapter Twelve

Denver, Colorado is still cool at the time we arrive. Doc has set everything up, as usual, and he'll be here within the next few hours.

The rest of the early morning in Cali was spent brooding. No one could sleep, and there wasn't much we could do aside from sit around and share funny stories about Rocket, which inevitably led to anger at the Reapers and Strata. At one point, I suggested going back to Akrasia to sniff around for some Reapers and see who we could interrogate, but Frances nixed that idea.

It wouldn't have done us any good anyway.

The Reapers are holding Rocket in the OMIB of their storage world. There's only one way to get to their OMIB due to the way the space is constructed – a Reality Splitter. Once we have that, we'll have to think of a new way to describe 'testicular torsion.' But we still have to get Sky Iron, and Chrono still has to actually make the weapon.

Gonna be a day.

"Thanks for picking me up," I tell Frances as soon as she approaches the baggage claim area. Rather than argue with security, I decided to make everyone's lives easier and check my keister in as baggage.

"How was it?" she asked.

"What? Being baggage? It wasn't too bad. I didn't get any airplane peanuts, but if I had, I wouldn't have been able to eat them anyway." I wish my mouth could salivate at the thought of a small package of honey-roasted peanuts. *Damn this body.*

The baggage claim area is bustling, and I've got my eye on just about every john who so much as walks with a limp. I don't mind someone pre-emptively striking my ass, but Frances is with me and her safety is my number one concern.

A driverless aerostaxi picks us up and promptly takes us to an UberFord in the parking lot of Super WalMacy's. The air is thinner, and my Humandroid scanner-majiggy lets me know just about everything I need to know about as we ride. Lots of facts, little substance.

"The meeting is scheduled for one," I remind Frances. "It's eleven and Doc isn't here yet."

"He'll be here. I can call Arnie and double-check that if you'd like."

"You're right," I tell her, "he'll be here."

We sail over I-70 towards the heart of the Mile High City. Mountains on the outskirts add a sense of majesty to everything. Their snow-tipped peaks remind me that as soon as all this is over, as *soon* as I'm back in my RW body and Strata is behind bars, I'm taking the epic-est of epic vacations. I'm pulling out all the stops and I'll do it on the FCG's dime if I can manage it.

~*~

"Food truck again?" I ask as the UberFord lowers to the ground.

Frances shrugs. "It worked last time. You know what they say, if it ain't broke ... "

"When will Doc be here?"

"Fifteen to twenty minutes, tops."

The Goat Cakes stands at the center of the grouping in all its glory. Plastered on the side of the food truck is a cartoon image of Sally, Doc's service goat, who looks utterly delightful in her chef hat and apron.

Once the UberFord has landed, a blinking light and a loud tone indicates that it is now safe to exit the vehicle. We hop out and the vehicle takes off again. We keep a low profile as we make our way through a small grouping of runners standing around a juice bar.

"Hey, are you the Goat Cake people?" The dreadlocked stoner gal manning the juice truck calls out to us.

"No." Frances replies.

"I like it when you get tough," I tell Frances as she fiddles with the series of locks on the back of the truck. Damn if Doc doesn't have a few locks, and that's not including the finger and retina scanner that she has to clear next.

"Shut up," she says playfully after she's opened the door. Nothing has changed about the interior of the food truck. As soon as the overhead lights come on, I catch a box of fresh pine pellets in the far corner, the bench on the left and the control center – screens, NV Visors, bits and pieces – situated around a u-shaped table.

I plop down in the bench nearest the command center. "Should I message Strata?"

Frances nods. "Let's see what he says."

Me: I'm in Denver. I will have my taxi drop me off at the Revenue Corporation headquarters at 13:00.

Strata Godsick: Have you brought legal counsel?

Me: No.

Strata Godsick: Have you come alone?

Me: What's with the fifth degree? I told you'd I'd be here and I'm here, alone.

Strata Godsick: Good. We have many things to discuss.

Me: The understatement of the decade.

Strata Godsick: I will see you at one. Check in at reception and they will take you to a conference room.

"Well?" Frances asks.

Rather than give her the deets, I simply share the message with her. Her eyes flicker as she sits next to me. She turns to me, takes my hands, and looks me dead in the eye. "You have to be careful what you say, Quantum. Rocket's life is at stake. Remember that."

"I know. I'll be as careful as I absolutely can be. I promise."

"You can't get mad at him, or try to ... um ... " She clears her throat.

"What?"

"You can't try to *do* anything to him; don't even threaten him. Everything will be recorded, even if he is alone. He's trying to bait you." She huffs. "I don't see what there is to even gain in this meeting. I hate to be negative here, but I highly doubt the two of you are going to suddenly come to some sort of agreement."

"You're right. We won't come to an agreement. I'm aware of that. But we have leverage – Luther – and he has Rocket."

"You forgot that Veenure died last night at the result of our operation. We still have no indication on how he's taking Veenure's death."

"There are a lot of unknowns, but I think we have a pretty solid case against him. Where to begin? Here's one: let's start with the bleached people and move to the fact he was trying to imprison me; that he definitely hired those goons to come after me when I woke up; that he assaulted you in Steam and put you in the hospital; that he ended up murdering most of those bleachies with the source code bomb he detonated in The Loop; that he sent Rollins to kill me in real life; that his daughter killed Zedic, a federal agent on official duty; that Luther has agreed to testify against him; that his group of meaty skullheads have kidnapped Rocket – seriously, what other evidence do we need?"

"I know you and Doc like to throw around the testicular torsion phrase, but I want you to be more careful than you have ever been, Quantum. Strata is a snake; he is a poison, a toxin; he's like you."

"What do you mean?"

"He won't take no for an answer."

I shake my head. "I'm not like that," I tell her, "people tell me no all the time."

"And what do you do?"

"I do it anyway? What?" I wave her concern away. "Don't get all dramatic here. We'll get him, and we'll be recording as well. As per our plan, I'm going to be myself."

Frances bites her bottom lip. "That's what I'm afraid of."

~*~

"Here," I tell the driverless aeros taxi. The aeros shifts into the next lane and begins its lowering process. Other aeros slow around us, the people in them oblivious to the larger issues swirling around them. Funny, that. I'm as ready as I've ever been; no nerves, no worries whatsoever. Frances may have her concerns but not me – in my current state, there is absolutely nothing that they can do to me.

Doc: You know the drill and we've been over what you should and shouldn't say. This is straight from legal – don't stray.

Me: Roger.

Doc: Get 'em good. Do what you do best.

Me: Will do.

I walk a few blocks just to get my bearings.

My Spidey droid senses tingle and I have the impression that I'm being tailed, but that may just be my imagination running wild. Strata is expecting me in person, not in Evan's e-skin.

There's the place.

The Revenue Corporations HQ isn't as ostentatious as I imagined it being.

There isn't a big Reaper skull on top of the building surrounded by flames nor is it gothic or foreboding in anyway. No moat, no turrets, no beefcake button men out front guarding the joint – the RevCo HQ is relatively simple affair, twelve stories, and clearly not one of the new, post-post-post-post-modern architectural 'masterpieces' that look like a bunch of geometric figures having an orgy after a long night of boozing.

Aside from a Zen-like entrance with small, polished stones along a walkway, the place is pretty inconspicuous. I don't even see the Revenue Corporation logo until I enter the lobby, where I'm greeted by a female humandroid in a tight pantsuit. Her hair is pulled back into a shiny ponytail, and she's got the bod of an anorexic runway model circa 1995.

"May I help you?" she asks as she scans me. No reception desk – the droid stands on a large black tile, the only black tile in the recently polished lobby. Across from her are three posh leather sofas with billeted armrests, which are situated under a large painting what I would describe as a moon exploding during a solar eclipse.

"I'm here to see Strata Godsick," I tell her, "the name is Quantum Hughes."

Her face twitches ever-so-slightly. "I see. Please, take a seat."

I do as instructed. The company's AI tries to connect with my system and I quickly deny it.

"Please allow for the Revenue Corporations Office AI to access your interface," the droid dame says in a harsh tone.

"Fat chance, lady," I tell the broad. "I'm here to see Strata and that's all this place needs to know about me. I do not give my consent for the Revenue Corporation to access my operating system. We good here?"

She stares at me in a strange way for a moment.

"Is that you in there, Strata?" I ask her blackened eyes. "If so, yes, this is me Quantum and yes, I'm using InterHead to power this droid. You'd have to be one of the world's dumbest dumbasses to think that I would come here in person. That said, I don't have a shyster with me and I got no weapons." I show the palms of my hands. "So let's get this over with. I got places to go and people to see. Unless you're going to leave me waiting. In that case, I'll let myself out."

The Humandroid clears her throat. "That will not be necessary." She takes a few steps closer to me and I ready myself for anything. The hair on the back of my neck doesn't prickle – I don't have any hair anyway – but my interface picks up the fact that the droidie could be a potential hostile.

Targeting overlays appear on various points of her body, places that would most easily disable her.

She turns. "Right this way, Mr. Hughes. And I'll ask you not to scan me as well."

I shrug. "Old habits die hard, lady. You got a name?"

She stops and looks at me over her shoulder. "No."

"Alrighty, No, it's nice to meet you."

The droid stops in front of a check-in station near the only door other than the entrance. She places her hands behind her back and a small section of the wall opens. Four b-drones zip out of the wall and flutter around me. Two start a full-body scan while the other two hover nearby, ready to fire.

Once I'm TSA-ed, I follow No through a motoglass door not unlike the door at Veenure's apartment complex. We make our way down a sleek, AppleSoft white hallway.

There are no other people or droids around, and as we approach a conference room, a message flashes telling me all livestreaming iNet correspondence has been disabled from this point forward.

It gives me no option other than to agree to this, so I oblige.

I've been over what I need to say with Doc, and it'd be better not to have Frances and him in my ear at all times. They'll be able to see the playback anyway – RevCo can't disable that without accessing my OS.

"Please, take a seat," the droid says as we enter the conference room. There are two chairs, and she indicates mine is at the far end of the oval table.

So I take the seat nearest to the door. "Strata requested that you sit in the other chair," she tells me.

"I like this one better, No." I cross my arms over my chest and lean backwards. "Nice chair. I'll bet this one cost a pretty penny. How many Proxima users would you have to run an insurance scam on to get a chair like this?"

She hesitates for a moment. "I will inform him that you have arrived."

"Yep, time to relax." I have my stompers up on the table by the time she reaches the door.

She turns, focuses in on my feet, and exits the room. It's times like this that I wish I had an RW inventory list so that I could equip my cigar, item 30.

A big fat Gloria Cubana would be perfect for Strata's imperial entrance.

~*~

I start whistling the theme to *The Final Countdown*, or at least attempting to whistle it. I think there may be a plug-in I'm missing in regards to musical ability.

I give up after about a minute and check the room out yet again. There's nothing remarkable about the room, and nothing that indicates there's a trap in any way. Not that it matters – no sweat off my back if Evan dies.

Sophia already went over what would happen if I were somehow disabled. I'd simply wake up back in the dive yurt to find Aiden carefully examining the swimsuit edition issue of *Assassins Illustrated*.

So I'm sitting real good right about now, ready to turn up the heat.

The door opens and a Humandroid in a blue suit enters. He holds the door open and
Mr. Godsick himself walks in, a scowl on his face

Strata is going for the Johnny Cash look in his all black suit and black shirt with an open collar. His head is shaved, his skin is paler than BramToker's vampiric tookus, and there's a small RevCo pin attached to the lapel of his suit.

I forget that he's a short guy. My RW avatar is at least four inches taller than the schmuck and knowing this stretches my smile even further.

The little bastard.

I give him my biggest, baddest, bestest, most insincerest, shit-eating grin. "Take a seat," I tell him. "Anywhere is good."

Strata starts to say something and bites his lip. He looks to his droid goon, nods, and makes his way to the far side of the conference table. Once he takes his seat, he collects himself and places both hands on the table. A quick vitals readout and I see that his blood pressure has spiked since entering the room.

"I believe the best thing for you and me to do is to get straight down to business."

"Shoot." I tell him, my feet still on the table. "But make it snappy. Like I told your hotbody receptionist, 'I got places to go and people to see.'"

His left eye twitches. A vein pulses at his temple and quickly subsides. "Will you take your feet off the table?"

"I was just getting comfortable," I say on the tail end of a yawn. "Fine, fine, if that's the way you want to do this, have it your way." I nod over at the Humandroid bruiser near the door. "Take a load off, buddy. Sit on the floor or something. Hell, there may be some room in Strata's lap."

The droid's eyes narrow on me.

"If you got something to say pal, say it."

"Is this why you've come here?" Strata asks, his voice dropping into a growl. "To mock me and my employees."

"Employees? Relax, Strata, nobody is mocking nobody. I'm here to talk about Reapers, if you're ready."

"I don't know what you're talking about," he says hurriedly.

"Oh, like you *weren't* the one prancing around like a poofty trophy kill in your skull mask with antlers when you dropped the source code bomb in The Loop."

He pivots. "The Revenue Corporation has a mission statement and clear bylaws. If you'd like to read them, I can have them printed and delivered to you."

"Sounds like a plan. I'll probably be out of toilet paper in about a week, so see if you can deliver around them. So where were we? Down to business, right?"

Strata glares at me as he says, "The Dream Team knows where my son is, of this I am certain."

"So you did see him handing the Reapers their asses in your storage world. Fun stuff. He sure beat the hell out of Victoria, but then again, he was always your favorite, am I right?"

Strata slams his fist against the table. "Keep her name out of your mouth! I haven't gotten to her yet and to answer your question, no, I did not see him in my 'storage world' as you call it. I don't really know what you're talking about."

I clap my hands together, nice and slow. "Bravo, Strata, bravo. You have somehow managed to maintain a straight face as you deposit onto the table the biggest sack of bullshit these offices have ever seen, and *need I remind you* that they see your skeletal Tim Burton-looking ass whenever you pay them the dishonor of visiting."

He grinds his teeth together. "I will ask you again, one last time, where is my son?"

"I was gonna go with 'up your ass and around the corner' but I figured I'd spare you the wise guy act. Hmmm ... your son is ... " I feign confusion. "I can't seem to remember. Sorry, pal. Maybe it was ... what's the name of that one Zompoc world? Dead City. Maybe I saw him there. No, it was Infected Zero. That's the world. I think he was there."

"I am growing tired of your little game," Strata says, baring his teeth.

"Yeah, and I'm growing tired of all the shit you've done before and after the time I was stuck in a digital coma. Where to begin? You sent the Reapers after me, we can start there."

"I do not know what you're talking about."

"You attacked us in Steam and nearly killed Frances Euphoria."

He shakes his head. "Again, I do not know what you're talking about."

"You killed the bleachies."

He shakes his head. "You've gone mad since coming out of Cyber Noir, haven't you?"

"You sent your biggest cock holster, Rollins, to my hotel to kill me. Oh, I remember one now. Your whacko daughter, under your wing, killed Zedic Woods. Then there's the fact that you continue to employ orphans, starting them on a one-way road to corporate totalitarianism at an early age. And how can anyone forget that your company imprisons people through a device you co-invented with Ray Steampunk. Lemme see, what else? How 'bout the fact that your goons are currently looking for a RPG metal that will give you enough power to destroy a Proxima world. Need I go on? Here's one, you're currently holding one of our team members, Rocket, Rudraksh Vilas Paswan, illegally. That's a new one right there."

"I DO NOT KNOW WHAT YOU'RE TALKING ABOUT!" He says, scrambling in his chair.

"Jeez, get a load of this guy," I say to the Humandroid. "You guys got an anger management class as part of your company benefits or something? It helps to let go, Strata."

He points a crooked finger at me. "You really are the same stupid son of a bitch that you were before you were stuck in The Loop, aren't you? Don't think I've forgotten just how much of a pain in the ass you were! I will … " he bites his lips and clenches his fists together.

"You'll what?" I ask cooly.

"I want to know where my son is, dammit," he says in a low voice.

"Well, we want Rocket back. Sounds like both of us has a dilemma the other can solve."

"I don't have … " An idea flashes across his eyes. "Fine, we can trade."

I fold my hands together. "Now we're talking. Rocket for Luther?"

"Yes," he says excitedly. His Humandroid counterpart starts to say something and he shushes him. "Rocket for Luther." He looks me dead in the eyes. "I'm serious. We will release Rocket when you give us information regarding Luther's whereabouts."

"I'll do you one better," I tell him, "I'll bring Luther to you."

~*~

I stroll my happy metal ass right out of the Revenue Corporation's headquarters.

A black van lowers and I get in the back. Everything has been stripped out, aside from a single bench against the sidewall. The van lifts into the air and it is at this point that I breathe a sigh of relief.

I smile, relax even further into my seat and close my eyes for a moment. My live feed from our conversation has already been sent to Solon, the Dream Team's lawyer, and the others. Testicular torsion, an operation and one-act play starring a cantankerous bastard by the name of Quantum Hughes and directed by a War Faun that goes by the name Doc was an utter success.

Me: We did it.

Doc: Watching the feed right now and … That's it! Confession!

Frances Euphoria: Woot! Woot!

Sophia: THIS IS AMAZING! YOU BUSTED HIS BALLS!!!!!!

I wait for Rocket to say something. *Nope, nada, zilch, squat.* I never thought I'd miss his banter and bullshit as much as I already do

"I got you back, kid," I whisper as aeros moves into a higher airlane.

Strata agreed to trade Rocket for Luther. We have video of Rocket being taken by the Reapers. The dots are connected, our case is built. A damn good case too.

The digital exchange is set to take place in twenty-four hours, and that means we have until this time tomorrow to get a Reality Splitter made that not only frees my stupid ass, but also is able to cut through the OMIB of Strata's storage world, where Rocket is being held.

And that's if it even works there. Sophia seems to think that it will.

Time is of the essence. If ever there were a time to stop screwing around, that time is now.

Our case is built, dammit, every board has been laid. But the foundation still needs a little work, and a home isn't a home without a happy family inside.

Rocket is part of that happy family, and if push comes to shove, I'll gladly trade what's left of my life for his.

Chapter Thirteen

After switching vehicles twice, I'm whisked away to Doc's Goat Cakes truck. The guy selling organic snow cones, whatever the hell that is, waves at me. He points to a sign that reads 'droids are people too' and gives me a thumbs up.

"No they're not," I say under my breath.

Then I laugh.

"That's what I like to see," he says, "a little good ol' fashioned humor!"

I stop in front of the Goat Cakes truck and give my surroundings a quick scan. Nothing out of the ordinary, which is good.

Me: I'm letting myself in.

Doc: We're aware that you arrived.

Me: Just wanted to make sure I wasn't being tracked or targeted.

Doc: You are.

I look left, look right. My Humandroid sensors don't catch anything, which means one of two things: either Doc is bluffing or he's hidden his defense system so well that even a Humandroid can't spot it.

I'm going to go with the latter.

Frances already has my droid dive rig set up, which mostly consists of cabling spliced together with electric tape, and Doc has his own spot set up next to me. I should have known a section of the bed folds forward to make a pretty swank ass haptic chair. Doc sits in it now, finishing a bag of white cheddar popcorn.

He chuckles to himself.

"What?" I ask. "I haven't even said anything yet."

"You got under Strata's skin, Quantum, and damn if you didn't do a good enough job for him to confess to hostage trade! I almost didn't think you could do it – not doubting you here, just saying it shouldn't have been so easy – and boy was I wrong! He's probably figured out by now that he's been duped; even so, he'll keep Rocket peachy keen at least for the next twenty-four hours." Doc picks at a bit of popcorn kernel with his tongue.

"I sure hope so." The jammiest bit of jams sits at Doc's control center, gearing up to be our in-game. I mentally instruct my Humandroid interface to scan Frances. My eyes dilate and for a moment, I can see her nude body through the outline of her clothing.

"Why don't you go ahead and take a seat," Doc tells me, "and don't either of you worry ... " He crumples up the bag of popcorn. "We *will* get Rocket tomorrow, we'll get you too."

"We'll *try*. We still have collateral, remember?" I turn my finger to my face.

"You're not giving yourself away, and yes, we have collateral. We have Luther's body. Not that we can really do anything to it, but I'm guessing Strata doesn't like the fact that we have it."

"My thoughts are that it's a big set up," I say as I relax onto the couch next to Doc. "I can't tell if he knows it's coming or not."

"He doesn't," Frances says. "We have him this time."

"Yeah, sez you." Doc wipes some white cheddar dust off the front of his shirt. "Strata knows we're up to something and we know Strata is up to something. It's as simple as that."

"I tend to agree with Doc there, Frances, we're both trying to get each other by the juevos."

The faun in his human avatar form muses, "Now, if I were the sorry son of a bitch, I'd have something done to Rocket to make sure he isn't able to join us at the last minute. I'd have all my henchmen ready to spring once we showed up with Luther, and just for shits and giggles, I'd make sure everyone is outfitted with a couple of permalog collars. It will only take them getting *one* of us to seriously put a dent in our forces."

"We'd have NPCs in this scenario too," I remind him. "Aiden, the Lobby Boys, the other Loopers."

He nods. "True, but that's what I'd do if I were Strata. I'd overwhelm us until you, Frances, Sophia or I get caught in a collar."

"We'd waste the Reapers," I say, "we always do."

"Yeah, but he'll be there at the drop off, strong as an NVA Seed with his Meridian Circle back at his McMansion powering his evil ass. Even if we put up a damn good fight, he'll get one of us, and once one domino falls … " Seriousness flashes across Doc's face. "But we won't let that happen."

"No we won't," I tell him. "Let's make this one count. Have you already contacted Chrono?"

"He's standing by in Tritania. As soon as we have the Sky Iron, we'll port there. Then we'll get your ass out and then we'll get to Rocket."

"Bada boom, bada bing. Wait." I eye them both. "Did you say I was first, *then* Rocket?"

"I did."

"No, Rocket before me."

"We have to test the Reality Splitter before we try it in Strata's storage world. Frances and I already discussed this. No need to feel guilty; this isn't about you, it's about him."

"He's right, Quantum, it'll be better to make sure you can get out first, then Rocket."

"So then I'm the guinea pig?"

He smirks. "Aren't you always?"

"But we have completely different scenarios. I'm supposed to, um, kill Dolly with the ax. Then I'll be able to log out because she'll no longer control the world. Rocket situation is different. He's being kept against his will."

"Aware of that. Chrono and I will use what's left to forge a Reality Butter Knife to test while you're gone. Who said it needed to be an ax?"

"I assumed. And a butter knife?"

Doc grins. "You heard me."

"How will we get his cuffs off him?" Frances asked. "No one went over that. I get that we'll cut the game time continuum of the storage world to get to him, but how will we get the cuffs off?"

"I have a pair too, remember, and I have one stipulation for an item going into my list," Doc says. "I must have a fundamental understanding of how it works. I can take them apart quickly. That won't be a problem."

~*~

No time for farting around once I arrive in the dive yurt. Aiden is in his recliner and has since added a lava lamp just to give the place a little flare. He reads the business section of the Tritanian Times, his feet in a pair of Salvatore Ferragamo branded house slippers.

"You day trading now?" I ask instead of saying hello.

He appears behind me suited up. He's in a black cutaway jacket that's frayed at the collar. Great big goggles with tiny windshield wipers rest on his head and for once, he hasn't gone with a blade or Gatling gun arm.

I flick my fingers and my black duds appear. I refuse to play dress up for Steam. "You ready to scoot? We're late for a very important date!"

A spawning point appears and we both press it.

We're whisked away, down the rabbit hole and out the other end. Our forms tornado into shape inside the contraband shop. Joel sits on a stool and Steampunk Santa and Sophia are having a heated discussion about, well, science. No idea what they're talking about but I'm pretty sure they're arguing.

"Not so, my adequately educated but accolade-driven young doctor! An OMIB-Palisade is neither a stationary object nor an object in motion. It is akin to a black hole, or perhaps more accurately, to energy. Neither created nor destroyed which is why I believe they are dangerous."

"He just came from one!" She throws her finger at me. "And you have no idea what you're talking about. *NONE* of that makes any sense. You see … " Sophia raises a finger and math equations appear.

"Let's not turn this into a scene from *A Beautiful Mind*," I tell her. "Are we good, where are the rigs?"

"The rigs?" Steampunk Santa *tsks*. "These, my boy, are *much* more than simply rigs! These are Steamsuit XO-76s, the only four that exist in Steam."

"And why are you letting us borrow them again?"

He furrows his bushy brow at me. "Have you ever heard the phrase no questions asked, no answers questioned?"

"No?"

"Good. Follow me."

Steampunk Santa pulls down on a rope and a square portion of the roof lowers, letting in the orange light from outside.

He unfolds the ladder and we follow the stocky weapons dealer up. Doc is the last on the ladder. It ain't easy climbing it with his goat hooves, and Joel ends up offering him a hand, which Doc steadfastly declines. It takes him twice as long to get up there, and once he does, he's met by ooos and aaahs from the Dream Team.

Frances Euphoria: DROOL. I always wanted to fly in one of those!

Four exoskeletal suits stand before us, each about fifteen feet high. Angular bars of steel jut from various points on their bodies in a way that loosely reminds me of the quills of a porcupine. Their heads are all Transformer, red eyes too, and their legs thick, like they're wearing oversized paint buckets for shoes.

Air hisses as the front shell of the first Steamsuit splits open.

"It's all yours," says Steampunk Santa.

"Just like that?" I ask as I approach the towering suit.

"Do you want a demo or something or do you think you can figure it out?"

"Pretty sure we can figure this one out." Doc shoulders past me and the front of the Steamsuit next to me splits open. He pulls himself up and situates himself in operator's chair. As soon as his body is secure, the vehicle's shell shuts and locks into place with a hiss of hydraulics. The identifier YoRHa 4S is stenciled across the front of the Steamsuit.

He's airborne moments later, steam billowing out of the back of the craft and the bottom of his big metal stompers.

"Well if it's that easy … "

Aiden one-hand cartwheels into the craft with YoRHa 9S stenciled across the chest. He lands in the operator's chair and the craft to closes around him, locking him in.

"That was cool!" Sophia says in a way that reminds me of Rocket.

Aiden's craft has a single, Slice Bang-ish weapon on his right arm which is so large he's forced to drag it on the ground behind him when the vehicle is on the ground. He lifts up into the air, does a twirl, and joins Doc.

Sophia gets into her Steamsuit, which is outfitted with giant rotating gears for arms and shoulder mounted sound cannons. Her craft closes in on her once she's settled and she hits the air moments later. Hers is marked YoRHa 2B.

Doc: What's taking you so long?

Me: Just saying goodbye to our friends down here.

I turn back to Joel and Steampunk Santa. "The detonators are set along the other two walls, Wall Titan and Wall Maria, correct?"

"That's correct," Joel says, his eyes fixed on the Steamsuits that are now airborne.

"And if we set some kablooey at Wall Rose, you'll be ready to kaboomski on your end, at a moment's notice, right?"

He nods. "If that means what I think it means, yes."

"Good. Then we'll get this done, you'll get your riot, and we'll get our Sky Iron. One more thing – any thought on how we get in good with the Steam Breeds? We kind of didn't go over that and while I do have a vintage Easy-Bake oven, item 282, we don't really have time for me to whip up something yummy."

Joel gives me a curious look. Finally, he says, "The Steam Breeds aren't too bright, but their leader controls the power source for the fourth dimensional tripwire protecting Wall Rose. Most will think you are one of them as long as you are in your suits. *Do not,* disembark or let them think otherwise. Unfortunately that's all I can tell you."

Frances Euphoria: I'm sure we'll figure out a way – we always do!

"Got it." I step up to the Steamsuit with YoRHa A2 stenciled across its metal chest.

"One more thing," Steampunk Santa says, "do not think for one moment that you will be adding these Steamsuits to your inventory list. I expect them to be returned once you are finished. Do not worry about wear and tear, however, Chacho and I know a guy who knows a guy who can fix pretty much anything."

"You got it, bub."

As soon as I'm secure and my head is against a leather headrest, the suit closes around my form. The lining around my arms and legs inflates ever-so-slightly to lock them in place and a brilliant display of lights flash across my face, accompanied by a beeping sound with each new letter. Text appears on my viewing pane.

[Welcome, Steamboy_889.]

[D-NAS interface initiating ...]

[Checking black box ...]

[Black box confirmed.]

[Weapon status green. Initializing ...]

[Weapons confirmed. Ammunition at capacity. Loading OS updates ...]

[OS updates loaded.]

[Syncing to D-Nas ...]

[D-NAS G2G]

"Yippie ki-yay!" I shout, and again, my voice isn't my own. What I hear now booming and bass-tacular, its sound increased by a series of tubes connected to a small gramophone at the front of the Steamsuit's throat.

Steampunk Santa gives me the double thumbs up. I have two large blades for arms, one of his which has a Gatling gun with a small map of Steam inlayed on the receiver.

"Um ... I want to fly!"

[Flight sequence initiated.]

The wings extended outward and lock into place with a clicking sound. With little hesitation, I lift into the air, as easily as a person would take a step forward.

[Flight mode status green.]

The control interface is completely intuitive, and after performing a few flips, air moonwalks, and a perfect *petit jeté,* I join the others.

Doc's voice sounds out in my ear.

"Nice moves, really, I'm impressed. Now that you're done acting like an asshat, are you ready to get this show on the road?"

Rather than answer, I zip forward, twist, and excrete a cloud of dark steam.

~*~

Grandstanding has been the way I've lived my life up until now in the Proxima Galaxy. It is my personal philosophy, a great way to win friends and influence people, my *raison d'être*. No sense in stopping now.

Sure, the Dream Team, or better, STEAM Team, could mosey on into the city at the entry gate and work our way through the buffed up chiselers until we find someone with enough sense in their noodle to give us what we want or …

We could land in the center of the place and start shooting the place up until their leader comes to us.

I choose the latter, and due to time constraints, the Steam Team goes along with my direction. I'm the first to land, and while the other three circle above me, I stomp my feet, do The Twist, kick up dust, bang my arm blade against the ground.

[Taunt mode initiated.]

Steam Breeds start to take notice almost immediately. They are wider than I am by at least three feet, but no one has brandished a weapon yet.

One superhero landing later – which leaves a crater, mind you – and everyone knows Morning Assassin means business as well. He poses up next to me with his Steamsuit's Slice Bang up and gives those gathering a long, slow nod.

Doc lands next, lightly, just for contrast, and crosses his arms over his chest. Sophia, true to her character, keeps her favorite passive aggressive place in the air directly above us.

"Take me to your leader," I tell the closest Steam Breed, who has a green indicator over his head telling me that he is an NPC.

He lifts his shoulders and sets them back as he puffs out his chest. "We no have leader."

Caveman talk? I look to Doc to confirm it, but all I see is his Steamsuit mask with its emotionless eyes.

"Come again, bub?" I ask in my booming, Steamsuit voice.

"No leader. Steam Breed no leader."

I consider this for a moment. "Good, okay. How's this? I new leader. You new follower. Understand?"

He shakes his head and veins on his neck bulge. "We no good. You not leader. We no have leader."

Doc steps up to the plate. "Wall too big. We no like wall. Wall must come down."

Aiden gives it a try. "We new leaders. We good. Wall come down. Bye-bye wall."

Our main point of contact speaks to the nearest Steam Breed in a hushed whisper. He turns to Aiden and says, "Wall good. You no good." He lifts his fists and the Steam Breeds, about twenty now, all pick up their fists as well.

[Hostiles identified. System ready to engage.]

Square targeting reticles overlay on their bodies.

"If that's how we're going to do this ... " Doc spins up his Gatling. I get my swords up, and I'm about to go all Kill Bill on the steamed-up mountains when an older Steam Breed with wire rimmed glasses pushes his way through the crowd. This one has a blue indicator, a player character – *odd.*

"There will be none of that," he says, and he already has brownie points in my book just for the fact that he isn't speaking caveman. He's a head shorter than the others and he has a long, white beard that's twisted off at the end. Both his arms are mechanical, a smorgasbord of gears, chains and pulleys, that are well-polished and better maintained than the Breedies around him. "I am in charge here."

"Your buddy just said no one was in charge."

"You asked for the leader. We Steam Breeds have no leader." He raises a single arm in the air and the others raise their arms to meet his. "But I am in charge."

Me: What the hell is he talking about?

Doc: I dunno. Let me see if I can get an angle.

"Well, nice to meet you Mr. In Charge," says the Steam Faun. "I'm going to be just about as honest as I can possibly be with you. We are part of Ray Steampunk's Wall Survey group and we need to get to that wall and do a quick survey."

He strokes his beard for a moment. "You can survey it from the other side."

"Yes, we've already done that, isn't that right, um, Dr. Wang."

"Affirmative," Sophia says in her booming, mechanized female voice. "The front side of Wall Rose has been surveyed and is in good condition. There were talks of foundational issues at Wall Titan, something we hope to examine further after we've examined Wall Rose."

"Steampunk sent you?" He looks suspiciously at all four of us. "As in the Ray Steampunk."

"That's right," Aiden says, "we are the group that was responsible for, um, repairing and extending the wall around Alcatraz."

His eyes narrow on Aiden. "Is that so?"

"That's right," I tell the old fart. "Now, as per decree of the lineage of Steampunk and all that makes this world rusty, cranky, and good, turn off the tripwire protecting the wall so we can … "

Tear down that wall. I almost say it, but bite my lip just in time.

"So you can what?" the Man in Charge growls.

"So we can survey and measure the wall," Doc chimes in.

I step forward. "Or should we call Ray Steampunk here to help us ask?"

Doc: !!! You idiot! Ray Steampunk isn't going to appear!

Me: He did yesterday when I asked him to come …

"Ha!" The old man laughs and the gears in his body grind against one another. "Ray Steampunk come here?" His followers laugh with him. Once they've calmed down he says, "Okay, tough guy, call Ray Steampunk."

"Fine, I will!" I raise my Gatling gun into the air. The barrel spins and I fire a few shots over their tents. The Steam Breeds bristle. "You heard the man, Steampunk, getchur ass down here! Hello, we need you here; this was your idea, remember!?"

Sophia: QUANTUM! Do not refer to Mr. Steampunk that way in front of his subjects!

Frances Euphoria: She's right! Have you learned nothing, *nothing* about dealing with royalty in Proxima Worlds?

Me: Royalty in Proxima Worlds? Fine, fine.

I lower my swords to the sound of more laughter from the Steam Breeds. Eventually, the boss hog raises his mechanical arms and the crowd quiets. "So maybe you don't have his ear in the way that you think you do," he says.

Dammit, Ray!

"That said, you wouldn't have your wonderful Steamsuits *without* the blessing of Ray Steampunk," the old fella muses, "which means he must be, in some shape or form, crafting this little quest you've found yourself on."

"So what are you saying, pops?" I ask.

"So let's make a deal: I'll give you what you want, if you give me something I want."

"What is that you want?" Doc asks.

"My daughter."

"What'd she run off or something?" I ask.

He shakes his head. "No, she's a prisoner at Alcatraz, the only Steam Breed there. Since you four helped build the wall around the prison, I figure you'd be the perfect ones to break her out and bring her to me. Once you do, I'll have the tripwire temporarily disabled, and you can complete your little survey."

Chapter Fourteen

The four of us zip through the air towards Alcatraz.

Rather than fly over Locus, we head southeast, which puts us directly above the rolling hills separating Imperium from the capital city. The skeletal remains of enormous steam-powered robots pepper the hills, their rusted carcasses a testament to the wars that have raged in this odd land. One in particular died reaching towards the sky, a final lament, which gives me the chance to do a little good ol' fashioned target practice.

[New target acquired. Engaging weapons mode.]

I nail it with a fresh dose of unforgiving metal from my Gatling gun.

Then I laugh.

I'm not the only one who has used the big mechanical hand as target practice, evident in the bullet holes peppered across its palm.

Doc: Howzabout conserving some of that ammo?

Me: I just want to get a feel for how to use it.

I keep noticing a flashing blue icon on the bottom of the Steamsuit's viewing panel. It shows the proximity of my Steammates with a series of lime green plus signs beneath them. Rather than ask what it does, I mentally select the icon and it enlarges, a small shadow box forming behind it.

[Initiate sequence?]

[Please verbally accept.]

"Um … initiate," I say just for the hell of it.

"Shit … SHIT!" Gravity tugs at my guts as my craft begins to wind and grind all around me.

Panels fly off the Steamsuit and begin rearranging themselves, temporarily exposing the harness keeping me inside.

Doc: Dammit, what did you press!?

Doc is next to me now, and I catch him out of the corner of my eye as my sword arm separates and moves up – *moves up!?* – where it latches onto to something else, evident in a loud cranking noise.

[System activated.]

[Initiating interlink.]

[Interlink complete.]

More gears grinding, more anger from my dream-mates, and more loud adjustments as metal parts click together like Legos. The outline of a new body forms in the lower left hand corner of my viewing pane.

"It's morphing time!"

[Interlink fully initiated. Steamzord online and operational.]

The Zord gods of yore have shined down upon us and somehow, through a simple voice command, I have joined all four Steamsuits into something that would give Ultimus Prime an eighteen wheeler-sized hard-on.

Proxima gravity pushes me back further into my seat. The Steamzord is a bit clanky, but it sure can scoot along! Thinking about this puts a graphical flight tracking display on my interface telling me everything from the weather to the speed and our current altitude.

The next realization hits me. "Wait, why the hell do I have to be the leg?"

Aiden's voice appears in my ears. "Sometimes you win, sometimes you lose."

"Which part are you?"

"I'm the head and the arms!"

"And Doc, you're the other leg?"

"Roger that. I can never get a leg up. Ha! I kill me sometimes."

"I guess that's just the way the cookie crumbles. Let's get to Alcatraz!"

Sophia's voice this time. "Aren't you going to ask which part I am?"

"I figured you'd be the ass."

"I have a front side too, Quantum!"

"So you're the ... ?"

"I'M THE TORSO YOU IDIOT!" she screams in my ear.

"So you're the *front ass*, got it."

"Front ass," Doc chuckles, "I have to hand it to you there."

"And let me guess, you have nipple cannons?"

She huffs. "They aren't exactly where the nipples should be, but ... yes. I have nipple cannons."

Frances Euphoria: Screenshots!

Me: Most definitely. Transfer me one with the nipple cannons in full view.

Frances Euphoria: Rocket will go crazy when he sees this!

The mention of his name reminds me of what we're trying to do and why we're trying to do it. "Enough fun and games, let's goose it!"

~*~

The Steamzord, aka Yours Trulies, is a mech to behold.

Not much I can do as the leg, but if the chance to kick ass presents itself, I most certainly will take up the offer.

Below us, a pair of herders on steamcycles circling a group of sheep see us and do a double-take. Their sheep scatter. We pass over the ruins of a castle and I catch a glimpse of our body pushing out a chemtrail worth of steam from the bottom of its feet.

Damn, I wish I could have been the pilot!

"How's our weapon system?" I call out.

"One big blade the size of a two-story building for my leftie; one Gatling gun for my righty," Aiden says through the intercom system.

"Plus a ton of guns on its chest," Sophia says, "just so you know."

"Nipple guns. We've been over this. You got an ass cannon too?" I ask.

I can feel her roll her eyes at me.

Doc says, "Aiden switch gun controls to my interface."

"Roger. You want the shoulder cannon too?"

"Nah, give that one to Quantum."

"Hey, why am I the last one to get a weapon around here?"

[Shoulder cannon has been synced to your interface. Verbally accept this change.]

"Hell yes!"

[User D must verbally accept the shoulder cannon transfer.]

"Hurry up already, sync!"

[User D must verbally accept the shoulder cannon transfer.]

"Yes, dammit, yes."

[User D now has control of the shoulder cannon.]

Story of my life – I hope that there will be a time when I don't have problem with AI. Instead of bitch, I take in more of the sights of Steam, which roll below my viewing pane like a montage sequence in an old flick. Damn, there have been a lot of battles here. Lovecraftian graveyards galore, to the point where it is almost apocalyptic. It'd be fun as hell to do a little exploring, but there's no time for that. Which gets me thinking ...

"Hey, how are we supposed to figure out which one his daughter is?"

"What part of *she's the only Steam Breed* there do you not understand?" Doc asks.

"I didn't hear that part."

"Selective hearing is a pre-existing condition."

I laugh. Damn that Steam Faun and his early 21st century jokes.

"We're going higher," Aiden says.

"Higher, standing outside the fire ... "

"You need to work on your singing voice," Sophia chimes in.

"I'll get to that next. First, it's time to test my shoulder cannon."

The shoulder cannon swivels so it is facing backwards. Before anyone can protest, I lock onto a particular fluffy cloud and trigger the weapon. A red, concentrated beam of energy tears through the cloud. A circular indicator appears, letting me know the weapon will take twenty seconds to cool down.

"Happy now?" Doc asks.

"I ... I think so. I may need to blast that cloud again. He keeps looking at me funny."

[Iron West beach is due east an estimated fifteen minutes away. You will soon be approaching the air space above Victoria. Would you like to know more about Steam?]

"I'm good."

[Crankcase Lake is known for its rust colored water. The water is high in Vitamin Steam and the black sands that surround the lake are used in moisturizers and body scrubs. Alcatraz, situated on a man-built island in the center of Crankcase Lake, was built after the Federal Prison of Peshawar was destroyed after the Binghamton Prison Factory Fire.]

"I said I'm good!"

[Due south of Crankcase Lake is Verne Island, known for its interesting and unique animals, such as the Galapagos steam turtle. Steam turtles are unique because they are a living creature that has formed a relationship with humankind. Humans are able to open their glass shells, climb inside, and steer the steam turtles to the bottom of the Sea of Steam where there are plenty of treasures and mysteries to uncover.]

"Please shut up!"

"Who are you yelling at?" Sophia asks.

"The damn interface won't shut the hell up! I'm just trying to enjoy my time in ... the foot. I guess that doesn't sound as cool as I hoped it would sound."

"Did you answer its question?"

I quickly glance at the third to last message.

[Would you like to know more about Steam?]

"No! I would not like to know about Steam, dammit!"

~*~

The Steamzord's AI is more or less quiet for the rest of the trip. In the meantime, I get a good dose of Steam scenery and chat with Frances over the messaging interface. Time's a-ticking, and I can tell she's just as concerned about Rocket as I am. Eye on the prize is an understatement, and it is with no remorse that I aim the shoulder cannon at the walls surrounding Alcatraz and fire off a blast.

[New target acquired.]

Here goes nothing.

"Quantum!"

Ha! I don't think there will ever be a day in my life going forward that someone doesn't shout my name. This one goes to Sophia, who's utterly beside herself after she sees the blast I've just put into the wall surrounding the prison yard.

"What?" I ask as Aiden skids to a halt midair. "If Ray Steampunk *didn't* want us to blow up the joint, he would have appeared back in Tent City and let old man Steam Breed know we mean business!"

"But there are bad people in there!"

"There are bad people in here too, Doctor – what's your point? Again, I refer you to my original statement."

"Good call!" Doc starts firing the Gatling gun at one of the guard towers. A panel on top of one of the roofs cranks open. Air Enforcers pour out in droves. Doc adjusts his trajectory and starts taking the little bastards out in great waves of bulletry.

Another rooftop opens and a surface-to-air missile launcher slowly cranks itself into position.

"I've got it," I say as the shoulder cannon reaches full charge.

Le boomski!

The prison's SAM launcher is a great ball of fire by the time my shoulder cannon has had its say.

"This is against protocol!" Sophia laments.

"Dr. Wang, shaddup and get to firing at the approaching air enforcers, preferably with your nip guns!"

Doc's comment seems to work.

Soon the Steamzord is rocking in the air as Sophia pumps the weapons jutting out of the machinery's chest. The prison takes a pummeling and Lake Crankcase quickly fills with floating, steam-pissing, bodies.

Everything is hunky dory until a nearby cliffside opens up and a towering Steam Enforcer pulls himself out.

He's not the only one. A different hill opens up and another big bruiser pulls out. They're everything you'd expect in a Steam Enforcer – big, dumb-looking, slightly golden because of brass accent points, ape-like because their arms hang closer to their feet, and armed like the Saudis after their latest weapons deal with the FCG.

The two Steam Enforcers immediately engage us with their Gatling guns. As soon as the first bullet hits, an HP gauge scrolls across the top of my viewing pane.

[Warning. Enemy combatants are engaging.]

"No shit, Sherlock!" I grumble. "Come on, come on, come on."

I lock my shoulder cannon onto one of the enforcers.

[New target acquired.]

Success!

Boy howdy does it feel good to fire a blast directly at the big bruiser on the left. The red beam does little to tear through its metal body, but it does knock it backwards into a spattering of trees.

It springs back up and a shield forms on its forearm. Meanwhile, Doc is continuing to shoot at the small, Rocketeer-like Air Enforcers swarming all around us and Sophia and Aiden are engaging the other Steam Enforcer.

Our Steamzord rocks back and forth as Aiden's blade meets the blade on the Steam Enforcers arm. The steel grinds as they try to overpower one another.

"Come on, come on ... " I say as the particle beam cannon charges.

The damn thing! It's cool down time is killing us. I'm tracking the incoming palooka and if it doesn't charge soon, the big bastard will definitely have advantage over Aiden, who is completely engaged with the Steamer up front.

"Hurry up!"

[The particle beam system is in cool down mode.]

"Um ... transfer backup power to particle beam cannon!"

[Transferring backup power to particle beam cannon. Please confirm.]

"Hurry!"

[Please confirm.]

"Confirmed!"

I cut into the incoming Steam Enforcer. The blast does little to tear through its shield, but it does send the rustier, beefier version of K-2SO to the ground. It also momentarily cuts our power.

"What the hell did you do!?" Doc shouts as we free-fall for a moment.

"Had to rearrange the backup power! Hostile was incoming. Shit, someone do something!"

"System backup reboot, standby power engage! Auto-shield sequence initiate!" Sophia cries out.

My viewing pane flashes.

[Backup power system reboot. Standby power engaged.]

[Auto-shield sequence initiating ...]

[Auto-shield sequence online.]

Everything flashes green and we swoop up and away from the lake just in time. Water sprays into the air and the tiny Air Enforcers rally their forces. They come at us full throttle, and the towering Steam Enforcers hang back for a moment, allowing the little guys to do their damage.

Their bullets ding loudly against the Steamzord's exterior defense.

Aiden swipes a good baker's dozen away with his mahoosive sword. Their bodies split in two and like a balloon having its air let out, they spin away.

[Shoulder particle cannon is nearly operational. Currently at 85% capacity.]

"Hurry, dammit!"

As Aiden and Sophia engage the small Air Enforcers, and Doc lays down a wall o' bullets at the biggest of the two Steam Enforcers, I bite my lip, waiting anxiously for the cannon to fully charge.

My target now stalks us, tearing up soil and root as it paces back and forth.

Suddenly, the Steam Enforcer drops to its haunches. As it gets into position, its head and mouth open up. A large, directed energy weapon protrudes from its mouth; a blinding red light spins around it as it begins to charge.

My reticle blinks.

Shit ...

[Attack system update. New target acquired.]

The reticle spins counterclockwise as it homes in on the Steam Enforcer's open mouth. As I steady the cannon, a cascading series of numbers starts up on my viewing pane. On the ground, a large charge swirls around the Steam Enforcer's body as it prepares a ...

Throat cannon?

Now!

I fire the blast. The Steam Enforcer swallows most of it and not three seconds later, its core pulses, glows lava-red, and explodes.

Frances Euphoria: Yes!

"Whoo hoo!" If I had a cowboy hat I'd toss it in the air right about now. One jolly steam giant down, one more to go. I swivel the shoulder cannon so that it faces forward and begin tracking the other enforcer as the cannon charges.

[Ammunition at half capacity.]

Before I can ask if this means *me* or this means the all of us, Doc answers my question: "We're at half capacity. Sophia, Quantum, and I will concentrate fire on the remaining Steam Enforcer. Aiden, keep swatting the flies. Let's finish the job!"

"Roger!" Aiden says.

"Affirmative!" says Sophia.

"Let's murdalize the big goomba!" sez I.

Doc and Sophia concentrate their fire on the Steam Enforcer. Aiden keeps cutting down itty-bitty Air Enforcers as he slides left and right in an attempt to dodge as many bullets as possible.

In any other galaxy, I'd experience nausea as everything whips past me and around me. Here, I'm in my element, watching anxiously *again* as the charging icon lets me know we are good to go.

"How'd you blow the last one!?" Doc asks as our target continues to block our shots.

[Shoulder cannon ready.]

"It turned itself into a mortar, opened its mouth, and I aimed for its tonsils!"

"Well this one isn't doing that!" Sophia's voice is like a shiv in my ear. I cringe and listen as she finishes. "We need to do something to it!"

"Just keep firing at it!" Doc shouts.

We waste a lot of ammo trying to take the last Steam Enforcer out, enough that we get a new warning about five minutes later.

[Ammunition at 25% capacity.]

"Damn!" I say as I fire yet another blast at the Steam Enforcer, which knocks it back but doesn't do much else.

Meanwhile, Aiden has more or less mopped up all the Air Enforcers. Their quickly deflating bodies rest along the shore of Lake Crankcase and a good many float in the water. The water is also filled with prisoners in orange suits. Some swim, others, try to use Air Enforcers as rafts, and others have made it to the shore, where they have begun looting the dead Air Enforcers and taking their weapons.

Still no female Steam Breeds.

"Someone do something Power Ranger-y!" I call out.

Aiden's voice this time. "Bean shooter mode it is!"

A prompt scrolls across my viewing pain.

[Reroute shoulder cannon power supply to melee weapon?]

[Please confirm verbally.]

"Yes!"

[Verbal confirmation accepted. Rerouting power supply.]

[Manual override initiated.]

[Confirm new artillery mode.]

"Confirm!" all four of us shout.

My charge bar disappears and automatic controls take over and lower the craft to the ground. The sound of gears whirring and metal on metal contact echoes in the leg cavity that holds my body. Light flashes across my face as parts move all around me.

"Frances, can you give me an exterior view of what the hell is going on?"

Frances Euphoria: All of you should now have a bird's eye view.

The bird's eye view shows Aiden lowered onto one knee – aka me – and hoisting the second largest missile launcher I've ever seen to his shoulder. My cannon is gone, as are Sophia's nipple cannons and Doc's Gatling gun arm. Everything has been transmogrified into a massive golden shoulder-fired über zapper.

I'd pump my fist if my arms weren't locked down like I'm in some sort of sarcophagus.

"Smoke 'em if you got 'em!" Doc hollers.

The Steam Enforcer charges at us. It continues to fire, its bullets cutting into our shared life bar.

A pixelated loading hourglass appears on my viewing pane.

[Steamzord Bot Banger initiating …]

"Bot Banger?" Doc snorts.

I almost say that's my nickname for Sophia, but I swallow the joke. *Damn, it would have been good though.*

The hourglass keeps rotating as the approaching Steamzord gets even closer.

"Come on, come on," I say as I watch the loading hourglass. The tiny squares slowly transfer from the top to the bottom. "Let's go!" I shout. The Steam Enforcer is almost on top of us and its bullets are still tearing into us.

"Charging takes time," Sophia reminds me.

"We're about to get a big foot in the face if we don't do something soon."

"Almost there!" Aiden says. "Come on ... "

"Patience, young Proxima learner," Doc says. His tone of voice as changed; he's completely in his element, and I wouldn't be surprised if there's a cheek to cheek smile across his face.

[Steamzord Bot Banger is now ready.]

[Fire at will.]

The power around me dims and a static line whips across my viewing pane.

"Shit ... "

Everything goes black and white.

A blinding orange light fires from the Steamzord Bot Banger.

I watch in the bird's eye view as the blast *completely vaporizes* the running Steam Enforcer. By the time the blast is finished, all that's left is a hazy cloud of drifting particles.

Chapter Fifteen

I'd love to pat our big Steamzord on the back, but I'm currently stuck in the leg, so no can do. Instead I go with the verbal congratulatory message.

"Before you start celebrating," Dec says, "let me remind you that we still have to find this guy's daughter and get her back to Akrasia. Frances. Some help here?"

[Ammunition at 18% capacity.]

[Steamzord cool-down mode initiating …]

Frances Euphoria: Here's a schematic of Alcatraz. I believe she's in the underground bunker, marked on your schematic.

Similar to what happens when I wear my reaper skull, a three-dimensional outline forms on my viewing pain. The target is buried in an underground bunker, which means we'll need to blast our way in.

"All right, who's ready to do some digging?"

Sophia barks in my ear, "Initiate excavation mode!"

[Appendage-based melee weapons will be disabled.]

Gears and pulleys clank above me as the Steamzord's arms rearrange themselves into two yurt-sized rotating saws.

[Excavation mode initiating …]

[Excavation mode ready.]

The Zord lifts into the air and the sound of rushing steam roars in my ears. We skip right over Crankcase Lake and head to the prison yard.

"How about a swan dive?" Aiden asks.

"Better than a cannonball!"

Aiden steers our craft up and hooks over and drops towards the ground. He lands hard on the badminton court and lifts both rotating saws into the air.

The ground shakes and a crack forms in the pavement.

We jump backwards just in time. The ground caves in and dust sprays into the air. My targeting reticle tracks the female Steam Breed as she leaps out the hole.

Frances Euphoria: That's her.

Doc's voice this time, "Melee weapons engage!"

[Melee weapons initiating ...]

More gear grinding and metal on metal contact as the Steamzord's arms return to their normal status.

[Melee weapons ready.]

I've got the She-Hulk lined up in my reticle, even though the dust has yet to clear. She's motionless as she waits for us to act.

"Hands where we can see 'em," Aiden tells her in his booming, Steamzord voice.

Seconds later, the dust settles and we're greeted by a solid slab of flesh and mechanical amalgam. The female Steam Breed wears an orange prison outfit that just barely fits. Her chest is a chiseled set of pecs that tells me she's been doing a lot of pushups in solitary confinement. There's nothing female or dainty about her, aside from the fact that she's wearing ruby red lipstick. The red indicator over her head flashes blue, then red.

She's a marauder and a player character, just like her old man.

"We've come here to return you to your father," Aiden says.

"My heroes!"

Her voice does not match her body in the least bit. It ain't quite as sexy as Dolly's, but it's pretty damn close. The visual that accompanies the sound is all off, however, like a poorly dubbed Samoan e-porn.

As expected, her ironic grin flattens. "My father sent you, is that it?"

"That's it," Aiden says, "and we will be escorting you back to Tent City."

"That's sooooooo far." She crosses her arms over her chest and huffs. "Like, too far. I'd almost rather stay here. How 'bout I stay here, tall and handsome."

Is she ... ?

No, I'm imagining things. She must know that there are four of us in the Steamzord.

A dwarf prisoner who had been hiding behind a large hunk of rubble pops his head up and takes off. The tween Steam Breed leaps into the air and comes down hard right behind him, causing the dwarf to stumble forward.

He faceplants on a jagged bit of rubble and steam sprays out of his mouth.

"Poor guy," she says as she picks the dwarf up by the back of his prison garb and throws him over her shoulder.

Frances Euphoria: She's crazy!

Me: Just like I like 'em!

"Aiden, any way you can let me do the talking?" I ask aloud.

"You always do the talking," Sophia reminds me.

"That's 'cause I have a way with words and my voice is simply buttery. Aiden, let me man the vox."

"Fine, fine."

[Steamzord vocal interface initiating ...]

[Initiated.]

[Please begin speaking.]

My voice booms out of our Steamzord's metal mug. "Heya, toots, we got places to go and people to see, and one of those people is your daddy, who's gonna be happy as a steam clam to see you, believe you me! So howzabout you make this easy on us?"

She turns to the Steamzord and gives it a curious look. "Are you going to make me go?"

Are we going to make you go? The nerve of this one.

"Pappy Steam didn't say anything returning you dead or alive, but I'm going to make an edumacated guess and assume that he'd be more interested in seeing alive. To answer your question: yes, we are going to make you, yes, it will hurt, no, it won't kill you, and as I said previously, places to go, people to see, plus I feel like you owe us for busting your ass out of prison here."

"I busted *myself* out of prison," she reminds me.

"Parsing matter, sure, I get it and I agree with you. So what do you say – you coming with us or are we making you come with us?"

"Fine, but we're definitely not walking there and if you can't already tell," she flexes her neck muscles, "I can't fly."

~*~

I'm sure a good many of the misguided denizens of Steam got an eyeful the day they saw a Steamzord flying through the air with a prison garbed Steam Breed riding horsey.

Now I know how Mirror feels.

"No cowboy shit!" I shout, but my vocal privileges have long been taking away. Nope, Aiden is back at the horn, or the gramophone, and he does little to provoke or entertain the tween Steam Breed.

Frances Euphoria: More screenshots. Rocket will love this.

Me: He totally will. That kid will be jealous as hell when he sees what we've been up to while he was held prisoner.

Frances Euphoria: Poor guy :-(

Poor guy is right, I think as we fly over a tiny village that looks like it hasn't had a drop of rain in ages.

The soil is dry, the grass is dead, and the river demarcating the town could barely be considered a trickle. Why's Ray so against lushness? Sure, the world can be Steampunk, but does it have to be a Dune-esque desert world in parts as well? The constant smog, the consistent dusk around Locus, the corrosion simply for stylistic purposes – it just seems like a lot of work for nothing.

I'd love to bitch to Rocket about that. If the kid were here, I'd fire off a snarky message about Ray Steampunk being a tool, a rusted tool at that, and how the God Emperor of Steam seems pretty damn insecure if you ask me.

But the kid ain't here, and no one else on the Steam Team wants to hear me grumble.

"Now that's something." Doc says as we pass over the remains of an airship. I forget that we're both getting the same view of the ground below. The rib-like, skeletal remains of the ship are gone before I can get a good look at them.

My mind wanders off for the next thirty minutes or so.

I briefly recall seeing the Lost Pines below and having to change altitude once or twice, but I'm all but zoned out by the time we fly over the one of the walls that keeps Akrasia from the rest of Morlock. I get the notion to fire my shoulder cannon in the general direction of the prison city's shopping district, but think otherwise.

Ps and Qs – *you gotta know when to hold 'em, know when to fold 'em.*

We blast the barrier separating Tent City and the rest of Akrasia and my control panel flashes.

[Initiating landing and undocking sequence.]

[Ready at command.]

"Um ... how are we supposed to drop the big broad off if we're separating?"

"I sent you a message about this like five minutes ago."

Sure enough, a written message from Sophia blinks on my viewing pane.

"Why don't you ever check my messages!?"

"I do," I assure her, without reading the message. "So what are we supposed to do?"

Doc says, "Affirmative, initiate landing and undock."

[Landing and undock initiating …]

Insert Transformer sound here.

There's enough clanging, clanking, and clunking to give a mechanophobiac the screaming heebie-jeebies. The tween Steam Breed jumps just in time and lands in the center of the courtyard in the center of Tent City.

Now separated, our Steamsuits land around her in a half circle. I believe I am the only one who strikes a cool pose as I cross my arms over my chest and ever-so-slightly turn my back to Sophia.

"Where's your daddy?" I ask as the big Steam Breeds gather. And yes, I almost asked 'who's your daddy?' but again, I'm approaching forty and it's time to up my maturity.

More Steam Breeds surround us.

Why do all these guys and gals look like they have a screw loose? There's enough Bubba and Cletus faces in the crowds to cast a Steam-based remake of *Deliverance*.

As he did before, the old Steam Breed pushes his way through the crowd. He opens his arms wide. "Samantha!"

Her name is Samantha? As they hug, I get to wondering about their relationship. If they are both player characters, are they actually father and daughter or mother and son and just playing a role? Perhaps they are friends, and one decided to be the other one's daughter.

Or they are lovers, I think after the geezer cups his big bio-mechanical hand around her ass and squeezes.

Frances Euphoria: This just got awkward really quickly!

Doc: No comment.

Sophia: Ewwww – they're kissing now.

Me: I'm trying to think of an 'apple doesn't fall far from the tree' joke here but I can't swing it.

"You four!" The Steam Breed Patriarch says after a little heavy petting and some more smooching, "I can never thank you enough for bringing my lovely Samantha back to me." He pats her on the ass again. "She has been thoroughly missed!"

The Steam Breeds cheer and clap their big hands together.

I step forward. "Look, pops, as much as we'd like to stand around and watch you fondle your, um, daughter, as I told her, *we have places to go and people to see.* So go ahead and tell us how to turn the tripwire off or better, have one of these clanky goombas do it for you."

"Of course," he claps his hands together and a few of the Steam Breeds leave. "I am a Breed of my word. It won't take them long to reboot the tripwire, but you'll have to finish your survey rather quickly. Once the tripwire is rebooted, it doesn't power on for two minutes."

"So we have two minutes."

"Yes."

Me: Sophia, fly back to the contraband shop and make sure Joel is ready to bring the other two walls down.

Sophia: Will do.

The Dream Team's biggest brain does a double backflip into the air and zips away.

"How long will it take them to do the reboot?" Doc asks. "How long do we have before the timer actually starts?"

"About five minutes."

"Got it." Doc lifts into the air. "Let's get to the wall."

Me: So five minutes to get the reboot going, and two minutes once it is going. Got that, Sophia?

Sophia: Got it. I'll be at the contraband shop in just a sec.

~*~

The clock counting down on my viewing pane tells me that we have thirty seconds until the tripwire is officially down. Doc, Aiden, and I stand before it in our Steamsuits, ready to zip across to the other side and bring it down.

There are a good dozen ways I could come up with to bring down that wall and I'd like to explore all of them in a fireside chat one day, but now ain't the time. As much as it pains me to say it, there is no time to get creative.

The clock is ticking, *literally,* and there's still a lot to be done including getting my ass out of The Loop and Rocket's ass out of Strata's OMIB space.

"Doc, you got a better idea about how we're going to do this?" I ask as the timer gets to zero. "I mean, I got ideas, but they're a bit on the creative side."

"Aiden and I already discussed it. Get ready to link up."

"Wait, again?"

The words type out across my viewing pane.

[Link sequence initiating ...]

[Initiated.]

Before I can protest, the top half of my body bends forward and my arms shoot forward. Something smacks again the front and back of me.

"This better not be a Human Centipede!"

I hear a locking mechanism twist and crank above me as the sound of chains grinding echo through the cabin of my Steamsuit.

[Steamgun system check commencing ...]

[Steamgun system operational.]

More clinks, clanks, clunks and a few clonks and I've had it up to here – wherever *here* is because I currently have no sense of equilibrium – with the Voltron treatment.

It's only after Frances provides a bird's eye view that I see what the hell is going on.

The three of us have lifted into the air and together, we've created a particle gun with the barrel the length of the Reaper short bus. I'm the base and pintle, Doc is the receiver and Aiden is the barrel.

"I'm throwing the BS towel in," I say aloud, especially because of the fact that I have again found myself in a position as far away from the action as possible.

Why the hell is it that I have to be the base again? I get no respect.

"Time's a tickin', boys!" Doc says, no doubt with a smokable in his mouth.

[Ammunition at 13% capacity.]

"Got it!" he cries out. "Aiden, you ready?"

"I want to fire the gun!" I whine.

"You just hold us nice and steady." Aiden says through the intercom system.

Ray Steampunk. I got the feeling that the golden poster child of Steampunk has a hand in this. First, I'm the leg, now I'm the pedestal

"Laugh it up, Ray," I mutter as the weapon charges. "Laugh it up."

The lights cutting through the slits around me dim. A blast that could be used as stock footage the next time the History Channel does a doc on Operation Crossroads plays out on my lower portion of my viewing pane.

Against all the laws of physics, our limo-length shooting iron holds its position in the sky. Even as debris litters down upon us, screams ring out from the city on the other side, and the shock wave reverberates in our chest cavities.

Me: Sophia, Wall Rose is down. Status on the other walls.

Sophia: Wall Titan and Wall Maria are down. I repeat, all walls are down!

Chapter Sixteen

We don't stick around for much longer after the walls come tumbling down.

The three of us zip up about as high as we can without breaking the hazy celestial dome. Sophia is already up there in her Steamsuit and for once I'm happy to see her, after all, *I can't see her;* rather, I see her Steamsuit and not much else.

My breath of fresh air is cut short by a series of explosions below.

A war has already broken out down there, and I'd like not to be the one that lets God sort out the losers this time. Fiery explosions shake the ground. Buildings are bombarded with bullets, weapons clank together as the Boilerplate Army tries to keep things under control, Marauders go crazy, and prisoners escape and kill anyone trying to stop them.

"What did Joel say?" I ask Sophia over the comms system.

"What do you mean?"

"I am assuming you asked him to meet us somewhere after the walls were taken down. Not gonna lie here, but I've sized up a lot of jabronies in my two subjective years trapped in The Loop – that twerp is the type of hombre that won't be down there on the front lines."

"Agreed," Doc says.

Sophia's Steamsuit actually nods. "Oh, are you asking where he said to meet us after we took down the wall?"

"Yeah, that's what I'm asking."

"He ... um ... He didn't say about that."

Frances Euphoria: I'm getting a reading on some new activity below!

A portal opens up in the sky and Reapers on steamcycles spill out.

Nothing atypical about this lot of Steampunked, skull-masked, trouble boys and girls with bulging muscles, world-inappropriate shooting irons, and enough leather to outfit every B&D fetishist in the Tri-State area.

I make a beeline for the Reapers before anyone can stop me.

~*~

I give the first Reaper the Cuisinart treatment.

He's Kibbles 'n Bits by the time I'm done scissoring past him, steam from his deflating muscles whistling in the air. Another jets up to meet me and I cut her in half before she can get her mutant hack ax up, and both sides of her body spin away, propelled by steam.

"Quantum!" Sophia shouts. "We have other things to do!"

Doc this time. "Five minutes, tops, and nobody die!"

Out of the corner of my eye, I see the Steam Team's deadliest faun twist in the air towards a gaggle of Reapers. He lays into the biggest of the bunch with his fist while shooting at others with his Gatling gun

Damn these Steamsuits sure get the job done!

I swear I'm having deja vu as a battle not unlike my first big battle in Steam plays out before my very eyes. A witch whooshes through the air, alchemical magic rippling around her arm as she attacks a

Boilerplate Air Enforcer. The enforcer has large pipes sticking out of the back of his suit which are spewing a foamy green substance. As soon the stuff touches her skin, the witch writhes and burns as she spirals towards the battle below.

Aiden lands on the ground and clotheslines a Reaper on a steamcycle.

Damn, that's gotta hurt!

Dust, explosions, steam, debris, rubble – the Shock and Awe Campaign has landed in Akrasia.

On the other side of the now crumbled wall, SRT Mondoshawans waddle towards the battle with boxy weapons. A group of prisoners in orange jumpsuits have taken them up on their offer. They wield whatever they can find, and it ain't long before the biggest prison riot since the Carandiru Massacre is well underway.

No time to soak in the mayhem – Gatling gun fire dings against the front of my suit. I find the culprit, a Reaper in a rusted AT-ST on the ground below, and I advance towards him. We collide and my life bar takes a bit of a dip as the Walker flat out explodes.

On the ground now, a Steam Breed rushes towards me with a dragoon's lance. I swipe the lance away with the big blade on my left and follow up with my right. The slice across his chest draws a thick cloud of white steam. I zip around him using the boosters and finish the job.

Aiden flies past, crash-lands into a building, and blasts off. Above me, Doc is firing short bursts at anything remotely hostile. Sophia floats above him, her arms crossed over her chest.

Frances Euphoria: Incoming!

Another portal in the sky opens up and I brace for more Reapers.

I'm taken off guard when I see Ray Steampunk in all his golden boy glory float out, his shimmery cape beating behind him.

Steampunk is in a polished golden cuirass with an offset flame on the chest and a pair of pearl white epaulets with matching gold tassels His legs are protected by gold and silver cuisses and his tootsies are enshrined in a pair of sabatons with elaborately decorated ankle plates joined by buckled straps.

"Enough."

The word echoes from the godfather of Steam in the form of a sine wave. As it balloons in size, everything the glittering wave touches returns to its original shape.

The bricks of Wall Rose, Wall Maria, and Wall Titan swirl in the air as they rebuild themselves.

The lifeless, deflated bodies on the ground regain their shape and re-attach to any appendages they may be missing. The windows of the contraband shops, the bail bond shops, the hat shops, the shiv shops, the umbrella shops, the ironic tabard shops, and the stained glass of the cathedrals swirl in the air as they rebuild.

Ray Steampunk lifts his hand in the air and all the Reapers rise from the crowd. About three dozen skull-masked Juggaloes squirm, struggle and kick as they try to logout.

Some cry like sissies once they realize their logout buttons are missing; those less cowardly take to their weapons. They fire upon the crowds only to see the bullets and blasts from their hack arms dissipate in front of them.

Doc lands his Steamsuit next to me. The front of the suit splits open and he hops out.

"I've got it from here, Ray," says the Faun of Steam as he equips his souped up golden goosinator hack. The hack boils saffron as it moves up his arm to his shoulder, as its symbioses spreads across his chest and latches to his other shoulder as a colossal three-barreled mutant hack takes shape.

Using his other hand to steady the weapon, Doc aims it at the Reapers.

ZOT!

His first three blasts take the goombas at the front of the pack. They're forced to log out and will only be able to log into the OMIB going forward.

"Hey, I want in on the fun! How do I open this thing?"

"It should just open upon command," Sophia's voice says in my ear.

"Open up!"

[I'm sorry, I am unable to interpret your command.]

"Ah, come on ... " Doc fires on another pair of sitting Reaper ducks as jealousy and anger spread through me. "Cut the crap, Ray, open up this dammed suit!"

[I'm sorry, Steamboy_889, your suit has been placed in sudden lockdown mode.]

"Reboot the system, let me out of here!"

[System reboot? Please confirm.]

"For the love of ... " I shake my head. "Yes, affirmative, reboot."

In the time it has taken me to manually get hold of my Steam suit, Doc has taken another two sets of Reapers.

[System rebooting ...]

Suddenly my pod opens up. I leap out, land, roll, and equip my 571, my Golden Goosinator hack. It spreads up my arm and I join Doc in blasting the hell out of the semi-frozen Reapers.

"What took you so long?" Doc asks. "I thought you lived for this stuff."

"Technical issues."

I take out the final row of Reaper whack-a-moles and lower my hack.

~*~

"Glad to see you turned a new leaf and are *finally* ready to help us," I tell the God Emperor of Steam as soon as we're done checking the Reapers' candyasses into the Smack Down hotel.

My hack is warm to the touch, but at least he isn't buzzin' in my ear like Hackie. I return it to my list as the thought strikes me. "Wait a damn minute, why the hell did you have us destroy the wall only to rebuild it?"

Faster than a flasher can whip open his trench coat and waggle his willy, Aiden, Doc, Sophia, Steampunk and Yours Truly are in the Lost Pines in front of Bjurstrom. The rogue steam mech is still in the crater that was opened up earlier, and while four of us normal folk are Steamsuit-less on the ground, Ray has maintained his holier-than-thou position in a golden bubble that floats three feet off the ground.

"Good," I say, getting the hint for once. "So you're finally willing to help us speed this along. The next step in the 'Bring Ray Down to Earth' intervention will be to get you to lower to the ground and talk to us mano y mano."

Sophia: Quantum, he helped us!

"And I'm simply trying to help him. Everyone needs a life coach."

Much to my surprise, Ray's sphere lowers to the ground and pixelates away. "You are correct," he says without moving his lips, "I have decided to help you."

"Well, it's about time, Ray."

"I realize that you have limited time."

"Correct, we gotta get Rocket out of Strata's storage space before tomorrow. Twenty-four hours, now twenty-three, no twenty-one. No less than that. I'm terrible with Proxima time. Point is – we gotta hurry."

Ray nods, his eyes black as ever. "And Chrono? Is he ready to forge the weapon?"

"He sure is, um, right Doc?"

Doc nods. "Chrono is standing by in Tritania."

"Good, and you will free Quantum from The Loop first, then Rudraksh, I presume?"

I glance downward. I don't like Doc's plan one bit in that regard. Sure, who wouldn't want to wake up from his second digital coma?

That said, Rocket doesn't deserve the dish he's been served and if I had to choose between getting him out and getting me out, I'd choose him. He deserves it more than me.

"There's nothing to feel guilty about," Ray Steampunk says as Joel's form materializes. "You should test the weapon *before* you try to use it to rescue Rudraksh."

"Not feeling guilty," I mutter.

"Ray Steampunk?" Joel drops to his knees. "I didn't think ... I didn't know!"

"Relax, Bjurstrom," Ray tells the sniveling grease monkey. "I understand why you did what you did."

"Wait, so he's Bjurstrom?" I ask Sophia.

"I thought we went over this," she says, "he's an extension of Bjurstrom's D-Nas."

"Why didn't we just call him by his real name then?"

She shrugs and I tune back to the conversation at hand.

"Why ... why did you stop it?" Bjurstrom, or perhaps Joel, or maybe Joe L., asks. "Why did you stop the destruction of Morlock?"

Ray Steampunk considers his answer for a moment and finally says, "Morlock and its Marauders and the Boilerplate Army keep the world of Steam in balance. This is not the real world, and the forces of evil can actually exist with little to no repercussions. This keeps this world sane, it makes the adventures treacherous and raises the stakes – all things necessary for those living and existing in a video game to continue to enjoy themselves. Virtual Entertainment Dreamworld, VE Dreamworld, that is what the Proxima Company specializes in."

"Then why did you let us fry the Reapers?" I ask.

"I didn't let you, they let you."

"What are you going on about now, Ray?"

"If you have a moment, watch any feed from the battle that took place in Akrasia. All perspectives show a battle between you and the Reapers and your team, The Dream Team."

"Steam Team," I correct him.

"That's a stupid name and you know it. Anyway, all the feeds show your team beating them."

Sophia's eyes grow wide. "So you can't be implicated!"

"Exactly."

"Even the Reapers' own feeds?" Doc asks.

"I am the NVA Seed," he reminds the Faun of Steam.

"Okay, so why are you going GoogleFace incognito then? Why not just come out with it?" I ask.

"Legal reasons, as I'm sure you can figure out on your own. I'll be much more useful to you if the Reapers do not know we're working together. Now, let's get to the cliffs outside Steam City. It is time to get the Sky Iron."

A golden sphere forms around each of us and the rogue steam mech. A blinding bar of pixilated light extends from Ray Steampunk and connects to the spheres around us. As if someone has just sucked us all through a straw, our bodies compress and our forms mesh together as we're zipped away.

~*~

The four of us take shape on the side of a high escarpment. The rogue steam mech forms below and immediately begins drilling at a rapid rate, spewing dust, rock, and debris into the orange dusk. Rock meets metal and metal wins, cracking and stripping at the stone as it makes its way to that big juicy vein of Sky Iron.

Ray Steampunk floats above us, his hands clasped behind his back as he watches his mining exhibition, the big show-off. At least he has finally decided to cut the crap and help us.

Frances Euphoria: Oooo pretty!

A rust-colored strand of liquid metal appears in the air above the burrowing steam mech. It twists up the cliff side, coils in midair, and forms itself around a spool.

"It's like copper?" I ask.

Steampunk doesn't answer. More veins of orange-brown metal lift into the air. They harden and coil once it reaches Ray Steampunk.

"How much do we need?" I ask.

"As much as we can get," Doc says, a cancer stick hanging out of his mouth. The 100% Red, White, and Blue Faun of War and Steam in that order ashes his cigarette. Aiden asks for a bump and Doc hands it to him. Morning Assassin coughs, exhales a plume of smoke, and gives the cigarette back to Doc.

"Never can get used to these things."

Sophia launches into a dissertation of RPG metals and how they're so valuable, and rare, and how just a few grams could pay for a home in Valhalla – I all but ignore her. Time's a tickin', and as much as I like seeing heavy machinery do what it does best, I'm feeling a bit antsy.

"This should be enough," Steam's biggest male diva says. "Definitely enough to forge a Reality Splitter."

The spool of Sky Iron drops before me and I added it to my inventory list, item 591.

Doc does the wrap it up sign and a spawning point shaped like a target appears before him.

"A target?" I ask.

"What?" he asks. "It works, doesn't it? Thanks for the help, Ray. We'll be in touch."

He nods. "I look forward to it."

~*~

"We really need to hire a trio of trumpeters," I say after our forms take shape in our Tritanian guildhall. "It would make our entrances oh-so-grand."

Our Tritania crib has been spruced up yet again. The walls are now teal, and across the room is a single sofa in tufted Cascadia Blue velvet, seated before a coffee table made from red ivory. The long table has been replaced by a small gym featuring kettle bells, yoga mats, foam rollers, hand grip strengtheners, and small plastic dumbbells.

A mirror has been installed on the wall behind the barbell storage rack.

"Dammit, Sophia." I say as soon as I take it all in.

"What are you dammiting me about?" she asks.

"You charging a membership fee for your little home gym?"

A toilet flushes and the door nearest to the home gym pops open Scotty steps out in an exercise outfit that would make Richard Simmons squeal with delight. The Scottish Assassin in a blue wrestling singlet with a golden lightning bolt across the front. "Oi, Quantum." he says as he returns to his kettle bell, showing me his thong.

Frances Euphoria: Ha!

"Don't you do it, Scotty!"

He crouches, grabs the bell and stands. He then runs it through his legs, giving everyone an HD view of his dimpled ass peppered in red hairs and zits. "Are you lot goin' ta sit there and watch me?" He focuses his bushy red eyebrows on us through his reflection in the mirror.

Sophia makes an icky face and turns away.

"You put this gym in?" I ask.

"Never mind," Doc turns to the exit. "Let's get to Chrono."

"Of course I put the bloody gym in. All the lads are in lock up and I figured it was time to do something about me weight. Lost half a kilo already," he says, nodding to the bathroom.

I shake my head and follow Doc and Sophia out. Aiden stays behind to spot Scotty while he tries for a bigger dumbbell.

Chrono, Zangief's younger Brazilian brother, steps out of his blacksmithery as soon as he spots us. He's in thick black apron, a flannel shirt, jeans, and a pair of black steel-toed boots. "You have the metal?" he asks, his eyes thirsty to see it.

I equip item 591 and toss it over to him. It disappears from my inventory list.

"Don't ... " Sophia sighs. "Never mind."

"Amazing," Chrono says as he examines the Sky Iron. "It is a lot less dense than I imagined it would be."

"Let's get to it." I look over my shoulder to find the Fantasy Faun also in some blacksmith gear. "I'll help." Doc pops the visor of his welding helmet down and struts right in to Chrono's blacksmith shop.

The big blacksmith follows and the two get to work.

"What am I supposed to do?" I ask the sky. Since we are in a protected guild-space, it isn't technically the sky of Tritania; rather, it is something almost OMIB-ish. Twinkle twinkle little star and whatnot.

"You can hang out with me," Sophia says.

Frances Euphoria: Ha again!

"I'll pass," I tell our guild's mind mage, who has, yet again, taken her favorite position in the sky a few feet above me. "Say, didn't Scotty say the other Brits were in prison?"

Sophia nods. "I think so. It's hard to tell with that accent of his."

"Then let's break them out of prison – that sounds like a great way to kill time." I turn back to the guild. "Hey!" I call out. "Aiden!"

Frances Euphoria: There's been enough prison breaks today. Sit down, shut up, and wait until Chrono and Doc are finished. If you're bored, you can go inside and work out with Aiden and Scotty.

The image of Scotty in his thong runs across my digital mind's eye.

Me: Pass.

Frances Euphoria: What about the sheep?

"Pippa? Well, Frances, that's not a bad idea." I mosey on over to Pippa's pen and lean against the fence. "Come here, girl," I say with my hand out. When that doesn't work, I equip my bouquet of Kadupuls, item 166. I wave the flowers at the sheep. "What? You don't like flowers?"

Meanwhile I hear the clink and clank of Chrono and Doc as they pound out the Reality Splitter. I really hope it doesn't take them long to finish the weapon, and I especially hope that the weapon looks badass, something that I'd be proud to hold over my shoulder a la Paul Bunyan before I tear into the very fabric of the game-time continuum.

"You aren't doing it right," Sophia shows me her open palm. One of her halal non-gmo nonfat kosher certified fair-trade organic granola bars appears in her hand. Pippa doesn't even look up from her grazing place.

I laugh. Nothing like a little equal opportunity sheep-snubbing to brighten the day.

~*~

Doc and Chrono rattle and clank for another thirty minutes or so. To kill the time, I equip my deck of Gambit playing cards, item 279, and start up a game of solitaire. Once I get bored with that, I equip my

Tamagotchi, item 214. *Damn, I never seem to make it from Babytchi to Marutchi.*

I toss the plastic Tamagotchi egg over my shoulder and start playing the knife game with good ol' item 33. I go with the most complex order I can possibly come up with. My hand spread wide on the ground, I stab the knife between my fingers, 4,2,3,1,4,3,1,2,4,1,4,2,1,3 …

I activate the AA and pick up the pace.

Frances Euphoria: You're obnoxious, you know that?

"I'm just killing time. Dope!" I stab myself in the web between my thumb and pointer finger. Blood gushes out and my life bar flashes.

Doc is the first to step out of Chrono's blacksmithery. He has a grin on his face as if he and Chrono have just discovered the Fountain of Free Beer. I throw my Bowie knife behind me and skip over there, bleeding hand and all.

"Knife game?" Doc asks when he sees the cut.

"It's only a flesh wound," I tell him. He frowns. "What? I was killing time. Where's the Reality Splitter?"

Chrono steps out holding an ax to behold. It ain't no rush job either. The Sky Iron and Chronoton have been forged and folded into a beautiful Damascus-pattern alloy. The ax is shaped like the SOG Tactical Tomahawk and features the two weight-and-metal saving holes bored through the head. The shaft is genuine unicorn ivory; the grip is wrapped in actual dragon skin and is capped in silver. It'd be the coolest cutlery you've ever laid your peepers on if it weren't for the fact that it is about the size of a fondue fork.

Frances Euphoria: It's so little and cute! It's like a Lumberjill Barbie accessory.

I clear my throat and roll my eyes up at the sky. "I was expecting something a bit, um, more manly."

"Pfft!" Doc shakes his head. "That's what she said, bucko. What the hell were you expecting?"

"Something anime-sized," I tell him. "But no worries, the size doesn't matter as long as it does the job."

"That's also what she said."

"Can I see it?"

"That's also what … yeah, you *can* see it."

Sophia snorts.

"Can I hold it then?"

He narrows his eyes and wrinkles his brow at me, scratches one of his faun horns and breathes loudly through his nose.

"Come on, Doc, don't bust my balls here. I was just ribbing you."

Doc nods, and Chrono hands the ax over in the most gentlemanly of fashions, arm bent at the elbow and the axe laid reverently across his forearm, grip first.

Hello item 591, my Reality Splitter.

"Now get to Cyber Noir," Doc says. "Sophia and I will put our feelers out to see if this stuff works in Strata's storage world. Once you've taken care of what you need to take care of there, don't log out. Spawn here instead, and we'll get to the storage world. In the meantime, Chrono and I will use what's left of the metal to craft a Butter Knife Reality Splitter."

I raise an eyebrow at Doc.

"What?" he asks. "We have to test it to make sure it'll work!"

Chapter Seventeen

I spawn in the dive yurt alone. My Loop gear takes shape on my body – trench coat, black shirt, stompers – I kick open the door and step out.

Kill Dolly.

I shudder at the thought and the Loop bristles all around me.

Everything is ominous, stripped of its life force, suspicious, unforgiving. The trees in Three Kings Park lean towards me, waving their mangled limbs. The broken park benches swell and waver, the rabid dogs in the woods howl at the nonexistent moon.

Welcome home, Quantum, I swear they all say.

The rain picks up.

It bullets down from darkened sky, plinks against my clothing. I hate to do what I'm about to do, but I know it needs to be done. I walk towards park's entrance, towards the trashcan fires surround by yeggs holding a séance.

The thunder rolls and the lightning strikes. I get the heebie-jeebies as I feel a pair of eyes on me.

"I know you can see me, Doll," I mumble, "and I'm coming for you."

One quick scroll through my list and my flare gun, item 24, takes shape in my hand. I scroll down and go with item 303, my Walther PPK/S. The gun goes in my hand and I stuff it in my trench coat.

I aim the flare gun up, squeeze the trigger, and watch the bright charge make its mark in the air.

I'm still not quite out of the woods, literally, but I know a taxi will be waiting when I get to the exit.

Something moves in the trees and growls. I ignore it as I move past, focused on bottling my emotions. Not long ago, Tritania's NVA Seed forced me into a scenario in which I had to let Strata and Dolly kill each other while I stood by and did *nothing*. I thought it was a bunch of malarkey, but as it turns out ...

A man's gotta do what a man's gotta do, I think, as I see the taxi ahead. *Even though it kills him to do so.*

The crumb-bum of a driver rolls down the window. "Where to, pal?" he asks as I approach.

"Whew," I wave his stench away. He smells like a locker room attached to the kitchen of an Indian restaurant. He belches long and loud, his lips flutter like Barney Gumble's. "Out of the taxi, Buster." I point the PPK/S at him.

"What's the big idea, Daddy-O?" he asks in grit-for-breakfast Loop taxi-driver voice.

"We're going to go over some hygiene strategies I tell him. Out, *now*."

"All right all ready, no need to get bent out of shape," he says as he steps out. "That taxi's yours, mister."

I cap him before he can grab his chain knife.

This one would have been a fighter, and I respect that, but now ain't the time to pay my respects. I step over the cabbie's body and hop into the driver's seat. I hold my breath as I reach to the passenger's seat and roll down the other window.

I need to get some speed fast, I think, *just to air this shit rod out.*

The engine huffs, wheezes, and cranks as the taxi wobbles away from the ground. Still holding my breath, I get the chariot in the air and take off towards the Mondegreen.

No time for a scenic tour neither.

I go straight there, avoiding the shenanigans and all the places I'd normally stop off for some giggle water with a side of cruel intentions.

I try to keep my mind blank, as cold rain sprays into the taxi. Dolly already knows I'm coming and she likely knows what I'm going to attempt to do. I'm surprised The Loop hasn't turned against me. With all the other vehicles whipping in the air around me, surely one of them will try to turn a fender bender into first degree murder.

Hell, I'm tense just thinking about it. I got my eyes on the other drivers now like I'm a small town copper in a one stop sign town.

I stay clear of anything on any of the buildings that could fly off and bring my beater down. Gargoyles, water towers, shabby rooftop gardens, the couple smashing nasties too close to an open window – all are suspect.

But nothing happens. No attacks, not even the usual aggressive driver.

She's the NVA Seed, I remind myself, *and she knows you're coming.*

Damn the memories I have of Dolly. The Maltese Falcon playing on a television in the background, her tight red dress peeling down to reveal her mammiferous attributes, the way she looked at me, through me even.

I swallow those memories down. My decision has been made and that same damn decision is the reason my ass is trapped in the first place.

The Mondegreen looms into view. Fortress Dolly is the same as it was the last time I tried to blast it open – protected by a hardened shell, impenetrable from any of the weapons in my list.

Until now.

I goose it. She knows I'm coming, and if there's one thing I'm good at doing, it's making an entrance.

~*~

I equip item 300, my suicide bomber jacket. Instead of putting it on, I toss it into the passenger seat. On top of it I throw item 105, my Birkin bag full of frag grenades and on top of that, I gently roll my Bomberman replica bomb, item 385.

I put the pedal to the metal for just a moment longer, activate my AA bar and bail like a paratrooper over Normandy.

The resulting explosion throws me back even with my AA bar keeping me in a slow-mo semi-floating state. I land on a rooftop, lose my balance, and faceplant hard.

My life bar takes a dip, but it ain't nothing.

I sprint to the edge of the roof and my Reality Splitter, item 591, pixilates together in my hand. I look at the bloom of fire and smoke at the front of the hotel, take a deep breath to settle my nerves, and leap off the rooftop.

I turn up the AA a few feet away from the pavement.

I land softly; the fire I've caused is already partially burnt out. The explosion did nothing to The Great Wall of Dolly, and I didn't expect it to.

I still need to test the ax. A quick look right and I see a hooptie parked on the side of the road. Parked is an understatement; its wheels have been stolen and it now rests on cinder blocks. I stroll over to the beater, bring the little ax back, and strike the trunk.

A slice in the game time continuum follows the bit of my blade. It makes no sound as it cuts through the trunk of the vehicle, a hot knife through butter.

"Whoa."

The gash remains in the air. On the other side is the OMIB, all twinkly and star-filled.

I take a step back from hooptie and admire the ax. The thought of what I'm about to do returns to me and I quickly lose my enthusiasm.

"It's gotta be done," I tell myself.

The exoskeleton surrounding the hotel bubbles and tendrils lift off as I approach.

"Bring it, Dolly," I say bitterly.

The first tendril flies at me and I cut it down with the Reality Splitter. It's like using a hot sharp blade to cut the leaf of an aloe vera plant or something.

I keep swiping and Dolly's Witchblades keep falling. The tendrils shrivel and smoke as they hit the ground, emitting an orange steam and hissing loudly.

"Sorry, Doll." I mutter as I knock an incoming Witchblade out of the air.

Two more come at me and one of the two tries to circle around back to give me the *Alien* treatment. AA bar goosed, I cut the first, spin around, cut the next.

Dolly tries to get creative and I match her creative with the sheer destructive power of the Reality Splitter. Tears appear at the corner of my eyes and I let them fall.

I hate doing this.

"I'm sorry, Doll," I say again. "So damn sorry."

Suddenly the barbed tendrils stop flying at me. They retract back to the building and mold into its surface. The exoskeleton over the entrances peels open in the way that resembles a cheesy nacho being lifted from the stack.

The door opens and I stop dead in my tracks.

"Quantum?" It's Picasso, the kid that helped me get out of The Loop the first time.

~*~

"I know it's you, Doll." It's not often that I turn on the waterworks like this. I wipe a few tears away and a few more after that. A deep breath in doesn't seem to help any.

Picasso shrugs and turns away from me. "Are you coming?" he asks.

It may be a trap.

I hate to think that way, but the possibility is there. I stay frosty as I make my way to the entrance of the hotel, my Witcher senses at code red. If a dust mite so much as sniffs they're getting a bullet between the eyes. I step into the lobby and …

Everything is cavernous, as if the crust from outside has made its way inside. The space is twenty degrees colder than the outside. There is no smell, which conflicts with the jagged rock face, and the only noise I hear is the static of an old television.

"Jesus, Doll," I say. The Mondegreen hotel has become about the saddest thing I've ever seen.

Picasso turns to me and his eyes flash orange. "She's upstairs."

"Doll, let's just get this over with. I know it's you … "

Picasso crumbles into dust.

" … MAKES her way lives her life does her things ALL OF THIS TO SAY every little sneer every little TEAR come away and FLY FLY FLY … world over world smolder world builder world destroy world WORLD cruel world at the end of the … CRUEL!"

"Uncle Carnie?"

The short, ill-tempered little monster stands at the stairway, twitching, ripping at his long sideburns. He's in a Mark Twain white suit that's soiled beyond belief and a little white top hat on his dome. "YOU don't know me YOU don't know me ALL OF THIS TO SAY … bluebirds crippled crows broken beaks of Maltese falcons SHUT UP nest eggs ROAST NEST ROAST NEST baited breaths life death LIFE DEATH all real all false all false all real." He pauses, looks at me and snarls. "All false real."

"Easy, boy," I tell the circus freak as I pass him. No smell from his soiled britches, still, I hold my breath.

"YOU AND ME tragedy you and me LOVER KILLERS you and me DIE TOGETHER you me DEATH UNITES us YOU AND ME travesty ... "

Cryptic little bastard, I think as I take the stairs, which are now made of rock. I know where Dolly is, and it pains me to think of what I'll need to do when I get there.

Just to be safe, I raise my finger to see if I can log out.

"What the ... !?"

The logout button is now available, glimmering in solid gold light.

"Dolly? You're letting me ... ?"

I shake my head and cast the logout button away.

"This is *not* how it ends," I grit.

My pane of vision narrows as I reach my floor. I sludge through the hall as if it were made of quicksand and stop in front of room 406. I suck the emotions I'm feeling in my chest down, wipe my tears away, and reach for the door to my home for two subjective years.

A spark moves up my arm as I twist the doorknob open.

~*~

Light from the television flickers across the space. *The Maltese Falcon.*

~~*You've got to trust me, Mr. Spade. Oh, I'm so alone and afraid. I've got nobody to help me if you won't help me. Be generous, Mr.*

Spade. You're brave. You're strong. You can spare me some of that courage and strength surely. Help me, Mr. Spade. I need help so badly. I've no right to ask you, I know I haven't, but I do ask you. Help me.~~

I whisper the next line. "You won't need much of anybody's help You're good. It's chiefly your eyes, I think, and that throb you get in your voice when you say things like … "

"Quantum."

Dolly rests on my bed in her Jessica Rabbit red dress, a hotbody at ease. She ain't sprawled out on the bed like I thought she may be, and luckily for me, her witchblade armor hasn't spread up her arms, nor is it advancing towards me with the hopes of shredding me to death.

"You can log out now," she says, without making eye contact with me. "You've won."

Something has changed in my painting of the sailboat at sea. Instead of braving the waves, it is now upside down, its hull exposed.

I take a step closer to her and I keep my ax at my side, ready for anything.

"You want to kill me now?" she asks.

"You know that's not true," I tell her.

"Then what is it you want? That weapon you hold can kill me, for good. No respawning."

She turns to her other side to reveal a bloodied arm. I nearly drop my ax and run to the bedside with item 158, my first aid kit. "Dolly, are you okay!?" I ask. "What happened?"

"You still don't get it?"

"Get what?"

Her voice hardens. "You attacked me."

"With this?" I look at the Reality Splitter and back to her. "You know I wasn't trying to do that, Doll, honest. Never. I'd never do anything to hurt you."

She glances at me and her eyes flash orange.

"You know it." I drop the ax and it plinks against the ground. "I couldn't ... I wasn't going to hit you with that thing. I just needed to get in here."

She stares at me for what seems like eternity. Finally, she says, "I've given you your logout point, Quantum. Go get your friend."

"I will, but I got a few things I need to say to you first." I take a cautious step towards her. "
You mind if I sit?"

She casts her head away. "Fine."

"Dolly, you saved me. You really did. Multiple times even. You did this because you loved me and I know that you know how much I love you. You're an NVA Seed; you can read my thoughts. I don't have to tell you how I feel. I don't have to say anything."

I reach out for her hand and she reluctantly lets me take it.

"But this, this can't happen. Not now anyway. I've been a total idiot, a total boob. I'm sitting here trying to do important things in the world out there and put a stop to some real evilness and at the same time, I'm running around like a chicken with his head cut off, getting into this, curious about that, doing things I shouldn't, playing with fire. You get my drift. So that's it. That's what I have to tell you. I love you, Dolly, and I don't want you to ever think I don't think about you or cherish you or miss every goddamn moment we spent together. But we can't do this right now. You know that; I know that."

A single tear forms and slides down her cheek.

"I'm sorry, Doll."

"Me too."

"I gotta be smart about this for once. I gotta be a different Quantum and you know that." I wipe my own tear away. "You of all people know that."

"I know."

I bend forward and kiss her on the head. "All of this is my fault," I tell her as I stand. "I'm aware of that."

"Wait." Dolly stands to greet me and takes my hand in hers. "I want to logout with you."

"You know you can't do that." I close my eyes to hold back the pain I suddenly feel. The gesture does little to quell the anguish in my heart. "You … "

Dolly holds the side of my hand as the logout button appears.

"Dolly."

"Press it," she says. "I mean it."

I raise my pointer finger, and look back to Dolly. A golden halo frames her head and the look in her eyes is soft, warm. We press the button together, but only one of us disappears.

Epilogue

It's going to take a lot of beers and some heavy duty soul-searching to unpack what I've just been through. As instructed, I don't logout completely. Instead, I stay on the Proxima menu screen and select our guild in Tritania.

Feedback anathema. Feedback ambrosia.

The tethered ends of a black hole engulf me and fling me forward. I see flashes of Dolly's face and the halo that formed over her head just as I logged out. I need time to process this, but now ain't the time.

Damn.

The game time continuum splits, the event horizon makes itself abundantly known. I materialize in front of Doc, Chrono, Aiden, and Sophia.

"Quantum!" Chrono runs over and gives me a big bear hug. I suck in a big breath, bottle the emotions that just poured out of me. It works, somewhat.

"Easy, pal!" I tell the big sweaty brute as I pat him on the back. "Did the butter knife work?"

Doc nods and throws his thumb over his shoulder to a tiny square cut into the game time continuum. "And now our guild has this hole. We should have tested it somewhere else. Anyhoo, it works, and I believe the knife or your ax, will work in Strata's storage world."

"We still don't know for sure?"

"Son, no one ever knows anything for sure. We couldn't spawn there to check it before you returned, but we're fairly certain that it'll work."

Sophia nods. "I am 90% certain. Doc is right around 80%. Don't worry, it'll work."

"And if not?"

Doc looks up to the darkened sky. "Don't worry about that for now. Frances and I have already discussed contingency plans."

Aiden approaches me. "How'd it go?"

"It went," I grumble.

Frances Euphoria: Look on the bright side, you can log out now!

"Did you … ?" Aiden places his hand on my shoulder and looks me dead in the eye.

"I didn't have to." I tell him with a gulp.

"Good."

"Here's what I don't want," Doc says, interrupting our bro-ment "I don't want another Royal Rumble at the Reaper Corral. I don't want us shooting, cutting, exploding, and pillaging our way through the storage world. We gotta get in there stealthy, cut into the OMIB, and find the kid and get him out. That is our only objective. The Battle of the Bulge between the Reapers and us can wait 'til later."

"Isn't the OMIB matched to the size of the storage space?" I ask.

Sophia's eyes go wide. "You … you actually listened to me!"

Doc's Atlas Sphere appears in his hand. "Yes, which means it isn't too big, yet big enough to be a pain in our asses. Luckily, we got our Atlas Spheres."

I scratch the back of my head. "I thought those were only good for finding logout points."

"They are good for finding logout points. They are also good for finding Dream Team members due to a little code Sophia installed in them."

Sophia raises a finger. "Um, it is much more than a little code, Doc. Actually, it revolves around a kink in an avatar's D-NAS. To explain how this is possible, you need to understand the basics of neuronal bit strings … "

"Not now, Dr. Wang," he growls. "In fact, we need you for another mission here."

"Oh?"

The Dream Team's CWO gives her a cheek to cheek shit-eating grin. "That's right. Log out and prepare for Quantum and Rocket's extraction. They'll be needing a ton of care once they're out of their dive vats. The ArachnaMed unit can handle most of it, but it'll be better if you're there."

Sophia's shoulders drop. "So I just have to wait for you guys to go do what you're going to do?"

"You are the only one in Baltimore. If Frances were there, she could take care of it. Instead, she'll run in-game."

"Fine, fine." Sophia dramatically lifts into the air, the ends of her long robes swirling around her. A logout point appears over her head and dramatically lowers over her, disappearing her avatar as it descends.

I clap my hands together. "Glad she's gone! Let's get suited up."

Aiden's black ninja uniform replaces his Tritanian guild duds. He equips a few guns, checks them, stashes them across his back or at his side.

Doc's furry goat legs and tactical vest turn black. Liquid body armor spreads down his arms and solidifies. Gloves appear on his hands, black paint under his eyes, followed by a balaclava with cutouts for his horns. He goes with his bone saw, a wakizashi on his back, grenades hooked to his belt and a Glock on each hip.

"If you two are itching to play dress up, you KNOW I'm down." I start from the bottom and work my way up with black stompers. Then I go with milspec liquid Kevlar pants, a bullet resistant vest with matching epaulets and my Zorro mask, item 305.

"Lemme borrow your black paint," I tell Doc.

He tosses it over to me and I smear it across my face, ears and the underside of my neck.

Frances Euphoria: A balaclava would have done that for you.

Me: Frances, when an artist is at work, you let him work.

Frances Euphoria: You're an artist now?

Me: Look, if any bozo can sell a picture of a blue square and call it art, I'm *definitely* an artist. My medium is the inventory list, thank-you-very-much. Now if you will, screenshots, for the kid. He'll dig them.

I equip item 572, my buster sword, and sheathe it across my back. My Robocop Auto 9, item 304, appears in its holster on my right hip. Darth Maul's lightsaber, item 251, appears in a sheathe on my left. For the main course, I go with item 128, my M41A pulse rifle. Nine-hundred rounds a minute? You betcher ass.

Chrono claps his big paws together, clearly impressed. "I've never seen you guys in your gear from other worlds. If I were a Reaper, I'd definitely be scared of you three!"

"Thank you, Chrono, and you're right, they should be scared. Now as I was saying … " A tracking reticle appears in front of Doc. "We'll use our Atlas Spheres to find him in the OMIB. I expect some Reapers will be guarding him, but not a lot. We'll need to move fast. Neutralize any enemies and get him before they can respond."

~*~

The three of us spawn in Strata's storage world on top of a warehouse. In the distance, I can see large Reaper Sentinels standing at attention, ready to engage or be whisked away to another world at a moment's notice. Onion-shaped pods with tentacles hanging from them fly between the stolen items. Lights on their bellies cut through the haze and a few carry items to be moved to other locations.

Doc brandishes his Butter Knife Reality Splitter. He turns it upside down, pulls his hand back, and stabs it into the air. The end of the blade disappears and he tugs his arm down.

"It works," he says with a grin. About a minute later, and Doc has cut a door into the world's game-time continuum. Sparkling stars and glitzy galaxies shine out from the other side.

"Who wants to go first?" I ask.

Aiden shoulders past and once he's in, he quickly begins to establish a perimeter. I take one more look at Strata's hazy storage world, spit, and waltz on in. "Damn," I say as soon as I'm past the Stargate, "OMIBs always trigger my agoraphobia."

The place is expansive, and instinct forces me to raise my finger and double-check that I can still logout. *Whew.* At least there's that.

Doc's atlas sphere floats over my head and flashes green. "Let's follow it," he says, taking the lead.

For a faun, Doc is pretty damn fast, and I nearly break a sweat to keep up with him once he's in full speed ahead mode. Aiden flits in and out of reality, checking for hostiles and traps.

Frances Euphoria: Sophia wanted me to inform you that everything is prepped and ready to go for your return to our world.

Me: Looks like comms work here. Good. Have her order me some pancakes, breakfast tacos, and a six pack of beer too.

Frances Euphoria: You aren't going to be able to eat when you get out, you know that, right? You're probably going to be sick and disoriented for at least a day.

Me: How long did it take me to go for a short stack once I was out of my digital coma?

Frances Euphoria: A week.

Me: Point taken. Tell her to order the stuff anyway just in case I get the craving.

Doc makes a gesture with his hand and the two of us duck. Aiden is back moments later, his weapon at the ready. I lift my M41A pulse rifle, rooting to start shooting.

"Less than one click ahead," says Morning Assassin.

Doc chews his lip as he considers this. "How many did you see?"

"At least twenty. They're on a large platform and Rocket is chained to a metal loop jutting out of the center of the platform."

"Quantum, you ready to be you?"

"Am I ready to be me?" I give him a toothy grin. "Is there any other way I should be?"

"Good," Doc says, "then you know what to do. They'll be able to spot you fifty feet out, just remember that."

It feels good to be the obnoxious asshole that I keep trying to keep bottled up yet who always manages to weasel his way out, and it is with great pleasure that I equip my Reaper skull mask, item 551, and stroll my happy ass right over to the group of skull and candy kids guarding Rocket.

Realizing that this will work better if I fit in, I pull up the storage world's avatar interface. I expected that the Reapers love some avatar customization, especially because many of them are losers in real life, and boy am I right.

"Think like a Reaper would think …"

Frances Euphoria: I can only imagine where this is going.

I up my muscles to Bane-like proportions; throw a black tank top over my chest and make sure nipples are good and hard; toss some chains over my neck and use a chain and a big lock for my belt buckle;

jump into a pair of knee-high stompers outlined in skulls and speaking of my legs, I shrink them a bit so my upper body appears even more disproportionate.

I equip my two hacks, item 554 and 571 respectively. The more garrulous of the two fires up in my head.

I feel like you've been ignoring me.

"Not now, Hackie," I tell my first mutant arm cannon.

Are you mad at me or something?

"Hackie, not now."

It seems like you've made other friends.

"Shhh!" I tell him as we reach a point about four hundred feet away.

If you've made other friends, you can just tell me. It's better that way.

"Trust me, Hackie, you're my only friend."

Both hacks spread up my arm and I flex my now clawed hands. The Reaper hack morphs into a shiny barrel. Hackie doesn't do shit.

Frances Euphoria: Who are you talking to?

Me: My mutant hack. He's feeling neglected.

Doc: Focus on the mission at hand!

Me: Roger. Frances mask my handle.

Frances Euphoria: Um …

Me: Or give me a Reaper name.

Frances Euphoria: That I can do!

Your name has been changed to John Hand.

"John Hand? That the best you can do?"

Frances Euphoria: It is the first thing that came to mind!

Doc: You should have named him Cray Neeyum. Get it? Ha!

Me: Can we at least make the name reference worthy? Boom. John Hancock. Done.

Your name has been changed to John Hancock.

"That's better," I say under my breath.

With my Reaper mask on, everything in the OMIB is gridlines, DNA strands, and Matrix-y mumbo jumbo. My souped-up disguise should absolutely not work, but I'm not really betting on it to work, I'm betting on the troubled turdburglers trying to go medieval on me as soon as they get wind of my sorry ass.

A pod hovering over the platform lifts and moves to greet me. A light shines from its front, illuminating my chiseled body.

A guy in a Reaper mask walking in the OMIB with two mutant hacks spread up his arm? Nothing to see here folks!

The onion-shaped pod thinks otherwise.

~~*Identify yourself.*~~

"John Hancock," I tell the pod.

~~*This name does not appear in the database of authorized users.*~~

"Yeah? That's because I'm the new guy around here."

~~*Your response does not appear in the list of authorized responses.*~~

"Yeah? Well look again, buster."

~~*Unequip your weapons and place your hands in the air, John Hancock.*~~

I keep my mutant hacks on and slowly lift them up.

~~*Unequip your weapons.*~~

"Not gonna happen."

Another pod flies over and shines its light on me.

~~*Unequip your weapons.*~~

~~*Unequip your weapons.*~~

"What part of no do you two fail to understand?"

Red lights on their side bodies began to blink.

"Great, here comes the cavalry."

Five or six of the Reapers leave the platform and make their way over to me. Their mutant hacks morph into big-barreled shooters as they fan out.

~~*Unequip your weapons.*~~

~~*Unequip your weapons.*~~

Once the first few Reapers are in listening distance I call over to them.

"Hey, amigos, these pods have gone off their rockers. Can you call them off?"

The first Reaper stops and moves his head back, as if he's looking at me funny.

"Bros, I'm here to relieve one of you," says I. "Whoever wants to go home early, feel free."

Frances Euphoria: Bros? Who says that anymore.

"Stay right where you are," the first Reaper says in his heavily masked, metallic voice.

"Fellas, what's with all the hostility? Can't we all just get along?"

A few more Reapers leave the platform. I can see Rocket there now, his head bent forward, both hands chained to the ends of a T-shaped structure.

Hang in there, kiddo.

"John Hancock?" The first Reaper says. "Why does that name sound familiar?"

Another Reaper in a whiny female voice answers, "That's the name of the guy who signed … something. Before there was an FCG."

I almost drop my act to give the two skull-faced clowns a history lesson, but I catch myself just in time. "Guys, what's with all the procedure here? I'm just doing my job."

"Unequip your weapons!"

~~*Unequip your weapons.*~~

~~*Unequip your weapons.*~~

Those two pods will be the first thing I destroy.

The female Reaper shouts, "Unequip your weapons!"

"I forgot how, honest."

More Reapers join them and surround me. I got about eight weapons trained on me, and if I don't spring into action quickly …

I cough the question. "You ready, Hackie?"

Ready when you are.

"Fellas, and ladies," I tell the gathered group of problem children, "I don't know what all the fuss is about … "

Doc: We're in position. Twelve have now joined you or are on the way over. Five still at the platform. Distract them for just a bit longer.

"Unequip your weapons!" One of the Reaperettes hisses. "Last warning!"

"Why would I do that? Reaper protocol states, and I'm quoting verbatim here. *All Reapers must have a stupid amount of weapons equipped at all times, even if they are unaware of how to efficiently use their weapon.*"

The biggest of the bunch pushes through the crowd. Rollins-lite glares me down and at the flick of his wrist, his hack spreads up his arm, forming a large, curved blade. He raises this blade until the tip is pointing the underside of my chin.

"You got some shaving cream too?" I ask him. "I've been at a five o'clock shadow since yesterday and the orphanage … "

"ENOUGH! Unequip your weapons or I will kill you now."

Doc: Ready.

"Cool, cool," I tell the skull-faced palooka. "Just keep your Skeletor Underoos on, got it? I'll unequip my hacks as soon as you give me a little breathing room, *sheesh.*"

"Good."

Off with his head!

He has barely removed his blade from my neck when Hackie, of his own volition, swings around and cleanly nicks off the lead Reaper's noggin.

"Damn, that was fast!"

AA Bar activated, I backflip *over* the Reapers who have gathered behind me and catch Rollins-lite's head spin into the air spritzing blood. My Reaper hack forms its mahoosive golden rimmed barrel and I fry the closest Reaper I can find.

They unload their weapons at me and I duck their first volley. Once they let up to reload, I use my AA to goose it and give me some dancing room.

Three follow and by time they arrive, I'm a tornado in a knife shop, spinning with both my hacks. I swiftly take the arms off one of the skull kids. He cries like a sissy-pants as an underslung barrel forms on my Reaper hack. I blast him, I blast another, cartwheel right, and bring Hackie up just in time to stop one of the Reapers from slicing my head off.

We go back and forth for a moment and I kick him where the sun don't shine. In the blink of an eye, a sharp spike forms on my elbow and I bring it down onto the back of the Reaper's head.

Feed me!

"Have at it, Hackie! It's an All-You-Can-Gorge Reaper buffet!" I say as I blast another skull-faced nut-job. An explosion on the platform catches my attention.

The Reapers who have been stalking me turn and race towards the platform. I start firing at the them, giving them all I've got. "More!" I shout to both my hacks. "Fry 'em!"

Hackie responds by forming a bad ass shoulder cannon to go along with his arm gun and its two cannons. The Reaper hack doesn't do much, aside from increasing its blast radius.

I use what's left of my AA to bangtail it to the Reapers advancing towards Doc and Aiden.

"Frances, update!"

Frances Euphoria: All platform targets neutralized. Doc is working on the cuffs, Aiden is providing covering fire.

A yellow portal opens up on the other side of the platform. I keep blasting at the Reapers running towards the platform with my Reaper hack and focus Hackie on the Reapers piling out of the portal.

"Shit!"

My AA gone, I slow to a crawl compared to the action happening all around me.

Frances Euphoria: I'm logging in!

Doc: Absolutely not! We need you on in-game we can handle this.

Frances Euphoria: I'm not letting you guys have all the fun!

"We've got this, Frances!" I say as I blast another glammed-out skull boy.

Frances Euphoria: IDEA ALERT! I'll Random Spawn Points!

Doc: Genius! Do it! DO IT!

Another portal opens up over my left shoulder; Hackie's shoulder cannon pivots to meet the Reapers leaping out of the portal, their guns a-blazing.

Nice! A few of the Reapers disappear as they run smackdab into random spawning points generated by Frances.

"More portals open and as the Reapers move towards the platform, their forms completely disappear. "Keep 'em coming Frances!"

Frances Euphoria: Got it!

I see flashes of light in front of me as Aiden steps in and out of reality, cutting heads and gutting Reapers. Behind him, Doc has Rocket's right cuff off, and now works on his left.

A Reaper breaks through Aiden's defense; Doc pulls one of his shooting irons and unloads the entire mag into the Reaper's skull mask and returns to the left cuff.

"Killer diller!" I'm nearly at Aiden now and there are enough Reapers around us to fill a Houston megachurch. No matter how many knuckleheads Aiden or I cut down, more appear, even with Frances' RSPs doing them dirty.

I keep cutting, blasting, flipping and spinning around like I'm auditioning for Cirque du Soleil. I'm seconds from being overwhelmed when I hear a chainsaw roar coming from either side of the platform.

The Reapers scatter as a wall of supersonic metal tears into them.

Doc's UA571-C remote sentry guns mow down Reapers that Aiden and I miss and we get back to doing what we do best: murdalizing. The name of the game is maim, the story of my life is an algorithm.

I slice, dice, shoot, and scoot, for the next several minutes to give Doc the cover he needs to rescue the kid.

My life bar flashes.

I look to Aiden and give him the same wolfish grin he always gives me as a Reaper's blade presses through my chest, jutting out the front.

Everything goes red.

I laugh as Hackie's shoulder cannon morphs into a sharp scythe that opens the Reaper's noggin like it's an over-ripe abscess.

Hackie takes over, and as I stand there skewered, he picks up where I left off.

Doc: Let's go!

I tilt my head just in time to see Rocket collapse forward, free from his cuffs. Doc catches him and both their forms pixilate.

Frances Euphoria: Log out! Quantum, LOG OUT NOW!

I glance once more to Aiden, who has lost his arm from the elbow down and is still engaging a Reaper. We lock eyes and he nods to me, telling me to log out first.

Bullets tear into my chest as my hand comes up. The logout button appears and everything goes black and white. I will wake up shortly in a vat of goo sucking air through a plastic tube. I will be weak again, a cripple to some, but I will be alive and sometimes, that's all that matters.

A sense of satisfaction rolls through me as I jam my finger onto the logout button and dematerialize.

Back of the Book Shit

Reader,

The eighth and final book in The Feedback Loop series will be release by summer of 2018. It's the finale, the big send off, and I want enough time to really get this one right. In the meantime, I will be releasing other books that take place in the Proxima Galaxy that are related in some form to The Feedback Loop series. The first of these releases is Fantasy Online Hyperborea, which is out now.

Inspiration

Weird inspirations this time around. I got back into gaming to get a better feel for what's going on out there and I was heavily inspired by Nier: Automata, which features a ton of mech and killer fashionable androids. This, Titanfall 2, and a childhood spent watching Power Rangers went into the Steamzoids used in the book.

Akrasia was based on Arizona's Tent City, which as of April 2017 is in the process of being shut down. For those who haven't read or heard of the place, a quick Google (GoogleFace) search will tell you more than you'd like to know. I suppose that is true about anything, nowadays.

Keep an eye on this space (i.e. the books I write). Later, before I release the final Feedback Loop book, I will publish a side series set in

Steam based on a woman named Cyn Oneida who retrieved the four Steamsuits for Steampunk Santa. It'll be mech-heavy.

The Proxima Galaxy keeps expanding

The Proxima Galaxy allows me the flexibility to write in both science fiction and fantasy, and I will continue to write within it for the foreseeable future. While the Feedback Loop is coming to a finish, I will continue to release works tied to the story told in these seven, later eight, books. The Feedback Loop is the foundation for what is to come, so by getting this far, you are completely primed and ready to see what else is possible in the Proxima Galaxy.

Kudos

To you, dear reader, thanks for journeying with me this far into the Proxima Galaxy and giving me the headspace to tell my story. Thanks to George C. Hopkins for the edit. Thanks to James-Andrew for giving a looksee. And Kay, as always, took care of the beta and did a bang up job.

Here's to the last and final part in The Feedback Loop series! **Set the date, summer 2018,** and be sure to catch up on my other books in the meantime.

Yours in sanity,

Harmon Cooper

Amazon Profile

 Be sure to check out Fantasy Online Hyperborea, a Tritania-based spinoff of the Feedback Loop series featuring several of the Feedback Loop's MVPs!

Fantasy Online Hyperborea is now available as an ebook, print, and as an audiobook narrated by Jeff Hays.

Enjoy the prologue on the following page.

Fantasy Online: Hyperborea (sample)

Copyright © 2017 by Harmon Cooper

Copyright © 2017 Boycott Books

Cover by Tom Shutt

Edited by George C. Hopkins (georgechopkins@yahoo.com)

Float over the Endless Sea,

Hyperborea, Polynya, and Ultima Thule."

--A famous Tritanian poem

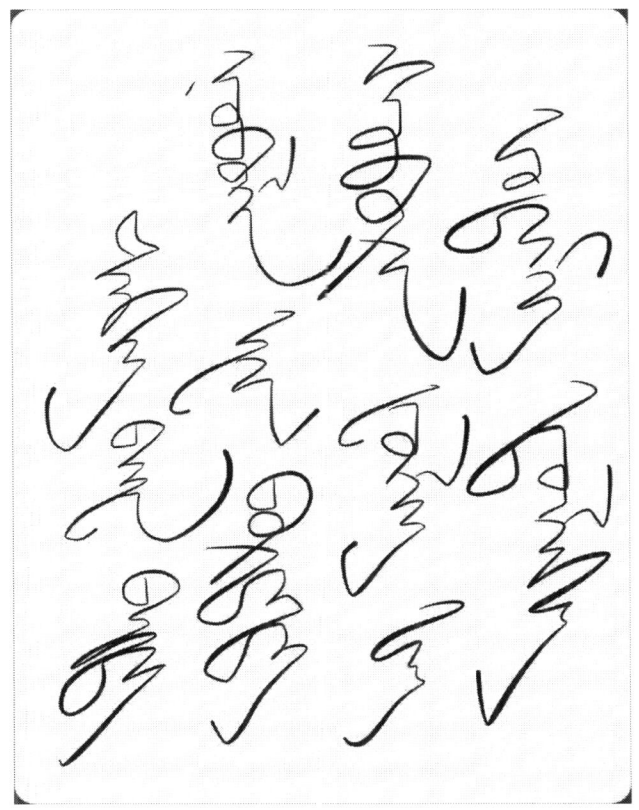

"Takha bae bitakh novlaa rakh Aya Bortaetae,

Huborakha, Polonkhya, Hutamae Dulekh."

--Written in Romanized Thulean

Prologue: Troll battles

At half the length of her body, Tamana's buster sword is meant to be held with both hands, to be used as both a shield and a weapon, but she's never been one to do things in a conventional way. She takes to the air, and following a perfect arc, she slashes through the enemy troll's poorly crafted leather chest plate.

-15 HP!

She botches the landing, still not used to her buster sword's weight, and cartwheels to the right. A fiery explosion suddenly flings the mountain troll backwards.

-5 HP!

Glancing over her shoulder, Tamana watches Ryuk load another black marble into his magic slingshot. He pulls back and lets go. A blast at the troll's hairy feet produces a cloud of dust and a scattering of debris.

"Both hands on the sword!" Ryuk shouts to her for the third time that afternoon. He pops off another black marble at the feet of the troll, causing more dust to obscure the air. Range isn't an issue with his magic slingshot; it propels the marbles with magic, not elastic, and it self-adjusts for range.

This is a good thing, as Ryuk is utterly terrible with his new avatar.

Tamana is by his side moments later, the strands of her long white hair beating in the wind. "My attack looked cool though, right?" she asks.

He has to smile at this.

"You chose a much stronger avatar than I did," he reminds her.

She winks at him. "You always were up for a challenge."

They lock eyes for a moment longer than necessary.

A smaller troll, likely the bigger troll's wench, flanks the two. Grimy dreadlocks cover her face and yellow man-bone jewelry clinks around her neck. She pauses, grunts, and charges.

Ryuk loses his footing and muffs his next shot. The marble explodes and a nearby bush bursts into flames.

Still holding her weapon incorrectly, Tamana side swipes her ironing board of a sword at the she-troll and manages to cut the wench's hairy arm clean off at the elbow. The she-troll shrieks as her black blood jets into the air.

-39 HP! Critical hit!

The dust clears. *"Doka duchaka!"* Maddened with rage, the savage male troll charges at the two with his fists held high over his head.

"I've got this!" Ryuk procures a clear marble from the pocket on his belt, pulls back, and looses it.

What the ... ?

The male troll freezes in place, his chiseled arms still held over his head. Ryuk glances back to Tamana to find that she's also fixed in place, her tremendous sword held awkwardly in the 'ready enough' position at her side. Turning to the dying female troll, he gasps once he sees that the blood spraying from her arm is pixelated, it too frozen in midair. From the grass that was moments ago blowing in the wind, to a bead of sweat on the side of Tamana's face – everything around him is completely stationary.

But I can still move, he thinks as he squeezes the handle of his slingshot.

Not knowing how long he has until time returns to its normal pace, Ryuk moves to the side of the alpha troll, takes a few steps back just to give himself some distance, reaches for a black marble and …

Time blazes ahead and the troll turns to him.

Taken off guard, Ryuk is seconds from being clobbered when the tip of Tamana's buster sword pierces the creature's chest, splashing oily black ichor onto Ryuk's face.

Instakill!

The troll slumps forward and Tamana kicks his corpse off her buster sword. She keeps the troll's blood on the blade as she turns to his smaller counterpart. One clean swipe and she finishes off the she-troll too.

-17 HP!

They are each awarded experience points and the guild coffers increase by about a hundred rupees. With a flick of his wrist, Ryuk checks their stats and swipes them away.

Ryuk Matsuzaki Level 2 Ballistics Mage

HP: 87/115

ATK: 40

DEF: 5

MATK: 51

MDF: 18

LUCK: 3

Tamana Nakamura Level 2 White Warrior

HP: 85/138

MANA: 68/79

ATK: 52

DEF: 19

MATK: 12

MDF: 38

LUCK: 3

"That was crazy ... " Tamana wipes the digital sweat from her forehead. She stabs her bloodied sword into the soil, something she's grown fond of doing since taking her new avatar. Glittery magic spirals around her hands as she lifts her arms into the air. A halo takes shape over her crown and a cloud forms over the two; iridescent snowflakes gently settle onto their heads and shoulders.

+45 HP!

"What did you do back there?" She asks, after they've healed up. "How did you freeze time? That's, like, a level 30 spell or something!"

Ryuk shows her one of his clear marbles. "It's these clear marbles. Like I told you, they're wild cards."

"You should have used more of those when we were leveling up earlier." She shoots him one of her knowing smiles that he's grown fond of over the years.

He shrugs her off. "I wanted to play it safe. I knew the black marbles were explosive, and they seemed the way to go." He returns the clear marble to the pocket on his belt. "That was *definitely* cooler than I thought it would be. Next time, I'll, um, do something a bit more productive when time freezes."

The question he wants to ask is on the tip of his tongue.

He holds it there, decides to go for it, decides against it. Tamana and Ryuk had been gaming together for years. Ryuk wants something more and sometimes, he thinks that Tamana does too. One of the main reasons he'd agreed to re-roll, to become a *resetter* and start the game with a new avatar was to show her how committed he was to her.

Now he needed to say something about it. "Ahem … "

Tamana's smile fades as the thought of real world responsibilities spreads across her face. "I really need to log out now and take care of some homework. I keep pushing it off."

Shit. He kicks a piece of rubble away. "Same here, but not homework – family."

"You're meeting your brother today?"

"Later today."

Her eyes fill with concern. "Be careful, Ryuk."

"You do the same."

"My homework isn't that dangerous!" With a laugh, she lifts her hand and the logout button appears, rimmed in glimmering gold. "See you soon."

"Wait."

"Yes?"

Ryuk pinches the bridge of his nose for a second, realizes he's acting oddly, and looks up at her, away, and back again.

"What is it?"

He swallows hard. "Do you want to get dinner with me tomorrow night? I'd really like that."

She shrugs him off. "Tomorrow night? Yeah, that'll work. Same place? I love the miso ramen there." Tamana cocks her head at him. "Why are you looking at me like that?"

Dammit, Ryuk thinks, *don't be awkward!*

"I mean, okay, how about I just come out and say it? Would that help?"

"You don't like ramen?" she laughs. "I knew it! You never finish your bowl."

"Not that." Ryuk wipes his hands on his pant legs. "Okay here it is. I wanted to know if you'd like to go to a nicer place, some place more romantic."

"More romantic?" Tamana turns away from him.

"Yes, like one of those Italian restaurants in Ginza. Or … " He thinks as his face fills with blood. "Tokyo Sky Tree. Yes! We could have dinner there."

Tamana gives him a curious look. "Are you asking me out on a date?"

"No!" Ryuk shuffles his feet. "I mean, not exactly, um, yes exactly. Yes. Sure, let's call it a date. What do you say?"

She gives him a warm smile and nods. "Let's talk about it later. Bye, Ryuk." With that, she presses the logout button and her avatar dematerializes.

Find out more about Harmon Cooper at www.harmoncooper.com!

Made in the USA
Middletown, DE
25 July 2017